Born in Portsmouth the author has lived in the South Wales valleys for the past fifty three years, and worked for a period in the coal mining industry prior to its decimation by the Thatcher administration.

Gaffers' Row charts the fortunes of the Morgan family through a key portion of the twentieth century, and centres on the conflict between Rhys Morgan and an immoral mine manager, which has reverberations for the entire Morgan family.

Gaffers' Row

Rory T Hunt

ISBN: 978-0-9556833-0-5

Published by Smart

Printed by Lulu

For my wife

Sioned

(Janet)

Acknowledgements.

Many thanks to

My wife Sioned for her patience and encouragement.

Alan and Carol Jones without whose help this book

would still be an unfinished project.

My Grandson Jonathan Parsons

for the cover design.

(www.jrparsons.co.uk)

Prologue

Monday June 2nd 1902

Dai Morgan wheezed his way to the top of the mound and squatted on the sun scorched grass to regain his breath, he coughed repeatedly dragging up the thick black phlegm that choked his lungs, and spat it at an irritating bluebottle that was imprudently harassing him. Below, two of his three offspring's swung on a rope slung from a stout branch overhanging the pond, and dropped into the almost still blue-green water. While his eldest son Gomer aged twenty attended primarily to watch over his siblings eight year old Moira and six year old Rhys. Moira and Rhys swung out in tandem, with Rhys having a length of rope attached to his waist so Gomer could pull the spluttering non swimmer back to the bank, while Moira swam alongside Rhys as an extra precaution. Dai knew that if Rhys had been a strong swimmer Moira would still have stuck beside him, and they'd have still swung out together. She'd been two years and ten months old when Rhys was born, yet now he stood a good two inches taller but this didn't prevent her fussing over him continually. Wherever Rhys was Moira wasn't far away, and on the rare occasions they were separated Rhys seemed like a bird with clipped wings. Rested Dai raised himself from the ground, and with a wave to his children started the final leg of his journey home.

"You're later today," said Sioned, dragging the tin bath in front of the fire."

Dai merely grunted his agreement as he wrapped a cloth around the handle of a bucket of boiling water and lifted it from the hob. "I met the new under-manager today; I'm not too sure about him."

"Why's that?"

"Well we all knew where we stood with Meredith, but this fellow I don't trust him, smarmy bugger tries to hard, comes over too nice."

"He's supposed to have an eye for the ladies."

"He'd better stay well away from you, manager or not." Sioned chuckled at the idea as she gathered Dai's clothes, while he dabbed his toe in the bath and immediately withdrew it. "Duw that's hot."

"I'll get some more cold," she said taking the bucket to the tap in the yard. Dai sat naked on a kitchen chair until she returned. "Try it now," she said after adding half the contents of the bucket

"It's ok." Kneeling over the tub he wet his hair. "Talk is he's going to preach in Saron."

Sioned picked up a bar of carbolic and rubbed it into his scalp. "Hasn't taken him long to set himself up has it?"

"Only been here a month."

"What he say to you then?"

"Nothing much, asked me my name, how long I'd been on the coal, and if I went to chapel."

"And you decided he was not to be trusted on that."

"He's a boss you can't trust none of them, but there's something about him not right." Dai got to his feet and stood in the bath, washing his upper body. "Nobody knows nothing about him, where he's from or where he worked, we weren't sure if he was even Welsh, but with his name Dafydd Siencyn-Pryce he has to be don't he?"

Taking the flannel to scrub his back Sioned added to the speculation. "His wife, she don't speak Welsh."

"Don't she? When did you meet her then?"

"I haven't, I've seen her once in the village, scrawny woman, skinny as a bean stick, but they said in the Gwalia she can't talk proper, only English.

"He'd be no good in the pit if he couldn't speak Welsh," he said as she left him to finish his lower half.

Gomer pulled Rhys to the bank, "We'd best make our way home, mam will have dinner ready."
Moira nodded in agreement while Rhys frowned, he was having fun and saw no reason for stopping just yet.

"Can't we have one more go?" He pleaded.
Gomer was about to refuse as Moira and Rhys prepared to swing for the final time, clutching the rope as they moved backward to get maximum momentum, as they leapt Moira wrapped her legs around him and they swung out over the water.

"You'll have to lift me on tomorrow 'cos it's my birthday," she shouted before letting go.

Rhys was as excited as Moira, and anyone unfamiliar with the closeness of the pair might have had difficulty in defining whose birthday was being celebrated. Sioned had as she always did on such occasions baked a cake, in the centre the name Moira was spelt in thick sugary icing, and around the edge stood an assortment of candles, the number not having any bearing to Moira's age but were determined by how many were salvaged from Rhys' cake earlier that year. The pair had raced home from school to open whatever present Dai and Sioned had for her. Rhys produced the wooden rifle his father had carved from a piece of solid beech for his birthday, and waved it in the direction of Gomer as he entered the kitchen, ruffling Rhys' hair Gomer feigned death from a hail of imaginary bullets.

"That's a nice cake, someone's birthday?" Gomer teased.

Much to Moira's relief the back door opened and the grinning black face of Dai Morgan appeared, she knew it wouldn't be long now before she had her present.

After tea the two children sat together on the front step admiring her birthday gift.

"That's really nice." Rhys wasn't saying it to be polite he meant it.

"Dad made it himself." Running her fingers lightly over the equine relief carved into the lid. "I'm going to have a real horse just like this one day." Fumbling in the pocket of her pinny she produced two turquoise glass beads and several milky white imitation pearls and carefully placed them in the box. "I'll keep all my treasure in here."

"Why didn't you want a party like me?" Rhys had asked her every day since she'd declined her mothers offer.

"I'd have had to invite people I don't like 'cos they asked me to theirs, and it's better when it's just me and you."

Rhys nodded in partial agreement he liked it when it was just the two of them, and he also liked parties. "But you'd have had more presents."

"Like you did, bookmarks and texts from chapel, no thanks."

Rhys new when he was beaten and didn't raise the issue of all the fun they'd missed and changed the subject. "Think Gomer will take us down the pond."

"No he's got to go to work tonight," said Moira studying the box once more.

"He might if you ask him 'cos it's your birthday."

That night after Gomer had left for work, Sioned sat in her chair, using the scraps of left over wool from the cardigan she'd knitted Moira last Christmas to darn Dai's socks. Dai sat on the step his children had occupied earlier, and sucked contentedly on his pipe. Moira and Rhys snuggled together in their bed and chatted in whispers about the day's events, especially Gomer finally submitting to Moira's request and Rhys' pestering, and taking them to the pond and the swing.

"Always be me and you won't it?" Murmured Rhys on the periphery of sleep.

Moira's reply went unheard. "Always and forever."

Chapter One
Monday 14th April 1924

'*Hundreds of Colliers are found to be in a state of drunkenness in and around Newcastle, for many workers Sunday has become a regular excuse for profanity.*' Dafydd Siencyn-Pryce, under-manager of Pentre Bach Colliery read aloud the newspaper report to his pit overman. "Any man in this pit who abuses the Sabbath will answer to me."

"It's unlikely any of our men would dare Mr Pryce, besides the pubs are shut on Sundays." Gomer hoped Pryce wasn't going to embark on another sermon.

"Evil will exploit any opportunity, the trouble these days men have more time on their hands than is good for them," continued Pryce waving the newspaper at Gomer. "If it wasn't for the conviction of God fearing people such as me keeping the devil's brew at bay and the working class in check the country would be in total anarchy." He paused, lowering the paper as his fervour subsided, then added, "I didn't see your wife in chapel yesterday?"

Gomer Morgan cleared his throat. "Our youngest was ill, so Gwen had to stay at home."

"Hmm, I assume she'll be present on Wednesday."

This wasn't a question, but a reminder of the unwritten rule, colliery officials and their families attended chapel on Wednesday evening, and at least one but preferably all three Sunday services, and if the official had any choral aptitude he attended choir practise on Mondays and Thursdays. To maintain their positions the officials made certain the pews were fully occupied.

"Oh they'll both be there, if not Wednesday then Sunday without fail Mr Pryce, it's only the girl was bad see."

Moving towards his adjoining office Pryce grunted incoherently, then before closing the door he barked. "And get a deputy sorted for pit bottom, but clear your choice with me first."

Gomer resumed writing his shift report.

Nerys emptied another jug of water over Rhys' back, exposing the ugly blue blemishes that couldn't be washed away. The glowing red coals hissed as she dodged the water he playfully flicked at her.

"What else did your brother say?" She asked passing him the towel warming on the hearth.

Rhys stood in the tin bath drying his upper body. "If Mr Pryce finds any of us drinking on Sunday we'll be looking for work. Old Gwyn up and down will have to watch his self," chuckled Rhys.

"That man shouldn't be doing that job, he's not safe." Nerys used the jug to empty the bath water into a bucket, while he stepped onto the mat and continued to vigorously rub himself with the towel.

"I've never known a man to drink so much and still be sober, and as long as he winds me up and down the pit it's no odds."

"Well it's not right him drinking with a job like that, he could kill some one."

14

"I'd trust him with my life."

"You do everyday."

Rhys completed dressing while Nerys wiped up the small puddles splattered across the flags, and then putting on his cap he went outside to sit on the scrubbed white stone doorstep where he could relax and enjoy a cigarette. He watched the figure ambling towards him, along the dirt road that fronted the row of terraced cottages.

"Shwmae brawd."

Welsh still being the language of both home and the workplace, and English still only having gained a minor influence in the area. Originally borne by an earlier influx of migrant workers the only place English was officially used was in the village school. Rhys made room for his brother to sit. A fluff of dust flicked up as Gomer spat the black residue of his chewing tobacco into the road.

"Well, you going to take it?"

Rhys gazed passed the pit to the mountains beyond. "I know I should be jumping at the chance, but I dunno."

"For Gods sake use your bloody head man you're twenty eight with a family, and here's a chance to get off the coal with tidy money, what more do you want? You like being on your knees all day slogging like a bloody slave? If you do you're a bigger fool than I took you for?"

"You're as much as a bloody slave as I am, and I have my self respect."

Gomer ignored the inference. "But I'm not lying in water all day in the two foot nine busting a bloody gut, I'd rather be called Pryce's lackey than be proud and fucked up."

"Its not that I'm not grateful to you, but I'd know one day I'd lose it with Pryce and then I wouldn't have a job at all."

15

"You think you'll have a job when Pryce finds out your involvement with the fed? I remember armed troops being sent to Pandy to force the miners back to work, the federation wasn't a lot of good to those that copped the bullets."

"Times have changed they wouldn't do that again."

"Don't be so bloody sure, money is power in this world, and we have little of one and none of the other."

"You joined the army." Rhys hadn't meant it to but it sounded like an accusation.

"Wartime 'twas different."

"You never talk about it."

"I saw things I'd rather forget but I can't, and talking don't help." He stood up ready to leave. "Do it for Nerys and the kids, prides ok when you can afford it. Its not that hard, just yes sir no sir, keep your head down and go regular to chapel. You never know you might even end up next door to me in Gaffers' Row."

"Tell me deacon do you go to chapel to worship God or Pryce?" Rhys made no attempt to hide his sarcasm.

"I do whatever's necessary to keep a roof over my family and food on the table, and I suggest you do the bloody same. I can't hold Pryce off much longer, if you don't want it Jimmy Whiz will jump at it."

Gwen swapped the iron for the one on the hob, her spit sizzling on its surface as she briefly held it close to her cheek, before laying a cloth over Gomer's Sunday shirt. "Iwan you make sure you scrub your neck." She called to the boy with his head bowed under the tap outside the back door. "So what's he going to do? I tell you Gomer's danted with trying to talk sense into him."

Nerys leaned forward resting her elbow on the table, her hand supporting her head allowing her long black hair to fall over her face to conceal her distress. "He's so stubborn I don't know what's wrong with him. We could be living in middle row in front of you and Gomer, three proper bedrooms, and even our own toilet.

Gwen put her arm around her younger sister. "Maybe you need to put your foot down. Perhaps if you told him you were pregnant it would make him come to his senses."

"I want to be sure first, and we've been arguing so much lately I've been afraid to mention I might be."

"Where's dad?" Iwan asked as he entered the room

"Gone down Uncle Rhys' allotment. I hope you're clean, let me have a look at you."

"I'd better be going, don't want to make you late for chapel." Nerys made her way to the door.

"Don't worry it'll be all right you'll see, just tell him he's going to be a dad again. Iwan go fetch Mari and your father or we will be late."

Gwen watched her sister disappear around the bend that led down to the hovels as she secretly called them, remembering how they'd lived with Gomer's father and mother, along with Rhys, and Moira, in the two up two down cottage. Then she hadn't minded the cramped conditions, not even when Iwan came along, except when it was her turn to clean six of the block of twelve toilets that served thirty-two houses. It wasn't the cleaning so much as carrying and emptying the foul buckets into the trench dug by one of the men. On more than one occasion the contents had slopped over onto her clothes and run down her legs into her shoes. That bloody Rhys needed a good kick up the backside, and if Nerys didn't do it she would.

17

Iwan soon returned having run all the way there and back, "Mam do I have to go to chapel, why can't I go and play with Huw and Elis they don't ever go?"

"What those two do is up to Aunty Nerys, but you're going."
Iwan new better than to argue, fearing his mother's tongue more than the threat of his father's belt. When he was fourteen he'd start work in the pit, he'd be a man then and decide things for himself.

Mr Dafydd Siencyn-Pryce colliery under-manager, deacon, preacher, pillar of the community, a man respected and admired by all, or so he thought, stood erect shoulders back firm in his conviction that this was his true vocation. Firmly gripping the sides of the pulpit he bellowed a warning of the dangers of Satan's brew, which led to mass fornication by the working class. With abundant relish he described in graphic detail the hellfire and damnation that would consume the less than righteous, only if they repented would they be welcome in the kingdom of heaven.

Gomer sat staring intently as if he were hanging on every word, when really his mind was elsewhere; he'd heard it all before as Siencyn-Pryce had sought to practise his sermon on him at every opportunity.

Iwan stared terrified as Siencyn-Pryce's intense black eyes burned through his skull, raping his brain and stealing its secrets, could he tell Iwan had committed a sin with himself yesterday? Soon he would be working for this man chosen by God to seek out people like him, no matter where they hid.

Gwen sat with her arm around eleven year old Mari, thinking you bloody hypocrite.

Rhys took his cap from the peg by the front door. "Gomer should be home from chapel, I'm just going up to see him, then I'll slip over the stables to pick up a sack of manure. I won't be long."

"And what you going to tell him, as if I didn't know?"

He reached out and placed his hand behind her neck pushing aside her hair and looked into her pale green eyes. "You know I love you and would do anything for you and the boys?"

"I know." Nerys waited for the but, she'd resigned herself to what he was about to say.

"That's why I'm going to take the job." Rhys felt himself thrown back against the wall as Nerys launched herself at him, her arms vice like around his neck pulling his head towards her. "Careful woman or I won't be able to go and tell him," he laughed.

Rhys was sure then he'd made the right decision, but by the time he'd walked up the steep track to his brother's house he was less certain. He paused outside the door and viewed the valley, picturing it without the mine sprawling across its basin with an imposing grimy iron pithead at either side, while high on the mountain the huge black spoil tip loomed menacingly over the village. He'd only ever been out of the valley once, when his Uncle Vaughan died. Maldwyn Pugh a local farmer had offered the loan of a pony and trap, so his father could attend the funeral in Porthcawl. The whole Morgan family, father, mother, Gomer, Moira and himself took the opportunity to have a day out, it was the first time any of them had seen the sea. The picture of the sleek schooner bobbing in the harbour made six-year old Rhys wonder to what far off lands it had been, had the crew had adventures with pirates or giant sea monsters? The spell the ship and the sea cast remained with him, then his greatest wish had been he'd had more uncles. Ten years later he'd have traded all the uncles in the world for the impossible, for Moira.

"Are you coming in?" Gomer brought him abruptly back to the present.

"Just thinking of the time we went to Porthcawl. Rhys followed him into the kitchen and sat in front of the roaring fire.

"You should be thinking of your family and taking the job I have to let Mr Pryce know tomorrow."

"That's why I've come, if the jobs still there I'll take it, that's if Pryce is willing."

"What about the union?"

"I believe we deserve better pay and conditions, not just trying to keep what we've got. It's time the coal owners stopped using us to protect their profits, but the last strike didn't do us any good we went back worse off, next time it will be different. One thing we learnt back in twenty one is other unions don't always keep their word, what we do we do alone. We won't forget Black Friday in a hurry, but you're right in one thing I have to put Nerys and the boys first."

Gomer's expression changed into one of relief. "Nothing wrong with being pro-union, just don't advertise it. I'm not anti-union, but where would I be if I ran around shouting the odds? I'll tell you where, on my arse out in the street and my family with me. Learn this if nothing else, they have the whip hand and you can't beat them and you'll lose every time. There's a time to keep your head down and maybe there'll come a time to stand and be counted, but don't offer yourself as a target." He went to the fire and lit a taper for his cigarette. "You want one?"

"Thanks." Rhys took the offered cigarette.

"If there's a strike a lot of families are going to suffer."

"It's got to come to a head sooner or later. I'm not sure I can sit back while others do the fighting for me? We all have families."

Gomer held out the taper. "Ask yourself if all the federation leaders are in it for the same reason?"

"Oh! Not that one again." Rhys complained but Gomer wasn't going to be put off.

"How many are there because they see it as a way to promote themselves? Can you tell who is genuine or who is using the union for their own ends? Because they're no better than the mine owners."
Rhys felt uncomfortable they'd had this argument so many times before.

"I'd better go I told Nerys I wouldn't be long, and I want to get some horse shit for my garden."

"I'll come with you; I could do with some fresh air."

Rhys really didn't want Gomer's company because of his assumption that as he was fourteen years Rhys' senior he was entitled to lecture him whenever he deemed necessary, and had done so frequently in the ten years since Dai and Sioned had died, and Rhys could do without another. "No more talk about the union then."

Gomer laughed as they rounded the colliery offices. "Remember when you dressed up that dead sheep in old clothes and a cap. I'd only just moved in to Gaffers' Row, if Pryce had found out it was my brother who'd done it I would have been moving straight back out."

"It wasn't only me, it was Gareth Jones' idea we were only eleven."

"Pryce nearly had a heart attack when he walked into his office and saw someone sitting with their back to him looking out the window."

"It was just a bit of fun."

"He didn't think so, that's probably the nearest he's ever come to swearing." Gomer was still laughing when they reached the stable.

"Maybe Pryce won't give the job to me."

"It's between you and Jimmy Whiz, perhaps you not being a regular chapel goer will work in your favour."

"How come? Jimmy's there every week without fail, and he's in the choir."

"Because Pryce will believe he'll be bringing another lost soul into the fold, and you're married which means he can save a whole family."

Rhys chuckled. "Yeah, and who's responsible for his spiritual guidance?"

Chapter Two
Monday August 19th 1924

The dust from the rag mat swirled around the back yard, Nerys stopped beating and turned her attention to the washing, moving part of it from its overnight soak in the tin bath and placing it in a bucket which she took inside, as she lifted it onto the kitchen hob the carbolic and soda mixture spilt onto the red hot coals sending a blast of acrid steam into her face. She was finding it hard to concentrate, not because it was Rhys' first day in his new job, ok it was only a trial, probation he'd called it, and she had no worries whether he could do the job, it was what Siencyn–Price said after chapel yesterday that bothered her. Once she had the washing out and the boys off to school she'd go and see Gwen, she'd know what to do.

Nerys pulled the front door behind her, she wanted to leave it open but was afraid Wil Hopcyn's dog would go in and cock it's leg as it had last week when she'd been cleaning upstairs, she knew it was Wil's dog because she saw it scampering out through the front door as she came down the stairs.

Wil had just shrugged his shoulders saying, "Dogs got to go somewhere, he don't know do he?"

Not yet midday and the ground felt hot beneath her feet, not since the summer she'd been carrying Huw had she felt this uncomfortable. She was less than half way along the street when her sister turned the corner, walking towards her.

"I was just coming to see you."

Gwen smiled. "You should be thankful I saved you a walk, I'm going down to Poison Corner and wondered if you wanted anything?"

Nerys' only want was her sister's ear, and although the local shops were not the appropriate place to discuss her dilemma, she accompanied her sister hoping an opportune moment would arise.

The Gwalia Stores was regarded as the second most important focal point of the community. Where the gossips in the chapel used whispers, nods and knowing looks, in the Gwalia everyone was discussed fully and in great depth, as long as they weren't present. Ironically those who entered and participated most vehemently were always the most reluctant to be first to leave.

The bell sounded its usual discordant tinkle as the half glazed door swung open, releasing a perfumed bouquet of numerous herbs and spices, combined with the sweet fragrances of freshly cured ham, strong cheeses and biscuits mingling with other discreet aromas seductively teasing their senses, enticing the sisters to set foot on the lightly saw-dusted wooden boards. Bronwyn overseer of the chitchat sat arms folded on a tall chair behind the far end of the counter, fronted by a display of opened tins containing an assortment of biscuits. Her husband Owain stood in readiness beside the bacon slicer.

"Morning ladies and how are we today?" Owain greeted everyone in exactly the same manner, his superficial smile baring a row of teeth more colourful than the flowers on his wife's cotton dress.

Gwen didn't like him and had even less time for Bronwyn and her clique. "I'm fine, but you don't look so good," she answered dryly. "Four pounds of flour two bars of washing soap, and a packet of starch. Oh! And some lamp oil please."

"I think we could have some thunder, gone very heavy, still a drop of rain might clear the air." Undeterred by her brusqueness Owain's attempts to initiate a conversation while he collected the goods, succeeded only in increasing the volume of hot air. At the far end of the counter beneath a range of buckets, sieves, and oil lamps three women stood close to Bronwyn, like witches huddled around a cauldron. They turned in unison and stared, almost challenging the right of the newcomers to be there. After a long silence one of them Glynis Hughes nicknamed Gabby spoke sarcastically.

"Surprised you still come in here, what with you coming up in the world, now Rhys' got a boss's job."

Nerys looked at the group of women as if they were the scrapings from her shoe, before locking onto her target. "There's two types of people in this village, those who try to raise themselves from the gutter, while there's others who know their place." Gabby's face reddened as she opened her mouth to reply then thought better of it.

"What's up Gabby not like you to be lost for words? Gwen chipped in as she picked her change up from the counter.
Gabby stayed silent until the pair had departed the shop; she'd lost too many verbal battles to Gwen in the past.

"That lot are pure evil, and Owain's just as bad as any of them, it makes my blood boil to look at them since I caught them running

25

Moira down after what she did." Then nodding towards the butcher's shop Gwen added. "And him, he's carried on as if it had nothing to do with him."

"What did happen? I know Moira was pregnant but no one ever talks about it." Nerys had remained ignorant of the details of Moira's death, she'd heard the rumours, but hadn't been privy to the juiciest of the gossip, probably because at the time her parents considered her too young.

"Not much to tell really, except it killed her mother and father. They'd hoped for a girl for years, and Sioned miscarried more than once, they were really grief stricken when one was stillborn. Then Moira came along and they both doted on her, she was always their favourite. Rhys and her were inseparable he was devoted to her, and her him, and she was such a pleasant girl no one could dislike her."

"Whenever I try to talk to Rhys about it he changes the subject, or goes out."

"Gomer was the same for a long time; I'm not sure which affected him more Moira's suicide or watching his parents giving up on life."

"Rhys will talk about his mother and father, but not Moira I think he feels guilty in some way."

"They were exceptionally close."

Nerys was about to push for more details when the sudden blast of the colliery hooter sent all thoughts of Moira from their heads.

Iwan tossed another stone into the stream, if he had to go to chapel on Sundays then he'd take a day off from school to compensate, not that there was much to do on a Monday. On the rare occasions he could avoid chapel he would go to Echo Valley, not to see the abundance of coloured damselflies and dragonflies, or catch the newts and frogs that inhabited the pond, but to conceal himself among the ferns and masturbate while spying on the couples that frequently courted there. He lay back on the grass, enjoying the sun before it succumbed to the advance of the thickening cloud. Stimulated by the memories of past voyeurism his hand fondled what gave him most pleasure. His enjoyment was short lived, he sprang to his feet, sliding and tumbling down the grassy slopes running full pelt towards the wailing siren that halted the heartbeat of the valley. By the time he reached the pithead the colliery's hooter had been silenced.

Squashed into a small yard between the office and lamp-room an anxious crowd of wives and mothers had already gathered, Iwan threaded his way between the tightly packed throng of sweating bodies, holding his breath in an attempt to evade the overpowering bouquet of accumulated body odours as he searched for his mother and aunt. Grave faced David Davis the surface foreman came out of the once white painted coal grey offices.

"What's happened Dai Dai?"

"How bad is it any body hurt?"

"Are my boys ok?"

The anxious women were rapidly firing questions before David Davis had a chance to speak, standing on the top step to the office he motioned with his hands for them to be quiet.

"There's been a fall in the two foot nine seam, how many men are injured we don't know but men from the other districts are there doing everything they can to bring them out. That's all we know for the moment." Dissatisfied with the lack of information a few members of the crowd shouted more questions.

"Anybody been killed?"

"How many are missing?"

"My boy it's his first day is he ok?"

While the majority stood in horrified silence, each in personal prayer, hoping that it was the other person and not their loved one who would be carried out. Nerys gave thanks that last Saturday had been Rhys' last shift on the coalface. Gwen repeated to herself over and over, as if in its thinking it would make it true. Gomer's job took him to all parts of the mine, and he'd probably been nowhere near the accident. Iwan looked up at the darkening sky feeling the sudden cooling breeze penetrating his thin shirt, a second droplet splashed on his forehead.

Rhys hoped he would be as sprightly at seventy; he increased his stride to keep pace with Bryn Jones the man he was to replace as pit bottom deputy. Siencyn-Pryce had allowed him two weeks to prove he could do the job, if he couldn't he'd be back on his knees shovelling while dreaming of Porthcawl and the ships that sailed to lands far away, and Moira, ever present Moira. Bryn and Rhys were patrolling the main roadway, making sure the hauliers and their ponies were not impeded bringing the coal to pit bottom. Where the roadway branched towards the Two Foot Nine district, they were alerted by Hywel Thomas's cries for help as he hobbled towards them. Bryn galloped off in the direction of pit bottom to raise the alarm, leaving Hywel to limp along at his own pace, while Rhys sped towards the fall.

The entrance to the workings were blocked completely, not with large rocks but fine shale that ran like sand as the men frantically dug into it, those without tools scrabbled with torn bloody hands. Rhys made a quick assessment of the situation, the tram rails that ran parallel with the stalls were a mass of broken timber and stone debris, immediately he ordered the men to stop digging and put supports in place before they were all buried, while he checked the heading for gas.

Jimmy Whiz screamed hysterically at him, "They'll be fucking dead if we don't get them out now."

"Put in some props or we'll all be killed." Rhys bellowed back.

It was twenty valuable minutes later when Rhys considered the immediate area to be safe, that construction of small tunnel was begun through the shale rather than just shovelling blindly, as had been the case before he'd arrived when every shovel full removed was immediately replaced ten fold. With room for two men to work at a time the tunnel gradually deepened, the debris being cleared by a line of men shovelling in a chain formation.

"Who's in there?" Rhys asked the now more stable but still shaking uncontrollably Jimmy Whiz.

"Will Thomas and his son Haydn, Dyfrig Harri, Eli Benbow, Geraint Jones, Bryn Williams and the boy who started with him today I don't know his name."

"Anyone else?"

"Mr Pryce and." Pausing to avoid completing the sentence he sucked in a deep breath, before continuing. "Your brother."

More would be rescuers arrived with their own tools, and two of them being senior fireman relieved Rhys of command, enabling him to take his turn in the stifling airless tunnel. He'd barely progressed eighteen inches when the stones slid from around his shovel uncovering a dirty pink hand. Together he and Gruff Roberts carefully cleared around the hand exposing the arm, shoulder and eventually a face. Rhys hadn't cried since Moira's death, he sat cradling Gomer's bloodied head while snail trails appeared on his own cheeks, runs of white mascara on his black face.

One by one the bodies of father and son Will and Hayden Thomas, Geraint Jones, Eli Benbow, Bryn Williams and his new young charge, then the fireman Dyfrig Harri were extracted. Along with Gomer they were laid head to toe between the tram rails, a headless arrow of death. The one time Gomer had spoken of the war he'd recalled the horror of collecting the dead and laying them in neat rows, saying one row was one too many.

Jimmy Whiz's eyes said far more than the one word he spoke. "Bastard." He stood accusingly in front of Rhys barring him from re-entering the tunnel.

Unable to meet his gaze Rhys pushed him roughly aside. "We've still got one more to find."

Crouched inside the hot the airless tunnel the falling razor edged shale sliced through his skin, the blood blended with his black sweat, forming pools around his knees. On the verge of exhaustion Rhys was about to be relieved when his shovel struck something solid, quickly he cleared the rock flakes to expose a huge stone that denied any further progress. He decided to veer the tunnel to the right and hopefully go around the boulder. Just a few more minutes and he'd have to let the next man takeover. Without warning his shovel sliced through the shingle into a hollow. The boulder had wedged forming a lintel over a triangular cavity, approximately two feet at its highest point, into which only a minimal amount of shale had trickled. Rhys peered into the void, then motioning to Gruff Roberts he hung his battery light on a wooden prop. Lying on his belly and holding his oil lamp at arms length inside the chamber, he slowly wriggled snake like forward. Gruff peered into the hole watching the swaying dim yellow light, hoping it wouldn't turn blue.

"Gruff, Gruff?"

"What Rhys?"

"Get a rope, and push it into me with a stick or something." Rhys panted. "And be quick."

After what seemed an eternity Gruff shouted. "Here it comes." Something hard slammed between Rhys' spread legs making him howl with pain. Ignoring his bloody torn finger nails he untied the knot from around the piece of wood. Gruff strained to see what was happening, fortunately pulling his head from the opening just in time as the retuning lump of timber shot past him, courtesy of Rhys' boot. Reinserting his head and shoulders into the hole he waited until Rhys' ankles inched to within his grasp, and using all his strength he dragged Rhys out. The two exhausted men crawled their way out of the tunnel.

Rhys was able to utter to Jimmy Whiz. "Pull the bloody rope, pull him out." Before he drifted into unconscious

Chapter Three

Sunday 7th June 1925

The tombstone read.

Sioned Morgan

Beloved Wife and Mother.

July 15th 1864 - February 9th 1913

Aged 48

David Morgan Devoted Husband and Father

November 3rd 1861- April 13th 1913

Aged 51

Moira Morgan

Much Loved Daughter

June 3rd 1893 – July 7th 1912

Aged 19

A Family At Peace

Rhys stood alongside a more recent grave composing an inscription for the yet to be erected headstone.

Gomer Morgan

Beloved husband of Gwen

Father of Iwan and Mari
May 2nd 1882 - August 22nd 1924
Aged 42
Forsaken By His Brother.

If he'd allowed the men to carry on digging perhaps, then that was something he'd never know, "I'm sorry brawd, I didn't help Moira and I failed you as well, but I promise I'll do my best for Gwen. She's been putting on a brave face for Mari's sake. She was worrying about losing the house, so me, Nerys and the boys have moved in with her. Since you went and Nerys lost the baby they've been inseparable. Pryce wasn't around to ask so we went ahead and did it anyway, we'll have to wait and see what he says. Iwan starts work underground tomorrow he'll be out on the main with me for a while. He could have stayed on top in the lamp room a bit longer, only Pryce caught him wrapping carbide in pieces of bread and throwing them to the birds, sky was full of bloody exploding crows, trust Iwan to get caught on Pryce's first day back. His hair's turned as white as Clawdd-y-Mynydd in the middle of February, and he hasn't been down the pit yet, rumour is his nerve has gone." Rhys glanced across the graveyard. "I'll have to go now, Pryce has cornered Nerys and you know how much she dislikes him. Perhaps I'll have some better news next week." Rhys made his way toward where his wife was in conversation with Dafydd Siencyn-Pryce.

"You settled in Mrs Morgan?"

"Yes thank you Mr Pryce, it's a lot more comfortable than the old house"

"You shouldn't have moved in without permission you know."

"I know we should have seen you first but you weren't in work and Gwen asked us and..."

Pryce interrupted. "I'll do all I can to make it official Nerys, you don't mind me calling you Nerys do you?"

"No I don't mind." He could call her anything he liked as long as she could stay in Gaffers' Row.

"We'll have to iron out the details, and resolve the other matter at the same time. I don't foresee any problems, do you?"
Rhys' arrival forestalled any reply Nerys may have considered.

"Fine sermon Mr Pryce, services haven't been the same without you." Rhys was surprised at how easily he pandered to the others ego. "If you'll excuse us we have to get the children home."

Rhys steered Nerys toward where Elis and Huw were playing with a group of boys.

"You two home and change before you ruin those clothes." She commanded.
Siencyn-Pryce stood high on his temple steps watching his flock disperse beneath a red sun slowly sinking behind the peaks of Clawdd-Y-Mynydd. His covetous gaze dallied on the woman with the hourglass figure gliding over the cobble road, and never once did he consider the husband whose arm she held.

Nerys found washdays a lot easier in this house, its large range enabled her to boil the clothes in the small bath instead of a constant change of buckets, and if she spilt a little water it sizzled on the hob without reaching the coals. The knock on the door startled her, who could it be this early? Not Llinos from next door she'd just shout and walk in, and anyhow Gwen was talking to her over the garden wall.

"Good morning Mrs Morgan, I mean Nerys."
Nerys' jaw dropped.

"May I come in?"

Nerys stepped back as he brushed passed her removing his bowler, the sickly sweet odour of excessive Pomade permeated her nostrils and aggravated the back of her throat.

"I trust you are well?" The thick lenses of his wire framed spectacles concealed if his eyes smiled as fraudulently as his face.

"Yes thank you, and Mrs Pryce how is she?" She only knew enough about his wife to feel sorry for her, eclipsed by the large shadow cast by such a small man. Her initial surprise quickly gave way to foreboding, she waited, whatever his pretence she knew his purpose, the difficulty being how to discourage him politely without inciting a punitive reaction.

He glanced around the room, picked the most comfortable chair and sat down. "I have some news for you Nerys." He paused as if expecting a response, but Nerys remained stone faced. "About the house Nerys, as I explained you shouldn't have moved in without permission."

"Yesterday you told me you didn't see a problem I had the impression you only had to rubber stamp it, if there is a difficulty I think you should discuss it with Rhys."

"Tut tut, let me finish. These houses are for senior officials and their families, the row in front is for firemen, and bottom rows are for colliers.

"I know that, and Gomer was an overman."

"True, but the important word there is was, and Gwen was only entitled to one months grace after Gomer's, er," he searched for an appropriate word. "Misfortune."

"So what about Gwen would you have thrown her out? Very charitable of you." Nerys wasn't prepared to listen to his waffling when she had no doubt as to the reason for his visit.

"Good gracious no indeed not, provision would have been made for a house in bottom row," he said indignantly then added, "As long as she was able to afford the rent of course."

"And what if she couldn't what then?"

"Well at that time it would have been up to Mr Llewelyn the Colliery General Manager, but I'm sure he'd have accepted my recommendation. Anyway her mother still lives over in Gelli doesn't she? So she wouldn't have been without a roof."

"Then why can't you use your influence with Mr Llewelyn now, or haven't you as much as you supposed?"

Siencyn-Pryce stood up stretching to his full height, a little under five foot and a half inch. He wasn't used to being talked back to and he certainly wasn't going to take it from a common miner's wife. He gripped his lapels with both hands as if about to embark on a sermon. "Now you listen to me madam the situation has changed, and I have no need to influence Mr Llewelyn or anyone else for that matter, at the end of the month Mr Llewelyn retires and I will be the new Colliery General Manager and what I say goes, you understand?"

For a second time Nerys was lost for words, so Rhys had been right it wasn't just a rumour about old Llewelyn, now this despot would have even greater dominion over them. She felt sickened by the smug smile spreading across his weasel features as he wallowed in his own importance. "So how long will you give us?"

His smile spread even broader. "The trouble is Nerys there are no firemen's houses empty at the moment, in fact James Wise has just been made up and he's also waiting for one." Nerys found Jimmy Whizz, being called James amusing but as Pryce continued her mirth was soon dispelled. "I'm afraid it'll mean moving back to bottom row for the time being, there is a house empty it does need a little tidying, you could say it's in need of a woman's touch."

" Which one is it? I haven't heard of anybody moving out."

"The one at the far end of Cwmdu."

"She'd have to be some woman, that place is nearly derelict it hasn't been lived in for as long as I can remember."

"That's all there is I'm sorry." He said in a most insincere manner, then pausing for his words to have maximum effect. "Unless," again he paused as if fanning the glowing embers of an idea. "No I don't suppose Rhys would be interested."

"Interested in what?"

"There's need of an overman in the Gelli Deg District and it'll be up to the new manager who gets it."

"And if Rhys were overman we'd be entitled to this house?"

"He'd be eligible for it then."

"But why would you promote so readily?"

"I'll scratch Rhys' back and you scratch mine, that way everyone's happy. My itch has been in need of a woman's attention for some time, not your fault entirely the accident interrupted our previous plans, but we can soon put that right."

"I don't recall ever making any plans."

"I often take an evening stroll along Echo Valley, I find the solitude helps me relax and concentrate on the composition of my next sermon, it would be helpful if next Tuesday evening you could assist me with my relaxation and the preparation of my lesson, and let me know if Rhys really wants the job."

For the second time in her conversations with Pryce Nerys' intended reply was disrupted, this time by Gwen entering the room.

"What do you want?" Gwen spat venomously.

"Ah Gwen so nice to see you, I just called to see how you were as I haven't noticed you in chapel lately."

"The only time you'll see me near that place is when I visit Gomer," said Gwen adamantly

Siencyn-Pryce adopted his most patronising and disingenuous ministerial manner. "I can understand your distress, we'd been standing together a few minutes before and it's only through God's mercy I was spared, poor Gomer was less fortunate, but I believe God must have selected him for a more worthy task."

"You self righteous sod you dare to stand there and tell me God saved you and left a better man to die." She motioned angrily towards Nerys. "Her husband not God rescued you, if it were God's work Gomer would be here and you'd be where he is. Gomer was an honest man not a bloody self indulgent hypocrite, now get out of my house and take your God with you."

Siencyn-Pryce had been totally unprepared for such an onslaught, and for the first time in his life was speechless.

"I understand, she's still distressed it'll take time." Were his parting words to Nerys as she hastily escorted him through the front door.

"Good God Gwen whatever got into you?"

Gwen stared straight ahead, her dark brown eyes emphasising the coldness in her voice, as she spoke calmly and dispassionately. "There's two men in this village that should have been put down at birth, that one would have been better left where your husband found him."

"And the other?" Nerys got the reply she'd anticipated.

"That waster Mostyn."

"You still on about Mostyn you think he's happy Moira killed herself? And Pryce is not everybody's cup of tea certainly not mine, but

38

just because he's alive while Gomer's isn't is no reason to hate him, he can make life very hard for us all." Nerys reasoned

"You don't know the truth about Mostyn and as for Pryce why are you standing up for him? If you knew what he's really like you wouldn't have opened the door."

"No I don't know the truth about Mostyn or Moira because neither you nor Rhys will tell me, and I'm not standing up for Pryce he makes my skin crawl, but I have to pretend to be polite because he's Rhys' boss."

"Well he's not Gomer's any more so I don't have to."

"Oh yes you do, If you want us to stay in this house you do."

"So that's why he was here, the house, you think I was gullible enough to believe he came to enquire on my welfare." Gwen forced a laugh.

Nerys' shoulders sagged, her voice barely louder than a whisper. "Yes that's why he came, and if we want to keep the house you know what he expects me to do."

Gwen nodded. "I know he tries it on with everyone." She put her arms around her distraught sister. "How longs he been pestering you?"
Nerys told what he'd suggested on this and the previous occasion, relieved to have someone to share it with.

"You haven't mentioned anything to Rhys?

"Good God no, Rhys would kill him."

"He should have left the bastard buried."

"We all make mistakes. What am I going to do Gwen?"

"First thing is to stop worrying and let me take care of Pryce. I've got the measure of him."

Chapter Four

Tuesday 27th July 1926

Rhys wallowed in the luxury of being able to stretch full length in a proper bath, just like they had in all the big houses, except this one still had to be filled by buckets, while the likes of Pryce would have hot and cold taps on the bath. At least this one along with the lavatory were connected to the drains, bet Pryce has an inside toilet as well.

As he soaked he puzzled, why had he been offered the overman's job, and why was Pryce prepared to promote him over others who were not only just as capable but senior? Would he be branded a brown tongue, an arse licker, or would people think he'd only got the job as a reward for saving Pryce? Whatever the reason there would be a lot of jealousy, and some would have the right to feel aggrieved, but as Gomer would have said, put your family first. Certainly it would solve any difficulties regarding the house; despite Pryce not mentioning any problems to him he knew Nerys had concerns. Then of course the extra money wasn't to be sniffed at. If he took the job he'd be afternoons regular for a while, a major plus of that would be he'd be excused chapel on Wednesday evenings though Nerys would be expected to attend in his stead. Now he had Gwen and Mari to consider as well, whatever people's opinion of him he had no choice regardless of the fact that a little more than twelve month ago his principles nearly prevented taking the fireman's job, when he'd made that decision there was no turning back.

His thinking was interrupted by Huw entering the scullery carrying the flush bucket they took with them each time they visited the toilet.

"Want me to do your back, Dad?"

Rhys leaned forward and gave Huw the soap and flannel. "Thanks. We've a little job to do this evening." Huw scrubbed and waited for details.

"You know the pen we built in the allotment last week? Well tonight we'll have something to put in it."

"What, Dad."

"You'll see but I'll need you, Elis and Iwan to help."

"I don't know where Iwan's gone; he bathed and went straight out."

"Probably with Gwyl Rees' youngest."

"Bethan"

"Aye, that's the one, he's been seeing her a lot lately. Well it'll be just the three of us then."

"No four, MarI'll want to come."

Where was she? They'd arranged to meet at half six, it must be close on seven now she must have been delayed. Settled beneath the canopy of a large oak, and in anticipation of the pleasures soon to be his he began feeling a little vexed by the longer than expected wait, but the result of a hard day's work and his face warmed by the evening sun dancing gently through the leaves Iwan drifted into a light sleep. The sound of approaching voices brought him wide awake; at first he

41

thought it was Bethan before realising she wouldn't be accompanied. Moving around the tree to where he wouldn't be visible he waited for the newcomers to appear into view. When the voices fell silent and no one came into sight, he stealthily moved toward where the sounds had originated, hoping he'd once again observe an unsuspecting couple in a favoured spot amongst the ferns where the ground fell away, creating a cosy leafy dingle. He wasn't disappointed and his excitement soon got the better of him, and what he'd fantasised of Bethan doing for him he did for himself. The woman was not visible apart from her raised legs between which the man thrust his bare buttocks rhythmically back and fore. The man let out a loud groan his whole body shuddered spasmodically, then momentarily he ceased all movement, before raising himself from the woman and pulling up his trousers. Realizing who he was Iwan slunk back into the undergrowth, but a far greater shock was the identity of the woman.

"Well boys what you think of her? She'll fatten up nice for Christmas."
Huw leaned on the enclosure gate, while Elis stood on the lower rungs stretching to stroke the animals back.
"Why did Mrs Harri give her to us, don't she like pigs?"
Rhys fondly ruffled Elis' hair. "Of course she likes pigs, and pork even more," he laughed. "But since she's been a widow she's finding it hard to look after it, so we're going to do it for her."
"I know, we'll call her Alice," suggested Mari.
"Why Alice?"
"I like Alice it's a pretty name."
"You can't call a pig pretty." Elis argued.

Rhys heard Huw mutter under his breath. "Because she looks like Mrs Pryce."

"Now Huw don't be disrespectful what has that lady ever done to you? Anyway the pig bears a far greater resemblance to her husband; if it were a boy we'd call it Dafydd. It'll be your job to make sure Alice has her aspirins everyday."

"Why's she got to have medicine is she sick?" Mari asked

"No not sick, she's got a few aches and pains and aspirin makes her feel better. C'mon I'd best get you three home and washed before your mothers get back, I don't know who is the muddiest you or Alice. Mari you can have the water first you're not half as mucky as those two."

Rhys was pulling the plug as Nerys entered the scullery.

"They must have been in a state for you to bath them."

"Aye, they were a bit on the grubby side, how's your mother?"

"She's ok I just wished she lived nearer, I know Gelli's not far but it's nearly five miles there and back and it looks like I'll have to go more often as she's not coping very well."

"Where's Gwen, I thought she went with you?"

"No Gwen went to see Delyth Thomas she's still finding it hard to cope."

"It was hard her losing both husband and son."

"Rhys I've got something to tell you, I know I shouldn't have done it I should have told you first, but I had to. Promise you won't get angry."

"It's that bad then?"

"You're not going to like it."

Rhys folded his arms around her and cwtched her. "I promise if I am angry I'll kick the dog."

43

"We haven't got a dog."

"Ok Alice then."

"Who's Alice?"

"Mari's name for the sow. Huw reckons she looks like Alice Pryce."

"She's not that bad looking, Mrs Pryce I mean. I hope Mari doesn't get too attached."

"Oops am I interrupting?" Gwen entered through the back door, the mendacity of her casual manner escaped notice.

"I want you to start afternoons in the Gelli Deg tomorrow they've hit a fault and lost the coal." Pryce was aware that he was handing Rhys a poison chalice, the men got paid for the coal produced and none would be happy working for the pittance of the day work rate.

"Very well, Mr Pryce, who's the fireman with me?"

"James Wise."

"Jimmy Whizz, bloody wonderful that's a great start." Rhys sighed.

Immediately Siencyn-Pryce seized on Rhys' remark. "Something wrong, something not to your liking?" Not expecting an answer Pryce carried on. "And where's that nephew of yours? He'd better have a good reason for not turning up today."

"He was ill this morning and I made him stay home, he'd spent all night out the back. Rhys lied; he didn't have an inkling where Iwan was he hadn't been home all night.

"Morgan, let's start as we mean to go on, you're an overman now and as such you and your family should be setting an example. Your sister in law has been absent from chapel for some time, and her son has been disrespectful to me on a number of occasions. If I were not a Christian man able to adhere to our lord's teaching and turn the other cheek, and thus spare Gomer's widow more suffering, young Iwan would have been given his marching orders long ago"

"I'll have a word with him he won't be a problem any more."

"The boy needs more than a word, if I were his father he'd have felt my belt buckle across his backside."

"I'll see to him Mr Pryce."

"See you do, my patience is exhausted, and while I remember I expect the congregation to swell by at least two this Sunday. Close the door on your way out."

Rhys gladly left the office and made for his allotment where he'd have peace to think before going home. What a bloody week this was turning out to be, first Nerys' revelation and now Pryce on his back.

"Don't worry Alice I won't kick you." His assurance wasted on the pig snuffling about in the mud.

"Where the hell has that son of mine got to? His bed wasn't slept in, and neither Huw nor Elis have seen hide nor hair of him."

"Perhaps he's with Rhys."

"Even so where's he been all night?"

Nerys had very little to offer. "You know what boys are like especially at his age, he'll be home with an excuse as long as Glyn Trwyn's nose."

"What did Rhys say when you told him?" Gwen moved the boiling water from the hob.

"Not much but he wasn't happy, I shouldn't have suggested it without asking him, it's put him in an awkward position. He's probably gone straight to the allotment, he usually does when he's got a cob on."

"Well what's done is done, but think how upset mam will be if Rhys says no."

45

"He won't do that."

"I wouldn't count on it everything else has gone wrong lately, Iwan disappearing, Pryce being awkward over the house, and now to cap it all you and Rhys."

"Me and Rhys will sort ourselves out, but you sure I won't hear any more from Pryce?"

"He won't bother you again, now he knows I'll expose him to his wife, the chapel deacons and the whole village, and he knows even if they don't believe me mud sticks."

Nerys seemed less sure. "I think he'd be confident enough to bluff it out, might even say I was chasing him."

"Trust me it's finished."

Gwen moved toward the open front door and called loudly. "Mari." Within seconds Mari's fair hair and freckled face appeared.

"What Mam?"

"Go down and see if your brother and Uncle Rhys are with Alice."

As quickly as she came Mari was gone again.

"You'll have to watch her; the lads must be noticing she's growing up."

"Good God Nerys she's only twelve.

"Haven't you noticed or do you think it's her vest in a lump? I didn't have a bust like that until I was pregnant."

"Mari's not stupid, I've put her wise to what boys are like."

"Like mam did with me, but I still got caught didn't I?" Nerys giggled.

"You were older."

"You don't think Rhys cared how old I was do you?" She laughed even more. "Take a look, Gwen, she's growing up."

46

"Don't look for trouble we got as much as we need just now."

Nerys became serious again, "You going to tell me about Moira?"

"Honestly there's not a lot to tell you probably know as much as me anyhow. Moira, she was a pretty girl, very small, dainty, didn't look her age. Well she'd been seeing a lot of Mostyn, and when she got pregnant he wouldn't have anything to do with her. So her father went to see him and there was hell of a row, they ended up fighting in the middle of the road outside The Bell. All the men left their beer and went out to watch, Mostyn was young and strong and poor old Dai didn't have enough wind to whistle. Mostyn gave him a terrible beating before some of the men intervened and carried Dai home. Gomer came home from work, saw his father and went berserk; I've never seen him in such a temper. He went and dragged Mostyn out of The Bell and if it hadn't been for Gethin Thomas and some others he'd have killed him."

"I don't think I ever heard Gomer raise his voice, Rhys can be quick when he gets a bee in his bonnet, but Gomer was so placid." Nerys shook her head in amazement.

"That wasn't the end of it, the whole village, well a lot of them anyway wouldn't have any thing to do with Mostyn and boycotted his shop. Then the next Sunday in chapel Pryce stood in the pulpit acting as judge and jury and denounced Moira as a harlot. Mostyn barged his way in pushing Pryce aside, he lifted the Bible in both hands and he swore he'd never been with Moira and the baby she was carrying had nothing to do with him. The place was in uproar the deacons lost all control, those that believed Mostyn argued with those that didn't, and some people even came to blows. Never been known before fighting in chapel, and Pryce threatened to sack all the men if they didn't stop at once. In the chaos Moira ran home and no one saw her after that, we

47

spent all night looking for her. The next day two boys Dai and Twm Thomas found her in Gadlys Woods. It finished her mam and dad."

"How do you know she went home?"

"She'd hung herself with the belt from Gomer's working clothes."

"Did Moira say the baby was Mostyn's?"

"Who else would it have been, they'd been walking out for six months?"

Feeling the question had provided the answer Nerys stood silently by the door and watched the plump fair haired girl sauntering along the road chatting to the muscular coal black man she'd adopted since her father's death.

"Is it true nan is coming to live with us?" Mari asked him unaware of the rift it had caused.

"So your Aunt Nerys tells me."

She missed the undertone. "But she says it's up to you."

"If it's up to me then I'll let you decide."

Mari couldn't disguise her excitement. "Really, you mean it, can I go and tell her it's ok then?"

"As long as your mother says so."

She slipped his hand and ran on ahead, her long hair billowing in the breeze.

"My decision huh," He almost laughed.

As Rhys opened the back door Mari came hurtling out. "I can go if Huw goes with me."

"I expect you'll find him down at Penny Well catching Sticklebacks." Nerys shouted after her.

Penny Well wasn't a well at all, but a part of the river where Rhys and a few others led by Guto Penny had built a dam so they could bathe one hot summer when they were children, it had been rebuilt and added to many times since, but the original name had stuck.

"Have you seen Iwan?" Gwen questioned Rhys before he was through the door.

"No I don't know where he is, he wasn't in work today."

"Where is he then?" She said under her breath.

Nerys busied herself fetching the hot water from the kitchen and emptying it into the bath, waiting to see what was his mood after last night. He hadn't spoken before he went to work this morning, his sullenness infuriated her, if he would just have a row and get it over.

Sensing the tension Gwen decided to make a smart exit. "I'm going to ask Bethan Rees if she's seen him."

Rhys stripped and got in the bath, maintaining his grim faced silence as Nerys revealed what Gwen had told her about Moira. She'd hoped he'd have opened up to her instead he continued bathing as if he hadn't heard a word.

"You could have told me."

"We'll never know the truth of it, but more than one person died that day."

"Why won't you talk to me about it?"

"I can't, it's not you, I don't want to remember, it was before I met you I was sixteen Moira was nineteen, she died and I still don't know why. It wasn't just because of the baby there had to be something else, and I couldn't help her." He passed her the flannel. "Here do my back." Taking the cloth she was about to broach the other matter when he precipitated her.

"I don't mind your mother coming."

Momentarily she hesitated from scrubbing. "I'm sorry I should have asked you first, but I honestly didn't think, I'd said it before I realised."

"I don't mind really, did you think I'd say no and that's why you went behind my back? That's what I object to, you not having enough faith in me."

"It wasn't like that."

Rhys stood up and continued washing his lower half. "No point in arguing about it now, let's forget it."

"I just felt so sorry for her she can't manage alone anymore. What would you have done if it were your mother?"

"I'd have asked you first."

"I'm sorry."

He got out onto the mat and she took the towel from him and gently started to dry him.

"Don't keep saying sorry." The towel fell to his feet as he pulled her to him and pressed his lips to hers. "Where's Elis?"

"Out with Huw."

Slipping one hand behind her knees he lifted her effortlessly and carried her through the kitchen and up the stairs.

Maude Williams enjoyed the company of her grandchildren, this was an extremely rare occasion all four at her home at same time. Iwan had arrived the previous night and refused to go home displaying reluctance to discuss what troubled him, she'd decided not to pressure him he'd tell her all in his own good time. "Have your parents had enough of you all?" She joked as the three new arrivals charged excitedly into the kitchen. In the melee Iwan was able to slip undetected out the back door.

"So when you coming?" Mari asked for the umpteenth time having allowed her enthusiasm to get the better of her.

"I've things to see to, and my furniture how am I going to move that? It'll take a while to get sorted."

"Uncle Rhys can borrow a cart from Mr Pugh and we'll all help." Mari couldn't understand why she didn't come today.

Maude smiled it felt good to be wanted. "All in good time, these two haven't said if they would like me to live with them."

Huw and Elis looked distraught at the idea that they didn't. "Of course we do Nan, that's why we're here," said Huw with genuine affection.

Elis not wanting to be left out added. "We all do even Alice."

"And who is Alice?" Asked bemused Maude.

Mari Huw and Elis between them told her of the sow that was sick and had to have tablets every day, and Huw reiterated that Alice looked like Mrs Pryce. While unobserved Maude's fourth grandchild strode purposefully away towards what and where he was unsure, all he knew was he didn't want to go home he felt too sick to face anyone after what he'd seen, especially her.

Chapter Five
Friday 28th August 1925

The day of Maude's move arrived sooner than anyone had hoped with the exception of Mari for whom it couldn't come quick enough. Tudor Gruffydd the colliery blacksmith and farrier had recently opened a small workshop adjacent to his house in anticipation of an increase in the number of motor vehicles resident in the village and surrounding district. Increasingly his spare time was occupied with carrying out servicing and repairs, not only on cars but the recently acquired second hand tractors belonging to a minority of reasonably successful farmers.

"We can do it late Saturday evening or very early Sunday morning. Owain is leaving his van with me from tomorrow dinner time and fetching it Monday morning, wants me to fit a sign on top of the cab, change the oil, adjust the brakes and grease the bearings, only take me a few hours."

Knowing the others reputation for never missing a chance to make a bit extra, Rhys sceptically asked, "How much is it going to cost me?" .

"Well," Tudor screwed his face as if making a difficult calculation. "Nothing if you do me a favour, can you drive?"

"I don't know I've never tried," Rhys raised an eyebrow waiting for Tudor to explain.

"Nothing to it you'll pick it up."
Rhys didn't share Tudor's confidence. "Why do you want me to drive?"

"I've got to pick something up on Sunday, it'll be a day out for you bring the family if you like."

"As long as I'm back for evening chapel, I daren't miss that, old Pryce doesn't seem too cheerful lately."

"What jolly old Pryce not on top form, not surprising when he's got to suffer disrespectful people like you. What you done to upset the miserable bugger?"

"Nothing I can think of, I only got to open my mouth and he jumps down my throat."

Tudor grinned, "Your own fault, don't open that big mouth so wide. You can't run with the hare and the hounds, you're his man now."

"I'm not his or anybody's bloody man," Rhys said indignantly.

"I read somewhere that either in Africa or was it India, well some bloody foreigners anyway, they reckon if you save a man's life he's your responsibility until you die, bet if you'd known that you'd have left the sod buried."

"I got an excuse; I wasn't sure it was him was him.?"

"There was no one else left to find so you got to take some blame. But don't worry we'll be back in plenty of time for chapel."

"Just to be on the safe side we'd better move Maude tomorrow then." Rhys didn't want to take the risk of it making him late for chapel; he'd have to miss the morning service as it was. "Where we going Sunday, and what we fetching?"

53

Tudor laughed, "Wait and see, wait and see."

Saturday evening Maude found herself bobbing along between Mari, and Tudor in the cab of Owain's van, her belongings wedged in the back together with Rhys, Huw, and Elis. Merion took a less direct route through the village, avoiding the road that past the Gwalia in case Owain should spot them.

"I didn't realise you had so much stuff Mam." Nerys joked as the back doors of the van were opened and the boys along with some of the smaller items spilled onto the road.

"I never throw anything away you never know when it'll come in handy."

"We'll find room for it; Rhys has emptied the front room for you."

Gwen led her mother into the kitchen. "You sure Iwan didn't give you a clue to where he was going after he left your place? He's been gone nearly a month I'm sure something has happened to him."

Maude sat by the table, she'd never needed a cup of tea so much. "No he just disappeared, there was something bothering him but I couldn't get it out of him, don't worry love he'll be back just needs to sort his self out."

"It's just like him, he's takes after Gomer rather keep it bottled up than say what's on his mind."

"There's not much you can do until he decides to come home, and he will when he's ready."

"Come and see, Nan, come and see your room." Mari came bursting through the door.

Gwen's anxiety loosened its grip, "You best go Mam she's been all morning fussing, and doing I don't know what in there."

Maude allowed herself to be tugged from her seat. "Steady on love you'll have me over."

Rhys came into the kitchen and placed a bowl on the table. "Are the kids up?"

"They're getting dressed." Nerys busied herself with the eggs on the hob. "There's tea in the pot, we've only had the chickens a few weeks but we'd miss the eggs now"

"There's another four in the bowl, I'm early collecting this morning I'm sure they haven't all laid yet." Rhys went to the scullery and put his head under the tap. "I think I might get some ducks," he gurgled through the splashing water.

"You'll soon have more livestock than old Pugh has on his farm."

Rhys re-entered the kitchen. "Aye and it looks like we'll need them."

Nerys turned from the range. "I thought it was settled," she said

"It is for the time being, but the governments subsidy runs out in March what's going to happen then?"

"Oh, Baldwin will have it sorted by then."

"I'm not so sure. What have the conservatives ever done for us? And the owners will still want longer working hours with a cut in the men's wages. If it comes to a strike we'd best be prepared"

"You always look on the black side," Nerys said scornfully.

"What other way is a coal miner supposed to look?" He quipped.

"Do you think it'll come to that, surely not after last time?" She looked worried

"We were sold out by the railway men last time, next time we'll know we're on our own."

Nerys placed his breakfast on the table, "So you do think there'll be a next time?"

"If there is I want to be ready, but there's no point in us worrying over ifs and maybes."

Mari entered the room closely followed by the two boys.

"You sure you don't know where we're going, Dad?" Huw asked as he yawned and rubbed his eyes.

"You won't be going anywhere if you don't shift yourself," Nerys interceded.

Elis sat by the table his head resting on his folded arms, "What's for breakfast?" He asked sleepily.

Huw and Mari voiced in unison. "Eggs again."

Quarter past nine Tudor arrived in the van with its gaudy new red lettered Siop Gwalia, set in a bright yellow tiara arcing high above the cab.

"No mistaking whose van this is," laughed Rhys.

Tudor pulled a face, "Like a bloody showman's wagon."

Rhys opened the rear doors, "C'mon boys in the back with me."

Nerys squeezed with Mari into the passenger seat pleased that Gwen had volunteered to stay at home with Maude, thus easing her conscience at leaving her mother the first day she'd come to live with them.

Rhys sat himself on the sacks of straw Tudor had thoughtfully provided, while Huw and Elis peered excitedly out of the two small windows in the rear doors, neither of them caring where they were going, this was an adventure.

The trip the previous day hadn't been long enough to be too disagreeable, but today Rhys soon felt quite battered as Tudor with great skill seemed to obligingly seek out every bump and pothole. One hour and ten painful minutes later the van drew to a halt, both boys waited eagerly for Tudor to open the doors, trying to guess where they were.

"Dad, I can see the sea."

"And boats."

"And a lighthouse." shouted Huw and Elis in competition.

Rhys new where they were, he'd been here once before with Moira.

"You stay here with the family and enjoy yourselves for a while, I have some things to see to. Its twenty five past ten, meet me over at that large building in the railway yard around midday."

Rhys watched the van turn the corner, what was Tudor up to? He didn't have time to wonder for long, small hands were tugging his sleeve.

"C'mon, Dad, come and see." Elis lead Rhys to the outer harbour wall, pointing at the small fishing boats stranded on the mud.

"Look Dad look at the boats," shouted Huw hauling himself up the harbour wall for a better view.

Nerys stood beside Rhys her arm through his while inhaling the fresh sea air.

"So where are the large sailing boats you always talked about?" She asked playfully.

Rhys looked disappointedly towards the inner harbour. "There was only one, it was over there, but there's nothing here now, not even a coaster."

He viewed the dock with a tinge of sadness; the only sign of activity was the shrieking gulls swooping along the quay and over the idle railway lines that would have once been full of coal trucks, finally perching on the neglected lock gates they'd claimed as their territory. Even the water seemed weary, lapping lazily against the slime green stone where once the majestic schooner had been moored.

"It's nothing like I remember; me and Moira sat here and watched the sailors working on the schooner."

Nerys hesitated, should she risk spoiling their day out by encouraging him to talk about Moira? "You were only six, everything looks different when you're young," she said sympathetically.

"True, but it was so much busier, everything looks so dilapidated."

Nerys took a deep gulp of the salt air, "I've never seen anything like it, only pictures in books. You can taste the smell, but it's not just a smell or a taste it's so." She struggled to find the word.

"Fresh?" Rhys offered

"No more than that, invigorating yet much more."

"I know what you mean," he laughed. "C'mon kids lets go and see the lighthouse."

Nerys squeezed Mari's hand, she hadn't heard a word, mesmerised by the surf capturing the late August sun and rolling it in tiny sparkling beads as it unfolded along the shimmering sand. "You awake?" Nerys joked.

Mari slowly turned to face Nerys, "Have you ever seen anything so big yet so beautiful?"

Rhys looked at his pocket watch and swallowed the last of his sandwich. "It's quarter to twelve, I'd better make my way to the yard. You finish the picnic." He rose to his feet brushed the sand from his trousers, put on his jacket and cap and made his way up the beach. The railway yard didn't seem any busier than the docks the sidings stood still and empty, between the tracks tall grass with large ripe seed heads swayed lazily in the breeze. He headed towards a big dilapidated corrugated sheeted building, with Great Western Railway emblazoned in large bold cream letters on a reddish brown background. Passing a row of derelict offices and workshops a face stared at him momentarily through one of the smashed windows, then instantly vanished as quickly as it had appeared. As Rhys reached the doorway it burst open swinging precariously on its one twisted but unbroken hinge, his path blocked Iwan slumped against the wall.

"Christ! What you doing here boy?" Rhys scrutinised his filthy nephew with a mixture of empathy and disgust.

"Iwan tried to push past Rhys but found himself held firmly. "I can do what I like you're not my father."

Rhys relaxed his grip a little, "Maybe but your mothers been worried sick for weeks, now you tell me what's going on."

Tears formed in the corner of Iwan's eyes and his head fell forward as he mumbled. " I can't, I can't tell you."

"Whatever you've done boy it can't be this bad."

Iwan raised his head and looked Rhys squarely in the eye, "What makes you think I've done anything, why has it got to be me?

"Then why else have you run away?"

"It's none of your business what I do, or where I go."

"I'm making it my business, I want to help."

"You can't help no one can, now let me go." He began to sob, "Just leave me alone."
Rhys let him go, and watched helplessly as Iwan slid to the ground his face buried in his hands.

Twelve thirty where the hell was Rhys, Tudor paced back and fore, peering round the corner of the building then examining his watch for the umpteenth time. "I'll have to go and look for him."

The other man took one last pull on his cigarette then crushed it beneath his foot. "Ok, there's no point in me waiting about, I'll lock up and be on my way." He held out a tobacco stained hand to Tudor. "Pleasure doing business with you Mr Gruffydd."

Tudor shook the man's hand. "Perhaps I'll be back for one of those," he nodded towards the Daimler charabanc and four Napier buses.

"Then you'll be disappointed they're not for sale."

Nerys rose to meet Tudor as he approached. "Do you know where he is?" He asked irritably as soon as he was within earshot.

"He went to meet you over an hour ago."

"Well he can't be lost I can see the shed from here, and the pubs are shut cause its Sunday, so where's the dull bugger got to?"

Nerys indignantly jumped to Rhys' defence, "Don't you call him a dull bugger, I'm sure he has a good reason for not being there."

"Aye, like I said, he's bloody twp." Tudor muttered as he turned and strode back to where the vehicles were parked.

"Fucking hell where you been?" Tudor made no effort to conceal his annoyance.

"I'm sorry I got waylaid." Was the only explanation offered. "This what we came for?" Rhys motioned towards the bus.

Tudor decided showing off his acquisition was more important than wrangling with Rhys. "Aye what you think of her?"

"Very nice, but what do you want with it?"

Tudor said proudly. "She's a Maxwell sixteen horsepower." Running his hand lovingly over the bonnet. "It did have fourteen seats but they were taken out and it's been used as a delivery van. I know it's a bit of a mess inside but Elfed the chippie is going to help me make and fit seats, and by next summer I'll be running trips here, and a daily service from our village into town."

Rhys viewed the inside of bus with distaste. "Smells like it's been used to keep pigs in, which one do you want me to drive?"

"You think you can handle this?" Tudor gestured towards the Maxwell, then seeing the flicker of doubt in the others expression he added. "Of course if you'd prefer the van? Only be careful I'd hate to return it dented."

"Better that than the bus getting damaged." Rhys joked. "It doesn't matter to me which, I can't drive either. You'll have to show me what to do."

While Rhys gripped the steering wheel as if he were preventing it breaking off, Tudor stood behind him clinging firmly to the back of the seat, and bellowing instructions as they jerked their way around the yard, dodging various piles and items of scattered debris until finally they arrived back alongside the van.

"Switch of the motor a minute there's something I've been meaning to ask you."

Rhys turned off the engine and waited.

"It's a bit awkward." The colour rising in Tudor's face.

"Before you ask, I can't marry you I'm spoken for." Rhys wisecracked.

Ignoring Rhys Tudor said dryly, "But Gwen's single."

"You're asking me if you can marry Gwen? You sly dog I thought you were a confirmed bachelor."

"No, not if I can marry her."

"I don't like the sound of this, i'm not sure if your intentions are decent?" Rhys' initial amazement had turned to amusement.

"Yes, no, Oh for Christ's sake shut up."

61

Rhys wiped his hand over his face to disguise his huge grin. "Ok start again, but I warn you I don't like the sound of it so far."

"Well I wondered if it was too soon for me to ask her out, you know after Gomer?"

"There's only one person can answer that and you'll have to ask her."

"You won't mind?"

"Why should I mind? My brother's not around anymore," Rhys' tone saddened momentarily. "But Gwen has a life to get on with, you mind you treat her right."

Nerys sat on a straw filled sack along side him. "I don't believe you just let him go what's Gwen going to say?" She looked up at him while the question hung in the air. Rhys didn't take his eyes from the road or the van with the children waving to him through the back windows, he wished he'd waited to tell her about Iwan until they got home; he needed all his concentration to drive.

"What the dickens was I supposed to do I couldn't force him?"

Nerys new he was right, at least he'd found a café and made sure Iwan had a hot meal inside him. "Why won't he come home?"

"Rhys was getting fed up with repeatedly answering the same questions. "I told you he wouldn't say, all he said was he came to Porthcawl because he remembered me talking about the ship, and he thought he'd be able to sign on one and go to sea."

"But why on earth does he want to go to sea? It's a good job ships don't come in there anymore or God knows where he'd have ended up."

"Well he didn't know that anymore than we did, he wouldn't say where he was going and to be honest I don't think he knew. I made sure he wasn't hungry and gave him what money I had, I couldn't do any more could I?"

"No I suppose not, but you haven't said what we are going to tell Gwen?" Nerys wished she'd seen him, she'd have made him come home.

Rhys thought for a moment before he answered almost in a whisper, "How about the truth."

They travelled a few more miles, each immersed in their own thoughts, until Rhys' sudden outburst of laughter broke the silence.

"What's so funny?"

"Tudor fancies Gwen."

"He what?"

Chapter Six
Friday December 25th 1925

Last Year had been bad enough her first Christmas without Gomer, but this year was even worse because Iwan wasn't there either. Gwen considered the girl carrying the chicken alongside her, if only she didn't look so much like him, did she love or hate her? No she couldn't hate her she hated him; sometimes she resented her but for what? It wasn't her fault she'd done nothing, and no matter how hard Gwen tried she could never be loved the same as Iwan. Gwen had surprised herself on how successful she'd been in concealing the truth, but now all she had left was a lie and this time everyone would know, how could she lie now?

"Why do we take the chicken to the bakery to be cooked?" It seemed strange to Mari when everything else was cooked at home.

"Two reasons, so everyone can see we're not having a pigs head, and because we didn't have an oven when we lived in bottom row, and Rhodri only charged tu'pence.

"But that was before I was born."

Yes, and it's still only tu'pence, you want me to carry it?" Gwen held out her hands but failed to take a proper hold, horrified they watched their dinner hit the ground with a dull thud and relieve itself of its limbs, the dish spun like a top finally coming to rest with a loud clatter on the cobbles, fortunately still intact.

"I thought you had it Mam." Mari automatically attempted to exonerate herself.

Gwen bent down and scooped the chicken back onto the dish carefully brushing away the particles of grime and grit. "We'll put the legs on and say Rhodri overcooked it, nobody will know." She carefully arranged the pieces so it once again resembled a chicken. "Wasn't your fault love, I was miles away."

"Thinking about Iwan?"

"Yes it's Christmas and he should be here, I miss him."

"Me to." Mari took hold of the dish. "I think it's safer with me."

Gwen had to agree. "You'd best get it home before anything else happens."

Rhys sat on the front step looking at his present and wondered where he would hang it. For the time being he'd keep it with his other treasured possession, the one that held the pearls and glass beads, Moira's box. He'd been irritated at the boy's rudeness when they'd laughed after Nerys gave it to him. He thought it was the best present anyone could ever have. It was the first Christmas present he'd had from Nerys and the first he'd ever had since he was a child. Gently he wiped the specks of dust that had dared to settle on the glass, she was still as beautiful as the day they married. Finding the fee for a photographer then had been out of the question and without Gwen and

65

Gomer's support the wedding would have been a meagre affair. He put the glass to his lips and kissed her.

"That'll be worn out," Gwen teased as she and Mari approached unnoticed.

Rhys mimicked a naughty child caught in the act as he innocently sat bolt upright. "Didn't see you coming."

"We guessed that."

Mari tried to ease his embarrassment. "It's a lovely photograph." She'd walked the four miles to the studio with Nerys for the sitting and again to collect it.

Washing dishes was women's work, and anyway there seemed to be some tension between Nerys and Gwen, he'd give them a chance to sort it out. Rhys settled back contentedly against the shed taking a deep draw on his cigarette, watching Alice foraging through the peelings.

"You're a lucky old girl, and you've got me into a lot of trouble." She took no notice, unaware that she should have been today's dinner for quite a number of villagers. Rhys had gained popularity with Mari for refusing to slaughter Alice, but the people who'd been promised joints and had their money refunded were more than slightly aggrieved. He'd hated killing the chicken, the pitiful way its eyes looked at him as it hung tied by its feet from the washing line, while a steady drip converted the grass beneath to a bright red glaze. The memory prevented him eating any and he'd contented himself watching the others enjoying the meat, with the exception of Mari who refused to eat animals of any kind. His peace was interrupted by the noisy arrival of the two boys and Mari, Huw and Elis had been up extra early and were tired and quarrelsome, Huw danced in front of the shorter Elis holding the whip high out of

66

reach, while Elis gripping the tops tightly against his chest with one hand, struggled vainly to reach.

"Dad, tell him," Elis whined.

"If you two are going to quarrel do it somewhere else, I came here for some peace and quiet."

They both new by his tone not to argue, and sped off yelling at each other. Mari sat thoughtfully beside him.

"Do you know what's up, is it something I've done?"   She asked.

"What do you mean?"

Mari shivered and pulled her coat tighter around her. "Oh nothing it doesn't matter. " She shivered again and stood up, "I'm going back to the house it's too cold here."

"You're right it is, I'll come with you."

Rhys pulled the gate closed. "What's bothering you?"

"Well every time I go into a room with mam and Nerys if they're talking they go quiet as if I've interrupted something, I feel as if I'm being whispered about."

"It's not anything to do with you, they do the same to me and nan."

"When we were washing up they couldn't wait to get rid of me."

"Where was nan?"

"Asleep, why?"

"They probably wanted to discuss what ever it is they're keeping from us. They'll tell us when they're ready, if you're that worried I'll ask Nerys about it tonight."

Maude and the children were in bed when Rhys made the decision to confront the sisters. "I don't know what the big secret is but it's upsetting Mari and I think your mother has noticed as well, if you don't want to tell us it's fine by me, but it's not fair to have Mari worrying she's being blamed for something."

Gwen's cheeks flushed as Nerys spoke, "You might as well say now it's got to come out sooner or later."

Gwen sat down by the table her words, "I'm expecting," struck Rhys like a punch in the chest. "Well say something if it's only to call me a tramp." Bewildered he looked towards Nerys for aide.

"She's about three months."

The only word coming to Rhys' mind was how? But he knew how. "Does Tudor know?" He finally asked.

Gwen's redness deepened. "No and don't you tell him, it's not his."

Rhys turned again to Nerys who shrugged her shoulders. "She won't even tell me who it is."

"I'll never tell anyone, so there's no point keeping on about it."

"Who else knows, does the father know? Rhys queried.

"No, anyway he won't care and you're only worried about what people will say. I know I've let everyone down, let Gomer down?"

As her tears gushed freely, Rhys haunted by flashbacks of Moira put his arm around her.

"It's not the end of the world."

Neither Rhys nor Nerys slept very well that night, both tossing and turning knowing full well that life for the family was about to alter. The gossips had made life unbearable after Moira's death particularly for his parents; he remembered the fights he'd got into at sixteen because of the callous teasing. Thank God Iwan wasn't here, but how would Mari and his sons cope with the snide remarks and sniggers from behind hands held in front of overworked mouths, why should they have to go through that? And then there was Pryce, he'd have a field day, exposing Gwen's shame in front of the village from the pious sanctity of his pulpit, while the self righteous deacons nodded in agreement as the whole family had it's nose rubbed in the dirt. He couldn't let that happen there had to be another way.

"But where do you think she could go?" Nerys didn't like the idea of packing Gwen off.

"I don't know I haven't thought that far, it's just an idea." Rhys wished he'd got it straight in his own mind before saying anything.

"Don't talk about me as if I'm not here, I do have a say in it."

"Well what do you think Gwen?"

"I think it's a good idea, no one would know and it would save a lot of bother."

"Who's being a bother?" Maude asked as she entered the kitchen.

Nerys moved over to the hob and lifted the kettle. "Sit down Mam, I'll make you a cuppa, you're going to need it.

Early in the New Year Gwen slipped discreetly from the village; no one openly queried why she'd suddenly gone to visit Maude's sister Enid, there was some speculation as to why she hadn't taken Mari with her. It was only the older villagers that had any recollection of Enid leaving the area half a century before to go into service with a family near Llandeilo.

"So your Aunt Enid is your family skeleton? Christ I think every one in this village is hiding something." Rhys wasn't as shocked as he pretended, after all his own family had their dirty washing aired in public long ago, and half the village's favourite pastime seemed to be trying to discover and expose the remainders secrets, and vice versa.

"Yes usual tale, young girl fell for a traveller's sweet talk and when he moved on he left something behind."

"What happened to the baby?"

"Still born."

"So how did she end up with a big house in Rhydamman?"

"She married a local shopkeeper, a widower a lot older than her and he was quite well off, they never had children though he had some by his first wife. That's all I know."

"So she married into a business and became lady of a big house?" I can't believe you never told me before."

Nerys looked slightly perplexed. "Don't know why I didn't, I've never given it much thought, probably because I've never met her, I don't even know where Rhydamman is, it all seemed a bit remote."

"And all this time I've been married into a wealthy family." Rhys joked.

"Aye, but the poor side." Maude opened her eyes she'd been awake for a while listening.

"How much older than you is she, Mam?" Rhys asked as she moved to make room for him to sit by the fire.

"Four years, I was twelve when she told me she'd fallen, my dad hit the roof, big chapel man very strict even after I was married." She cast her mind back, then chuckled. "Wasn't willing for me and Gwyl to be alone, wanted Gwyl to sleep downstairs and used me and Megan sharing a room as an excuse. Megan said she didn't mind sleeping downstairs but he wouldn't hear of it." She laughed again. "Until we went and got rooms with old widow Beynon who lived the other side of the village, then he came and ordered us back home."

70

"Who is Megan?" Rhys had never heard of her before either.

"My younger sister she died when she was eleven with consumption."

After a brief reverent silence Nerys continued. "How did Enid end up in Rhydamman?"

"My mother had a cousin there who was unable to have children of her own, her and her husband were going to bring the child up as theirs."

"They must have been terribly disappointed when it was stillborn?"

"Disappointed huh, relieved more like it, they didn't want a black kid and they soon got rid of Enid, didn't exactly throw her out but made her unwelcome."

"Black! You never said it was black."

"As midnight."

Rhys was absorbed with the conversation and was about to ask why she didn't come home but Nerys was ahead of him.

"My father wouldn't have her back, and I don't think she wanted to come anyway. She got a job looking after the local shopkeeper's children, two boys one was five the other a baby barely a year old, in no time she married him, and that's about it.

"And they didn't have any children of their own?" Despite already having been told Nerys wanted it confirmed she didn't have any cousins.

"No they weren't married long, no more than a couple o' three years when he died, Enid brought up the children by herself.

"And you've never been to see her?" Rhys queried.

"No nor her me, we write once or twice a year Easter and Christmas mainly, I'd like to see her again before I go."

"No rush then." Rhys added light heartedly, before turning to a more serious problem. "Tudor keeps asking me for Gwen's address, he can't understand why she's not written to him and I don't know what to tell him."

"Why she told him she was only going for a few weeks I don't know." Nerys' comment was directed at her mother.

"We thought he'd forget her, after all they weren't serious, she only saw him a few times."
Maude's underestimation of Tudor feelings rankled with Rhys.

"Well she may not have been, but Tudor seems to be under a different impression, he reckons he's going to drive over to Rhydamman and see her."

"He's not is he?" Nerys and Maude both looked horrified.

"He will, when he gets something in his head it takes a lot of shifting."

"She'll have to write to him and soon." Nerys looked again to her mother. "We'd better write and tell her."

"If it's not too late, he's already asked Owain for a loan of his van."

"You got to stop him Rhys."

He gestured, his hands held out with palms upwards. "And how am I supposed to do that?"

Tudor had expected a more positive response from Rhys, after all how often did someone offer to take his family to see relatives?

"Its not that we don't want to go, only I think we should let Gwen know we're coming, and have you thought Enid might not like us all turning up uninvited."

"Ok I see your point." Rhys' hopes that he was making progress were soon thwarted as Tudor added, "Perhaps it would be better if I went alone."

"You're going then?"

"Yep, to true I am. Owain said he'd lend me the van if I do the next service for free, and I'm not giving him the chance to change his mind. You're welcome to come if you want."

"Have you considered that Gwen might not want to see you, and that's why she has stayed away and not written? After all she's been gone over three months, and if she wanted to hear from you she would have got in touch. Perhaps she doesn't think as much of you as you do her."

Rhys wished he hadn't been so forthright; Tudor looked both hurt and embarrassed his anger spilling into his voice.

"I've known Gwen since we were that high." Holding his hand below waist level. "And she's not the type to just bugger off without an explanation, so don't tell me there's nothing, you're hiding something."

"Maybe she needs time and she's still missing Gomer, that's all I'm saying." Rhys' attempt to minimise his earlier statement made little impact.

"I don't know what you're trying to say Rhys, but whatever it is I don't believe you, I think you're lying and I'll find out the truth on Sunday.

"Before you go rushing off to Rhydamman go and have talk with Nerys and her mother."

"Why, what they going to say?"

"You'll find out when you ask them."

Nerys was slightly taken back to see Tudor when she opened the door. "Rhys is not here he's down the allotment Alice is not well her arthritis is worse its this weather I've never known so much rain it's a wonder we're all not washed away." Only when she paused for breath did she realise she was blabbering.

"I'm fine Nerys nice of you to ask, how are you?" Tudor said cheekily. "I've just left Rhys, he suggested I should come and see you."

Nerys tried to regain her composure, "What on earth for?"

"I don't think he'd want me standing on the doorstep discussing it."

"I'm sorry making you stand in the rain, come in." The particles of mud Tudor kicked from his boots against the step, formed brown rivulets in the cobbles.

"You can take them off right there, I'm not having a trail of mud through the house."

Tudor reluctantly slipped off his boots, revealing a pair of toeless socks.

"I was going to throw them away when I took them off." He said as if that made them acceptable.

"Well there's nothing there to darn, take them off you can have a pair of Rhys'."

Nerys went to the dresser took a pair of thick woollen socks from the draw and tossed them to him. "Here put those on."

"I wanted to ask you about Gwen? " Tudor sat holding his old socks.

"Give them here let me get rid of them before they walk out on their own." She took the socks and tossed them on the fire, then crossed the room and shut the door that lead to the stairway. "I know, but I can't tell you a lot I've written to her asking her to write to you, you should have a letter next week."

74

"I'll see her before then I'm going to visit Sunday."

"Why don't you wait a week see what she says in her letter? Just turning up there could be a waste of time."

Tudor shook his head. "Why won't you tell me what's going on? I know there's something and I'll find out anyway in a couple of days."

"You want a cup of tea?"

"No thanks just the truth."

"Then I'm going to need one." As Nerys turned towards the hob the back door opened and Mari appeared.

"Hello Mr Gruffydd."

"Hello Mari, I'm just asking your Aunty Nerys if she wants to come and see your mother Sunday."

Mari immediately became excited. "Can we, are we going to see her?"

Nerys' glare told Tudor he'd spoken out of turn, why just added to the mystery.

"We don't know if we're going yet, I'll have to talk to Uncle Rhys, now take this tea into nan, and let me and Tudor have a chat." Nerys waited until she'd left the room before she turned on him. "Thanks that's just great, trust you to open your mouth in front of her."

"I only asked her if she wanted to see her mother, what's wrong with that?"

"I'll tell you what's wrong."

"I think it's about time someone did."

"Oh Tudor why couldn't you just let it be?" She sat opposite him. "There's no easy way to say this, if I told you Gwen doesn't want to see you again what would you do?"

"I'd go and ask her why on Sunday."

75

"I thought as much," she took a deep breath. "Gwen left because she didn't want to bring shame on this family, she's having a baby." The colour drained from his face and he sat motionless, Nerys reached across the table and caught his hand breaking the spell.

"A, a, and she thought I wouldn't stand by her?" He stuttered.

"You're not the father."

If he heard he wasn't listening and leapt from his seat. "I'm buggered if I'm going to wait till Sunday I'll go tomorrow, I'll take the flipping bus."

Guiltily Rhys made his way from the allotment, aware he should have gone to the house with Tudor and not left it to Nerys. She was busy with the children's tea but found time to give him a, you wait until later look, but there was more to worry about than the edge of Nerys' tongue. Trouble at home and even bigger trouble at work, the government had accepted the report of the Samuel Commission to withdraw subsidies, with a recommendation miner's wages should be reduced by between ten and twenty five percent while the working day was lengthened. The prospect of a lock out had become almost a certainty, as the deadline for compliance with the mine owners terms loomed closer; people were going to have much more to concern them than Gwen's morals.

Chapter Seven
Sunday 25th April 1926

Plas Amman

Rhodfa Garnant

Rhydamman

16th April

Dearest Tudor,

I'm sorry I haven't written before, I've not had much practise at writing letters, and this is the hardest I've ever had to write. I've sat down several times and tried to put pen to paper, but find the result is never what I intended to say. This time however if I'm again not able to express myself as I wish, I'll still send the letter because you deserve to know the truth. I am extremely ashamed of myself and would dearly love to be able to go back and undo what I have done. If you are wondering if you are the father, because of that one time when I came to your house, then put it out of your mind. No matter how much I would have wished it to be true, I didn't know then, but I do now that I was already with child. There is no possibility that the baby is yours. I cannot ever reveal the identity of the father for reasons I can't possibly explain, except to say, this child was not conceived through love, although I will love it when it is born, because a baby cannot be accountable for the sins of its parents. I'm sorry for any pain I've caused you, and believe me I am truly very fond of you. I can see no benefit in you coming to see me or contacting me, as what is done cannot be altered. I know you are a good man and will not seek revenge out of spite, so I beg you keep the reasons for my departure from Pentre to yourself, not for me but for the sake of my family, who have caused you no hurt. I wish you well in all you do.

I'm so sorry.

Gwen.

Tudor had read the letter over and over and could have repeated word for word from memory. His first emotion had been anger and he'd screwed it up and discarded it, only to later retrieve it from the hearth where it had luckily fallen when he'd aimed it at the fire. He'd intended driving over to Rhydamman on Wednesday afternoon the day he'd received it, but he'd been unable to obtain the parts necessary to complete the overhaul on the bus's engine. He'd known it made sense to wait until he could borrow Owain's van, and no matter what argument he had found to the contrary he'd had no choice. Carefully he folded the creased letter and put it in his inside jacket pocket, in a few hours he'd have all his questions answered, wouldn't he?

"They'll be here soon didn't Nerys say about midday in her letter? It's gone half past now." Enid seemed as anxious as Gwen but for different reasons, why she'd left it so long was unexplainable, she'd had time and the desire to visit her sister but for many years, she'd put it off afraid that the people of Gelli had long memories, eventually it became something she'd do one day, subconsciously aware she never would.

Gwen's stomach churned at the prospect of having to explain, not to Tudor though that was going to be tough, it was Mari whom she feared facing. She stiffened at the sound of tyres crunching on the gravel drive, then the slamming of doors, she held her breath and waited for the bell. She controlled the urge to hide when she heard the voices in the hall, sitting stiffly upright in her chair she waited, the door suddenly flew open and Mari came bursting into the room flinging her arms around her mother's neck.

Rhys would like to have gone to Rhydamman he was curious about Maude's sister and where she lived, what he hadn't relished witnessing was the confrontation of Tudor and Gwen. It was no surprise to the others when he volunteered to stay at home with the boys, reasoning at least three of them would attend chapel.

Huw and Elis didn't understand why they couldn't all go, and why chapel was so important, a ride in a van was far more exciting than listening to boring old Pryce. After their initial protests, and having watched the van

79

pull away without them, they sulkily made their way toward the allotment. Left behind with orders to muck out Alice, and then get scrubbed for chapel, could the day get any worse? They dawdled over their chores but discovered new motivation when their father and Mrs Harri paid then a visit. Huw noticed the unease between his father and Mrs Harri, whom he had never liked since the time she clipped him around the ear when he had an urgent need to relieve himself against her garden wall.

Later while on their way to chapel Huw asked, "Dad, why did Mrs Harri come to see Alice?"

"Well it is her pig."

"Then why don't she come and clean her out?"

"We look after her so we get a share in her when she's." Rhys couldn't bring himself to say it.

"When she's killed?" Elis could.

"You're not going to kill her, are you?" Huw was horrified.

"I'm not, but Mrs Harri knows someone who will."

"You can't let them." Elis again chirped in.

"Not down to me son, I'll do my best to talk her out of it but Mrs Harri won't leave it to me again, I let her down Christmas."

"Well we won't eat her," said emphatically defiant Huw.

If Huw and Elis were upset at the prospect of Alice's slaughter then Mari would be absolutely distraught. Rhys wished he'd never taken on the blasted animal, without Doc Richards agreeing to provide a constant supply of aspirin in return for the promise of a sizable joint, Alice would have been dinner a long time ago.

For once Rhys was glad to be inside Saron Chapel, even Pryce's sermon was sure to be easier on the ear than the boys concerns for

Alice's welfare. The service started with a hymn then a short prayer and a second hymn, before Pryce started his oration.

"Why is it that some people in this village, in this chapel, think the Lord is blind to their sins. Do they think that the sins they commit are lesser sins than those of others? Or that God will overlook their waywardness because he is a loving God? Yes God is a God of love, a benevolent God, but only to those who repent, and seek his clemency. Jesus taught us to turn the other cheek, but ask yourselves can we expect God to continually turn the other cheek to our transgressions? Jesus said, 'let he who is without sin cast the first stone', if you are without sin then you are truly unique, but if you have been casting stones, are you without sin?"

Pryce scanned the room his piercing gaze lingering in turn on each of the congregation, until they lowered their eyes from his. "Yes I have heard whispers, heard rumours." He pointed to the row of sanctimonious deacons seated on the pew reserved exclusively for the chapel hierarchy. "Even the servants of this house, God's house have been sniggering, the poison seeping from their partially open lips. Is that how God has taught us to behave? I challenge each and every one of you if you believe you are as Jesus Christ without sin then step forth and expose who it is that has been the topic of the illicit conversations. Reveal who it is that has brought shame upon themselves, upon their family, upon the village and upon this chapel, our chapel, your chapel, my chapel, God's chapel." He paused, his passion inflamed eyes scanning each member of the congregation in turn, affirming his authority. "Then the burden is mine, as I am God's minister, and as his chosen envoy I must in his name pursue salvation for all those that have fallen by the wayside. Once more it falls again on my mortal shoulders to do what is necessary, for regrettably so often in the past I have had to endure this task. It is my duty, nay my mission to unearth and challenge iniquity and immorality, an undertaking in which I gain no pleasure save that of being a bridge, a bridge by which a sinner can cross from wickedness to salvation, and for them I am prepared to bear the arduous weight of their malevolence. You are all witness to our Lord having again selected me to do his bidding, and once more I am disposed to be his alacritous but feeble servant."

 Breaking off for a moment he took his handkerchief from his top pocket and wiped the rivulets of perspiration from his face. "It would be difficult to be unaware of the scandal that has gripped the community during the past week; even word of it has reached the ears of my lady wife, a fine virtuous woman, who has been an example to us all in the manner she conducts herself, by strictly living according to the good book." He held the Bible aloft, his piercing eyes locking onto one person. "Come forward and admit your errors, throw yourself at the Lords feet and beg his mercy through me, and through me our Lord will illustrate his abundant compassion, he will forgive your lapses by showing you the path to deliverance and true contentment. You have been weak and forsaken his teaching and like Eve have led some unfortunate feeble man astray, and conceived out of wedlock. But God's generosity knows no bounds and he'll welcome the child you bear into his church, and it will not be judged for the sins of its mother."

Catrin Williams didn't wait to hear anymore and fled sobbing out of the chapel; Pryce was committed to finishing and bellowed even louder.

"Catrin Williams you've chosen not to take God into your heart and declined his compassion, but God and I will wait for no one can survive in this world or the next without him." The door slammed closed, Pryce lowered the Bible and spoke in a sombre authoritative tone. "So that Catrin can be brought back to God's teaching, and for him to reclaim her tormented soul, she shall be excluded by this righteous congregation, shunned by all, no one should speak to her or offer her shelter or sustenance, her family must cast her out until she accepts the Lord and humbles herself in front of him. I will be here to help her when she comes, as she will, but the greater the moral and physical influence we exert on her will be for her benefit, and thus it will be sooner she'll seek God, and redemption."

Before he had finished speaking Rhys leapt from his seat charged up the aisle and flung the chapel door open so hard the handle made a deep impression in the mortar.

Huw and Elis ran to catch up with him. "Wait for us, Dad."

"You boys go straight home, change your clothes and wait for me."

"Why, Dad, where you going?"

"I have something to do, now do as you're told."

Huw and Elis had never seen him in this mood, his expression told them something was dreadfully wrong, and if they weren't careful finding out what could be painful.

Rhys went in the direction he suspected she'd gone, in his youth he hadn't been wise enough to anticipate Moira's intentions but he was determined history wouldn't repeat itself. He found her wading into the river at Penny Well, the water already up to her neck when he reached her. She struggled kicking and arms flailing, but he was too strong and lifted her easily, carrying her to safety high up on the grassy bank.

Nerys looked about the hallway while Enid and Maude hugged tearfully. She'd never been near anywhere so grand, the half Wainscot panelled walls led up a wide oak staircase accessing a large balcony landing. From the high coved ceilings on both floors the cut glass chandeliers deluged the halls and stairway with a scintillating vibrancy.

"This is my youngest." Her mother's introduction jerked Nerys back into reality and moving cordially forward she gently took Enid's offered hand.

"Nice to meet you at last, mam's told me so much about you."

Enid smiled. "Has she now."

Maude introduced Tudor who felt an uncomfortable outsider in this family reunion.

"We'll all go and see Gwen then we shall leave her and Tudor alone they have much to discuss." suggested Enid.

Gwen embraced her mother and Nerys, but her eyes were fixed firmly on Tudor, as he hovered just inside the door.

"Come along lets give these two a chance to talk, you can tell me what's been happening in Gelli and Pentre all these past years." Enid ushered Mari and the two women across the hallway into another room. "Make yourselves comfortable I'll go and organise some tea. It's Lowri the housekeeper's half day off, but she has prepared a tray for us."

Mari could hardly wait for the door to close. "Mam's having a baby why didn't any one tell me?

"Your mother asked us not to, not for a while anyway, she wanted to tell you herself when she was sure." Nery's tried to assure Mari she hadn't been excluded.

"What does Tudor think about being a father?"

Nerys and Maude exchanged a questioning glance. Maude spoke first.

"Your mother is telling him now, I hope he'll be pleased but you'll have to ask her."

"I don't suppose he's come all this way for our benefit," added Nerys.

Mari fell silent, as the door opened and Enid entered carrying a tray.

"Help yourselves." She placed the tray on a small table in the bay window. "I'll just pop some in for Gwen."

Tudor stayed silent long after Enid had left. He stared unseeing out of the window, and wondered how posh people sliced the bread so thin, and why sandwiches were cut into triangles? One bite and it was gone.

"Sugar?" Gwen offered him the sugar bowl.

"No thanks I've cut it out," he said prodding his thickening waistline. "Anyway it looks like it will soon be a luxury."

"At least you'll have your bus to fall back on."

"And who's going to ride on it if they're not in work?"

They fell silent again, Tudor put down his cup stood up and paced to the window.

"How can I expect you to come back to Pentre with me when you can live like this?" He motioned with his hand. "I've never seen such a fine house let alone been in one."

"I'm here only as long as my aunt will put up with me, I don't think she sees it as a permanent arrangement."

"Then come back with me, I love you Gwen and I'll be a good father." He stooped in front of her almost on his knees.

"Why haven't you asked me who the father is?"

"Because you'd tell me if you wanted, and it's not that important to me, I haven't come here to accuse or blame you, I'm here because I want you I always have, I'll look after you and the child just say you'll marry me."

"In time you might resent me and the baby and think I've married you just to give the child a name."

"No Gwen, I know you have feelings for me perhaps not as strong as mine for you, but you wouldn't use me like that."

"Wouldn't I? If I wasn't like this." She patted her stomach. "I may have even asked you to marry me, but I am and it's more complicated than you can imagine."

"I promise you I won't imagine I'll just accept. There's no way I'm letting you go the future will be pointless."

"If only."

"No ifs, it can be you, me, Mari and the baby, a proper family."

"More tea?" Enid held the pot above her sister's cup

"Please." Maude swallowed the last of her sandwich. "And where are your stepsons now?

"The eldest Joshua takes care of the businesses, I have little involvement with any of the stores or the undertakers, funeral directors he calls it. He comes once a week to keep me informed as if I'm still in charge, but we both know who's at the helm, I was only ever caretaker until the boys came of age. His family are grown up, though I don't think they ever saw a lot of him what with the business, council work and various committees. He's due to become mayor again next year, so that will take even more of his time."

Mari studied the ceiling once again, she'd come to see her mother and had only been allowed a brief few minutes before being ushered away. "Can I go and see the garden?"

"I'm sorry we must be boring you, us old women wittering on, of course you can."

"And the other son where is he doesn't he help?"

"Dewi, I don't know, I haven't heard from him for nigh on thirty years. He disappeared owing money too nearly every public house in the

86

town, and leaving two girls pregnant. One here in Rhydamman and another just up the road in Bonllwyn, she went away, her family refused any offer of help and has never acknowledged me since. There was talk he was messing with a married woman from Llandybie, and her husband had threatened to kill him if he caught up with him, I think he'd have been at the back of very long queue. I paid the debts, more for this family's sake than his, I haven't heard from him since, and if I'm honest I hope I never do. Dewi gave the Jenkins family a bad name, and a lot of locals used poor Joshua as a whipping boy for a long time, perhaps that's what gave him the determination to succeed."

"What happened to the other girl?"

"Lowri became my housekeeper her son has grown up and has a family of his own; he does a few days a week in my garden just to keep it tidy."

"She never married?"

"No she only ever loved one man, and was convinced one day he'd come back for her."

Pulling the front door closed behind her Mari looked up deciding there was little prospect of rain from the thistledown floating high above, and wandered around the side of the house where a leafy pergola ran through the centre of the walled garden. She didn't hear him because of the rustling foliage awakening in the gentle spring breeze.

"Hello." She jumped at the sound of the unexpected voice. "I'm sorry if I startled you." A freckled face crowned by a mop of ginger hair poked it's self through a gap between the climbing shrubs.

"Oh! I didn't see you."

"Hang on I'll come around." Within seconds a red headed gangly youth entered the pergola. "My names Geraint, my father looks

87

after the garden and sometimes I help him." He explained as he steered Mari towards a wooden bench.

"Where's your dad now?"

"Said he was going to see to the rose beds, while I tidied up here. You with the grocer?"

Mari puzzled for a moment and laughed. "The van, yes I came in the van but we're not grocers, my mam's staying with," she paused thoughtfully. "I suppose it's my Great Aunt Enid, we borrowed the van to visit."

"Your mam she's Mrs Morgan then?"

"Yes and I'm Mari."

She had lost track of the time, she was here to see her mother not flirt with the gardener's son, he was nice though, in a funny sort of way, and even if he was younger than her he seemed a lot more mature than older boys she knew. She slipped in through the back door made her way to the room she'd left over an hour earlier, only now her mother and Tudor had joined Nerys Maude and Enid.

"Mari." She felt the comfort of her mother's arms around her once more. "I've something to tell you." Mari viewed the smiling faces of her great aunt, her nan, and Nerys, but it was Tudor who held the largest grin, and she anticipated her mother's next sentence.

Both Nerys and Rhys spent a sleepless night tossing and turning, aware of the others restlessness but neither wanting to talk. Nerys lay reproaching herself for doubting Rhys, and not instantly placing him above suspicion for the condition of the girl sharing Mari's room. Of course he wasn't she told herself for the hundredth time, his explanation had been perfectly plausible. The idea was ridiculous but each time she relaxed her mind wandered into the realm of ifs, buts and maybes.

Rhys' reoccurring dream woke him once more. In it Moira and Catrin became intertwined, and it was Moira he carried from the water, Moira whose life he had saved, Moira who wept on his shoulder while he told her everything would be all right and he'd not let anyone harm her again. Each time he woke the pain was as intense as that felt by a lad of sixteen, and reality proved more graphic than any dream, Moira was dead.

Chapter Eight

Saturday 1st May 1926

I feared it would come to this, the pits shut and the men have been locked out. Pryce is drawing up a rota for us officials to carry out safety inspections, so hopefully there'll still be work when it's all over." Rhys tossed his tommy box and water jack onto the table. "Christ almighty what a bloody mess."

"Does it make that much difference if it's a lock out or a strike? It's the same which ever way you look at it." Nerys pushed Rhys' things aside and set a mug of tea in their stead.

"Aye, but with a lock out the bosses are calling the tune, shows they aren't bothered if the pits working or not. Pryce reckons that the owners are out of pocket and will be better off with the pits shut."

"Pryce will say what he's told, he's just a mouthpiece, the owner's puppet."

"There's a meeting outside the Gwalia at eleven."

Nerys poured herself a mug and sat opposite him. "Why there, it's an unusual place to have a meeting?"

"Owain, Mostyn and Doc Richards are the only ones in the village with a wireless, apart from Pryce and a couple of his cronies, and the union are making an announcement."

"Hasn't Elfed got one in the Bell?"

"Aye, but he reckons it's broke."

"Bet if it was during opening time it would soon be mended. So what they going to say?"

"If I knew that there'd be no need for me to go," Rhys said derisively.

Allowing for his anxiety Nerys let it pass. "Will you be back in time to go with Tudor?"

"I doubt it, anyway I expect they'd like some time alone."

"No chance of that, I'm going and Mari's not being left behind."

"You think it's a good idea Gwen coming back before the baby's born?

"With a baby or one on the way there'll be no denying the gossipmongers, they'll have their day no matter what."

"I know it's been awkward for you having Catrin here."

"Awkward's not the word I'd use, then what did you expect running out of the chapel after a pregnant young girl and bringing her back here?"

"I expected you to understand."

"Oh I do," then added with a shade of irony. "It's the rest of the village that needs convincing."

"Not only them, don't forget Pryce."

"I realize why you did it. Thank God you did no one else would have, Pryce had made sure of that."

"Pryce is setting up a work rota, I'll be at the back of the queue because I went against him and he won't forget it."

91

Her knuckles whitened as her fingers tightened around her mug.

"That's all we need," she sighed. Then instilling some sham enthusiasm into her voice. "Would it matter if you missed the meeting you'll hear all about it soon enough? And we could all go with Tudor there's plenty of room on the bus, it will be nice to get away from the village for a few hours."

Rhys knew she was right; it would be good to forget work, Catrin and Pryce for a while. He slid his hand across the table and clasped hers. "I'll go and tell the boys to get scrubbed." Before closing the back door he popped his head back around. "Has Enid got a wireless?"

Catrin's knuckles rapped again on the brown painted door that remained firmly closed, all her life she couldn't remember it ever being bolted. The response had been similar when Rhys had brought her here last Sunday, except this time she heard her father's subdued voice telling her sister to be quiet. With her head bowed she hurried back to her refuge, not glancing at the villagers who turned their backs and spoke in overstated whispers. Responsive to her anguish Maude rose from her chair and put her arms round the girl as she entered the kitchen.

"They'll come round love just give them some time."

"No they won't they hate me, everyone hates me." She nestled closer tears flooding from her owl like brown eyes. "They wouldn't even speak to me."

"I know love, I know," Maude sighed remembering how her father had been with Enid.

"If I stay here and have the baby the gossip will be even worse when I come home, so it's better me and Tudor are seen as a couple and when the baby's born the scandal will have run its course." Gwen moved over for Nerys to sit alongside her.

Tudor nodded his agreement as he moved the bus out through the gates of Plas Amman. "Pryce will never allow us to be married in his chapel, not without a public humiliation or making us beg his forgiveness."

A wry smile crossed Gwen's face and she spoke loudly, so Tudor could hear her above the noise of the engine. "Maybe he will then maybe he won't, and maybe we won't give him the satisfaction. Anyway I always thought it was God who did the forgiving, and even Pryce can't stop us going into town, to the registry."

Tudor laughed, causing him to be careless as he released the clutch, jerking the bus out onto the main road, nearly unseating Nerys in the process.

"Careful or you won't have a baby to worry about." She warned. Rhys paid little heed to the conversation; he sat midway in the bus away from the children who were noisily bouncing on the back seats. To say he'd been impressed by the luxury of Plas Amman would have been an understatement, and he judged it to be far to superior to any house in or around Pentre, even the colliery manager's house was no comparison. However she'd achieved it Enid had done extremely well for herself, she had been polite and not in the least patronising, yet he'd felt inadequate and ashamed he amounted to so little. Would Nerys view him as failure because he couldn't provide her with the luxury enjoyed by her relative? He looked at her and Gwen as they chatted happily, evidence of how much they'd missed each other's company. It was good that Gwen and Tudor had resolved their differences; that was one less worry. The lockout was another matter; he'd expected a strike not the owners to seize the initiative. The news on Enid's wireless had been heartening if only offering a smidgen of hope. The Trade Union Congress had announced that a General Strike in defence of miner's wages and hours was to commence in two days time, providing the Miners Federation agreed to the TUC taking over the negotiations, there was still a possibility someone would see sense. Then there was the problem of Catrin, he hadn't stopped to consider the implications when he ran after her from the chapel, and it would have made no difference if he had, but now his name was associated with a pregnant girl and where there's smoke there's fire, the mudslingers had made certain the slander reached his ears.

"Dad, Dad."

He looked round questioningly at the owner of the tiny hand shaking his arm, "Yes son."

"Auntie Enid said me and Huw could go and stay with her for a holiday, can we?"

"Sometimes people say things just to be polite they don't always mean it."

"She did mean it, she did, didn't she Huw?"

"I think she did Uncle Rhys she asked me as well," interrupted Mari, who had been sitting silently opposite Rhys recalling Geraint's wicked grin and the kiss he'd planted firmly on her lips.

"Well then it'll be up to your mothers."

Gwen's return to the village did little to relieve the pressure on Rhys, in fact it had quiet the reverse effect. Instead of transferring attention from the episode with Catrin people nodded knowingly saying. "It must run in the family all of them sex mad." While at the same time hoping Mari might give them justification for future gloating. Some had the effrontery to openly warn her that she'd be next, that was if her lusty uncle hadn't already seduced her. Both Huw and Iwan were in constant scrapes with other boys, either because of the taunts concerning Catrin, or the suggestion their father was also responsible for Gwen's predicament. Nerys however outwardly carried on as normal ignoring the tittle-tattle she could do little about, but when anyone openly tried to embarrass her as they did one day in the Gwalia, she took satisfaction in making them eat humble pie.

It was her third visit to the shop since Gwen's return, twice before the usual clique had stayed in condescending silence throughout the time she was there, and Owain had merely served her without any of his usual smarmy conversation. When she'd closed the door and stepped onto the pavement she trembled with rage at the sound of raucous laughter from within. On those occasions she'd successfully fought the urge to turn back and give them all a piece of her mind, common sense telling her payback was sweeter when delivered with forethought. The shop was full Bronwen and Owain were both busy serving and the usual group of crones were huddled in the corner. Nerys waited her turn to be served, or be the butt of a remark. Theresa Owen better known as the Mouthy Midget made the error. "How is Gwen?" She asked sarcastically then added. "And Rhys and Catrin?" With an unmistakeable emphasis on Catrin.

Owain, Bronwen and the other customers waited with baited breath either for Theresa to continue her offensive or Nerys to respond. Slowly Nery's turned and faced the group, she smiled but her eyes remained cold as she picked out her assailant.

"Oh they are all fine thanks I'll tell them you were asking. How is your family Theresa and yours Glynis? Must be hard trying to make ends meet at the moment, but then we're lucky Rhys being an official gets some work. Still you're better off than most with your girls bringing in a few shillings. What is it they do exactly?" She paused for a second

95

before icily delivering the killer blow. "In the evenings outside the Custom House in Cardiff." Then redirecting her attention to Bronwen who possibly for the first time in her life remained open mouthed but speechless Nerys remarked, "I'll call back when you're not so busy." Casually opening the door she left the shop and paused momentarily outside listening, then jauntily went on her way content with the total hush she'd created. The allegation she'd made were based on Tudor's assurance that his brother who had left the colliery after the explosion and found work in Cardiff docks, had witnessed Glynis and Theresa's eldest daughters picking up men outside a disreputable pub in that area of the city, and Theresa's daughter had offered him her services for four shillings and when he declined she renewed her offer for half a crown.

"Can you believe it, the TUC have sold out, after twelve days they've accepted the Samuel proposal without any assurances against victimisation, and even Lord Birkenhead has said 'The way they surrendered was humiliating.' The paper says, 'The only redeeming fact they could see was the Miners Fed weren't party to it.' " Rhys flung the paper across the room in disgust. "That's it then we're on our bloody own again, bloody TUC government and owners all in bloody league." He stormed out of the kitchen, violently slamming the door. Catrin sat in silence never having witnessed Rhys in such a foul mood waiting for Nerys to speak.

"Don't worry, he'll be ok when he comes back, he'll go for a walk and get it out of his system. He'd hoped the unions would stick together seems they can't agree amongst themselves." Nerys looked as dejected as Rhys had been angry, she forced a smile. "Well things can only get better," she said unconvincingly.

She treated it like any other Sunday, and it had almost slipped her mind, so she didn't really expect Rhys to remember their anniversary though he always had in the past. They were both preoccupied with more immediate problems, thankfully they were able to keep the family shod and fed and that's all that truly mattered. She'd taken the children home from chapel while Rhys went to visit his brother's grave as he always did when he was troubled, she wished he'd talk his problems over with her instead of informing her when he'd made a decision. Maude had the dinner well in hand when she arrived home and the boys were sent to change their clothes. Mari had gone to visit her mother again spending an ever increasing time at Gwen and Tudor's, Nerys suspected she planned to move there after the wedding although the subject had not been broached. Maude poured the tea as Nerys sat down and kicked off her shoes.

"They were killing me, thank God I only have to wear them to chapel." She said rubbing her swollen foot. "You made up your mind, Mam?"

Maude sipped her tea and shook her head. "I'd like to go it's a nice house and we'd be company for each other, we have a lot to catch up on but my family is here, you, Gwen, the children, and with a new grandchild soon it seems a bit silly to cut myself off."

"She's family as well, she's your sister, when you want to come back your room will still be here."

"I know but too many years have slipped by, we may be sisters but we're also strangers."

"You know we don't want you to go but it would be a nice change for you."

"I wouldn't mind going for a little while, a holiday I've never had one, holidays are only for the rich."

"Do that then and come home after a week or two, and if you wanted to go again for a while you could."

"We'll see, I've got to welcome my new grandchild before I can even think about it."

The rota system gave Rhys three shifts one week and two the next, which kept his family off the bread line. Each shift he'd run the gauntlet of a few angry colliers who were blind to the fact if the pit was to ever reopen some men had to work. How did you reason with men who had nothing before the strike and less than nothing now? How could you tell men whose families looked to them to provide that they had to suffer, while you only tightened your belt? How did you justify that you would gain equally from the daily misery they endured? These questions constantly ate at him but like it or not Rhys knew what he had to do, talking things over with Gomer always helped.

"You're right as usual brawd, look to your own first."

Before leaving the graveyard he chatted to Moira. Ending as he usually did apologising for his lack of understanding and failure to appreciate the depth of her despair. On his way home he stopped by the allotment where he picked the best of the flowers he'd saved for today. Alice ignored him completely when he peered over the top of her pen, continuing to pursue the pleasure of snuffling in the mud. The remainder of the way home he reproached himself for what he had to do very soon.

Rhys was even less comfortable the next day, and he found great difficulty in displaying any humour. The blooms he'd picked yesterday for Nerys were now doubling as a bridal posy for Gwen. His preference would have been in going to town with them rather than using Huw and Elis as an excuse to stay at home. He helped Nerys, her mother and Mari onto the refurbished bus, sporting its gleaming new green livery with T. Gruffydd Omnibus Co. in bold cream letters along each side. Its smartness mirrored by the groom in his Sunday best sat beaming in the driver's seat. Behind him sat Gwen in the empire style pale blue cotton dress she'd made for today, that did little to conceal her condition.

Not having long to go she joked. "The registrar may be registering a birth as well as conducting a wedding if you don't get a move on."

Choosing to carry a bible along with the flowers, she believed God would be present and bless their union, regardless of it not taking place in chapel.

The bus disappeared from view and Rhys grudgingly made his way to the allotment, It had to be done before the boys came home from school for their dinner.

Maldwyn Puw was leaning over the sty sucking on a blade of grass protruding from the gap between his crooked teeth. He pushed back his cap and remarked. "She's a good size you'll get some nice joints off her."

Trying to overcome the sickness churning in his stomach Rhys opened the gate. "Let's get on with it."

Chapter Nine
Wednesday June 9th 1926

Catrin rested on the Windsor chair she'd dragged into the coolness of the scullery, away from the oppressive heat of the kitchen fire. The front and back doors were open wide as an invitation to any meandering breeze, her fidgeting to obtain any comfort was thwarted by chronic backache. Until today the weather had remained satisfactorily cool, but now summer mercilessly gave free rein to what it held in reserve. Closing her eyes she raised the bottom of her dress slightly higher than modesty would have intended, and leaning forward as far as her swollen stomach would allow, she used it to fan her face.

"For God's sake Catrin must you show all you got?"
Startled she dropped her clothes tucking them between her knees.

"Oh! Nerys I didn't see you."

"Good job it was only me and not Rhys, that would have been a shock for him."
Embarrassed Catrin started to rise from her seat.

"Stay there I'll make a cuppa, Rhys'll be home anytime."

Having struggled from the chair Catrin followed Nerys into the house and seated herself at the kitchen table. "How is Gwen, any sign yet?" She asked as Nerys filled the buckets of water to heat ready for Rhys' bath.

"Be anytime now, I'll go back as soon as Rhys gets home."

"She's lucky to have you and your mother." She'd liked to have her own mother when her time came but there seemed little prospect.

"If it's anything like when she had Mari, she'll be no time, popped out as easy as winking."

"I hope it's the same for me I'm terrified."

"I told Rhys after I had Huw he could have the next one through his ear."

"Was it that bad?"

"At the time I would have murdered Rhys, but you forget otherwise no one would have any more, when Elis came along I think I expected it to be as bad or worse, but he was no bother, well not compared to Huw." She disappeared into the kitchen with one of the buckets, and returned after a few minutes with a cup of tea. "Here and don't worry, the birth wouldn't bother me half as much as having to look after it, two is enough for me."

"Hope I can look after this one." She patted her stomach.

"When me and Rhys first got married Mrs Owen next door had fourteen and lost two others, like a machine churning them out she was. That's how it was, quite a few large families were brought up in bottom row"

"Still is, Mrs Evans next door to us." The realisation that us didn't include her any more wasn't pleasing. "She's got twelve, seven boys and five girls some of them are twins though."

"Who's had twins, not Gwen?" Rhys' black face appeared in the doorway.

"No silly we were just chatting."

"No news yet then?"

"Not yet I was just saying to Catrin it won't be long. I've put your bath water to warm and there's some bread and cheese on the table, I'll just slip back over see how she's doing."

"How is Mari?" Asked Rhys wistfully

"She's still upset with you."

"She'll have to speak to me sometime."

"I wouldn't count on it being soon."

Catrin eased herself free of the chair. "I'll come with you I can't sit around here all day."

"Wash my back if you like."

"There's enough gossip already without you adding to it," said Nerys picking up the black shopping bag that accompanied her everywhere.

"I was joking."

"You'd better be." The dourness in Nerys' voice unsettled Catrin.

Mari had never been so glad to see anyone as she was when she saw Nerys and Catrin coming towards her. "Nan sent me for the doctor but he wasn't in." She gasped having run all the way to the doctor's house and back.

"Where's Tudor?"

"Still out in his bus." Her breathing becoming less laboured.

"We'll have to manage then, not as if she hasn't done it before." Nerys hoped her confidence would soothe Mari's trepidation. "Catrin you're about to find out what you've let yourself in for."

102

Removing some of the recently installed seats had proved to be a good idea, the Maxwell now had a duel purpose with room for freight and passengers, though space was limited for either. He picked up small jobs fetching and carrying for some of the farmers and shopkeepers in the area, with this and his workshop he was getting by. More often than not payment was in goods rather than coinage, and when he could he sold things on to purchase fuel. Tudor had failed to enthuse about today's task Gwen's time being so close, if it hadn't been a cash job with the prospect of more work he'd definitely would have been happier staying nearer home. Gwen had finally persuaded him telling him there was nothing he could do, and if the baby came well Nerys and her mother would cope, and he'd just be in the way. So reluctantly he found himself steering the bus into Cardiff's dockland.

Having abandoned his brother's futile directions, and after a few wrong turnings he finally stumbled across his destination. A row of single story dirty red brick offices contrasting with a new brilliant white sign with large black lettering that read, Brogden Enterprises Importers and Exporters fixed above a pair of heavy dark oak panelled doors. Inside the building was equally tatty, with dirty cream gloss painted walls, similar to those of the colliery offices. Having explained his business to a clerk sitting behind a desk piled high with several stacks of invoices and files, he was shown into another room where another man sat behind an equally large paper mountain. The man spoke without introducing himself, glancing up sporadically from the document he was studying.

"We're transferring our operation from our Barry Depot over the next month or so, you'll be required once a week on a Friday to collect files and other materials and unload them here, starting today, Thompson will give you the details."

Within five minutes of arriving Tudor was back on his bus searching for the dock exit. If he hadn't taken another wrong turning he wouldn't have seen him, working in a gang with five others unloading timber from the hold of a ship onto the quay. His first instinct was to stop and approach him, instead he swung the bus around in an arc and headed about his business.

Huw, explained what they were going to do. "Go to the lav and put some in this bag."

"But I don't want a pooh."

"Well we need a bag of it and you've got to get it, that's only fair I got the bag."

"It's your idea you do it."

"I don't want to go either."

"Can't we use sheep or dog's there's plenty of that about?"

"Suppose dogs'll do as long as its soft, you got to pick it up though."

They didn't have far to go to find an ample supply of suitable dog dirt, Elis with Huw's instructions and the use of a couple of twigs as chopsticks scooped enough to half fill the paper bag.

"This'll teach her to kill Alice," said Huw as he carefully placed the bag on the step and took a couple of matches from his pocket. "When I light the bag, you knock the door and run."

He struck the match against the step, bang, bang Elis knocked and gave the door an almighty kick for good measure, then fled, the flame flickered and died. Hurriedly Huw struck the second match and put it to the bag, the edge blackened and began to curl as the flame took hold. He'd barely reached the safety of Elis' hiding place when the door opened. Gwladys Harri intent on stamping out the fire on her doorstep was oblivious to the four hysterical eyes peering around the corner.

Rhys had just finished emptying the bath when the boys came home in a fit of laughter.

"What have you two been up to?" He asked hoping it was nothing and it wouldn't rebound on him.

"Nothing, Dad, just mucking about."
At least they were still talking to him, they'd been upset about Alice but had acknowledged he didn't have a choice, unlike Mari who amidst a flood of tears had fled out of the house calling him a murderer and swearing never to speak to him again. Whenever they were alone Mari found an excuse to be somewhere else.

"Your mother left you some bread cheese and cold pork."

"I'm not eating Alice," said Elis with Huw nodding in agreement.

"Suit yourselves that's all there is, eat it or go without." The blooming pig was more trouble dead than alive; he'd lost count of the people who knowing Alice's need for medication believed it humorous to ask for a slice of Alice because they had a headache. Even after Mrs Harri, Doc Richards, and Merfyn Puw had been allocated their share, Rhys still retained a sizable portion of the carcass. Maude and Nerys between them had cured the meat, while Mostyn had offered to buy any or all, but had to content himself with the head and trotters.

It was Catrin who brought the news. "It's a girl, and they're both ok."

"Is Tudor there?"

105

"Arrived same time as the doc, when it was all over." Catrin manoeuvred herself into a chair. "Nerys was amazing she knew exactly what to do."

Rhys' expression signalled he never doubted she wouldn't. "Let's hope she's around when your time comes."

"I've booked her and her mother for the whole week it's due."

"You didn't notice Huw or Elis on the way back?"

"No haven't seen them." Groaning she leaned forward.

"Hang on Nerys is not here." Wisecracked Rhys

"Don't worry it's only my backache. Nerys said she'll be home soon as the doc's gone."

"Think I'll walk over and meet her."

"Missing her are you?" Catrin laughed. "There's something been puzzling me."

"If it's about babies ask Nerys."

"No nothing to do with that. The day I ran out of the chapel and you followed me how'd you know what I was going to do?"

"I didn't for sure, but a long time ago my sister did something similar and no one was there to help her."

"She killed herself?"

"Yes, she was pregnant, that's how I guessed what you intended, I might have been wrong and looked foolish but I had to make sure."

"I'm sorry I didn't know."

"No reason you should, you'd have been a baby."

"What was her name?"

"Moira she was nineteen three years older than me, but I should have been there, I should have realised."

"How can you know what someone else is thinking?"

"I should never have let her run off alone; I should have gone after her she'd have come after me."

"But you were young yourself."

"I was your age, and you're about to be a mother, I was old enough and I let her down, we all let her down. When it came out in chapel I froze, maybe it was shock I dunno, whatever it was I watched her run out and I did nothing.

With Rhys' help she ungainly extracted herself from the chair. "Coming to live here is the best thing that ever happened to me, thank you." She reached forward and embraced him kissing him on the cheek, when he expected her to pull away she snuggled closer, and the cwtch lasted longer than he felt easy with.

"Can't turn my back for a minute can I?" Nerys stood glowering in the doorway.

Immediately he entered the allotment he knew that someone else had been there, the chickens were running free range amongst his seedlings, the gate to the run and henhouse door were wide open. Shaking the corn tin he counted the birds as they came hurrying into the run for their breakfast, six seven, eight, four missing, someone would have a full belly this week. The duck house seemed to be untouched, but on inspection proved to be empty. Resolving to get a proper padlock but not convinced that it would have made a great difference, he made his way home to break the news.

"If I knew who it was I'd string the bugger up, losing the chickens is bad enough but all the ducks were in lay."

Nerys picked up her bag. "No good complaining they're gone, we'll just have to keep a close eye on what's left."

"I'll go and see if Owain has any padlocks and what price they are, probably be cheaper to give the chickens away. You off to Gwen's?"

"Yes, I'll slip over see how they are doing, and how mam's coping."

"I'll come with you and see my new niece and try and patch things up with the old one."

Rhys endeavoured to use the walk to Gwen's house to clear the air.

"You don't honestly think there's anything between me and Catrin?" ."

"You tell me what I'm supposed to think? You bring a pregnant girl home to live with us, the whole village is talking about you and her and the way you ran after her from the chapel. I get pointed remarks from everyone who feels like having a dig, I even had blooming kids following me and chanting three in a bed and the little one said roll over, and then yesterday to top it all I come home and find you and her cwtching."

"You can't blame me for the malice in people's minds."

"I don't but I know what I saw, and I know why you went after her, but do you realise what it been like for me?"

"You're right I didn't stop to think it through, if I had I'd still have gone after her, not because I don't care for you but because she'd be dead, and I wouldn't want that on my conscience." They walked a few thoughtful steps then Rhys added, "And yesterday she was just saying thanks for what we've done for her."

"What you've done you mean."

"We've done," He corrected. "You took her in as well, you want me to be like her father and throw her out?"

"Of course not, it's just that she seems to becoming over attached to you."

108

"And you think I can't be trusted, the girl is worried and upset and she's grateful to us, to both of us."

"Don't be silly that's not the point."

"The point is no matter what Catrin does if you trusted me we wouldn't be having this conversation."

"And if you considered my feelings and put me first, instead of the union, Catrin, or whatever else you get involved with we wouldn't be having it either."

With nothing resolved they walked the rest of the way in silence.

Sara looked to Rhys like any other baby, he failed to understand how a wrinkled elfin featured new born could be said to resemble a parent, but he made all the required noises. "Isn't she tiny like a little doll, she's got her mothers nose."

Maude and Nerys fussed in turn with Gwen and the baby while Rhys turned his attention to Mari, his attempts at conciliation were greeted by a stony contemptuous stare. When Tudor tried to arbitrate Mari calmly walked out of the room leaving Rhys feeling like a one armed juggler with all the balls in the air. He thought it odd when Tudor being a non-smoker then suggested they go outside for a cigarette.

"I need your advice."

Rhys searched his shirt pocket and produced half a roly, he lit it motioning Tudor to continue.

"You know I was in Cardiff yesterday, seeing about the work my brother put me up for?"

"Aye, how'd it go?"

"Ok I got the job sorted, it could prove to be quite profitable. Anyway to cut a long story short I saw Iwan working on the dock unloading a ship."

Rhys' eyes widened, "Have you told Gwen?"

"No that's the problem, I don't know if I should."

"If you don't and she finds out I wouldn't like to be in your shoes. Did you speak to him?"

"No, I did think to but left it."

"So only we know you saw him?"

"And Steffan, I told him but he already knew Iwan was working there."

"Knows how to keep a secret your brother, you going there this week?"

"Yes every Friday for the next few weeks at least."

"Ok I'll come with you and see what he has to say for himself, and then we'll tell Gwen." Rhys shook his head it was just what he needed, another ball to juggle.

Rhys assumed nothing else could go wrong, until he met Tudor for their trip to Cardiff. He found Gwen and her new born firmly installed on the bus.

"You're not going anywhere without me," she said defiantly

"You told her?"

"No Mari heard me and you talking."

"It figures, take her home."

"Don't talk about me as if I'm not here."

"Good God Gwen you only had that baby the day before yesterday, let me and Tudor go and have a word with him."

"No he ran away once and if he knows we've found him he might vanish again."

Rhys frowned at Tudor. "Sorry but she's your wife, you two sort it out between you, I've got enough problems of my own. But my advice is to put it off at least a week he'll still be there."

Rhys withdrew from the argument with Gwen refusing to budge and Tudor resolved not to move the bus.

"You're back early." Nerys hoped that going with Tudor would have given him chance to think about them, but she soon realised their differences would have taken a back seat as his head would have been full of Iwan and Gwen and if not them Catrin or Pryce, but not her.

"Gwen's got it in her head she's going, so I left them to sort it out."

"Gwen can't go she should be in bed, didn't my mother stop her?"

"Didn't see her or Mari."

"You didn't think to get my mother to take her in?"

"Tudor was there, it was up to him."

"Uffern, cachwr ti."

"Don't swear I hear enough of that at work."

Nerys knew he disliked women swearing, and did it to emphasise her annoyance.

"You drive me to it sometimes," she said slamming the back door as she left.

He sat in silence wondering whether he should get the boys up for school, when he heard Catrin stirring in the room above. A few minutes later she waddled into the kitchen.

"I've called the boys not that they'll take any notice." She poured herself a cuppa and settled on a chair next to him.

"I don't want you to get the wrong idea." Rhys began awkwardly. "But I think you should try again with your father."

"She flushed slightly. "Its Nerys isn't it, she doesn't want me here?"

"No don't be silly you know you're welcome here, but maybe your father will have had a change of heart now he's had time to think."

"If you throw me out I'll have nobody."

"Don't be silly nobody's throwing you out, but perhaps your family deserve another chance."

"They know where I am."

Rhys felt the conversation was getting nowhere and was glad when Tudor came hurrying through the back door."

"Nerys coaxed Gwen off the bus on the condition you would come with me."

"That's what we were doing in the first place." Walking to the doorway he shouted up the stairs, "If you two are not down in one minute I'll be up there to get you." Then gesturing to Catrin, "You'll see to them?"

"Of course I will you get off."

It was close to midday when Tudor pulled up at the rear of Brogden's offices. "You go and find Iwan if you like I can manage here." Not wanting to be held to account if Iwan did a bunk he considered it prudent to leave it to Rhys, and if he were persuasive enough to convince Iwan to come back with them then they'd both benefit from Gwen's gratitude.

"Just point me to where you saw him."

Rhys had no trouble locating him, the gang had completed unloading a consignment of pit props from a Norwegian vessel, and were sat well spaced apart on the timber eating their lunch. Rhys successfully skirted around the stacks of props so he could approach and sit down alongside Iwan before he noticed him. He'd been sceptical of Iwan's reaction but he merely looked up as if Rhys' presence was normal saying.

"Hi what are you doing here? "Holding out his sandwiches. "Want one?"

Rhys shook his head. "You know why I'm here your mother sent me."

"How is she?"

"She'd be a lot better if you'd come and see her."

"How about Mari she ok?"

"She's fine but misses you. They both want you to come home."

"How'd you get here?"

"I came with the chap who delivers to the Brogden's office, you know him Tudor Gruffydds"

"Blacksmith?"

"Aye him, he's got a bus come van he fetches stuff over from Barry."

"I worked there for a while."

"You never found a ship."

Iwan shook his head, and although they sat in silence their conversation continued, while Rhys absorbed the smell and sounds of the docks that reminded him so much of Porthcawl, and Iwan chewed pensively on his lunch.

"What time you going home?"

"Depends on you, we can wait if you want."

"You expect me to come with you?"

"That's why I'm here."

"Why did she send you?"

"She wanted to come but we stopped her."

"It's my last day if you'd come next week I wouldn't be here, I was only taken on for a month."

"Where you going from here?"

"Nowhere in particular, thought I might try Bristol, but Cliff over there," he nodded in the direction of one of the other men. "He's from Bristol, said there's even less work there."

"Might as well come home then."

"Perhaps, if you're still around about six."

Rhys caught the others arm. "Don't make me wait for nothing, she'll be devastated if you don't come."

Iwan shrugged. "Wait if you want but don't count on it."

"Why are you so intent on hurting your mother?"

"I don't want to hurt no one, it's just how it's worked out."

"One thing you'd better know before you see Tudor."

"What's that?"

"Him and your mother are married?"

If Rhys had expected a reaction it was denied him, displaying no emotion Iwan casually stood up.

"See you later maybe," he said and set off to catch up with the rest of his gang who were moving towards a ship moored further along the jetty.

Chapter Ten

Monday 18th October 1926

Thank God it was Monday, the prospect of facing the pickets was preferable to spending another day at home. Maude no longer needed at Gwen's had arrived home yesterday, just as Catrin went into labour. Rhys had spent the hours between Sunday morning and evening services with Tudor in his workshop, not that Tudor needed any help, since Iwan's return he'd dogged Tudor's every step. Huw and Elis had taken the opportunity the birth created to disappear, missing their tea but more importantly chapel, they'd arrived home tired and hungry with an endless list of excuses which they tested on a too busy to bother Nerys. Later Rhys half heartedly chastised them, who could blame them dodging chapel?

Many of the jeering faces who'd become a regular feature at the colliery entrance were not at their morning posts, the few who had turned out were busy shouting the odds at an unscheduled meeting a few yards up the road. On reaching the lamp room Rhys understood why he'd not been subjected to the regular early morning abuse.

To be in full view of his assembly Siencyn-Pryce stood raised on a wooden box as a make shift pulpit, and was fervently engaged in modifying the story of the prodigal son. "And you are the first of my sons returning to the bosom of my family, for we are a family bonded by our work, together we are united by the toil we share, and welded by our faith in the one true God. So do not think you have betrayed your brothers, for God has illuminated the path of rectitude for you to lead so those still blinded by avarice can follow."

Bloody hell thought Rhys, isn't it enough they've been starved back without him humiliating them. The men dispersed each with their head bowed fearful of the reflection they'd see in another's eyes.

Rhys eyed one of the men his shoulders slumped as he slunk into the lamp-room, normally a proud man who even if misguided held his head high in a manner that said he was any miners equal. Rhys felt little sympathy for him. Have you been humbled enough to love your daughter and grandchild? Now you've broken faith with your workmates, can you see no ones perfect? I hope you can for Catrin and Nia's sake.

Rhys addressed the boots poking from beneath the car raised on wooden blocks. "There's a steady trickle every day, you may as well come back, next week there'll probably be a flood."

Tudor crawled out, adjusted his dislodged cap, then wiping his hands with an oily rag he shook his head. "We can manage another week or two I'm a lot better off than most, if work keeps coming in as it has the last few days I may never go back."

Rhys afraid his envy of being free from the colliery and Pryce would become evident changed the subject. "Where's Iwan? How's he and Gwen?"

"He's gone down to catch the Gwalia before they close, Gwen wanted something or other. They're getting on ok but." He screwed his face in puzzlement. "I dunno."

"What?"

"I just get this feeling the boy's keeping something back."

"Perhaps he needs time to get used to his mother remarrying."

"No he seems fine about that, and I think me and him are getting on really well."

"Has he said anything to Gwen about why he went?

"No, and Gwen's so glad he's back she won't push it."

"Aye, I could see she's made up. How is Mari? She still hasn't spoke to me 'cos of that blasted pig."

"I think she's missing you but to proud to admit it."

"Our house seems a lot emptier now she's back with her mother."

"She's a big help to Gwen what with the baby and all."

"Anyway I'm off down to see Catrin's parents, maybe I can resolve that one."

"Don't like an easy life do you?"

"Rhys grimaced. "Whenever was life meant to be easy?"

Iwan was half way home when he met Rhys. "Shw'mae, Iwan I've just left, well I suppose he's your stepfather."

"You mean Tudor, I've only ever had one father and he's dead."

"I thought you and him got on ok."

"We do, he's a good man and deserves better."

"Let's take a little stroll; I'd like to have a talk." They walked together, each deep in thought, Rhys wondering how to ask, and Iwan anticipating the question and considering his reply.

117

"I'm thinking of joining up." Iwan volunteered in a manner that sought neither advice nor approval.

"Navy?"

"Yeah, I'm going to see the world there's got to be more than this." He waved in the direction of the pit.

"What's it with you and boats?"

"Must be the tale you kept telling about the schooner in Porthcawl."

"But I saw it, and it didn't make me go to sea."

"Perhaps the story became more colourful in the telling."

"Cheeky bugger, you saying I exaggerated?"

"No, you just tell a good story."

"Have you told your mother?"

"No only you. I can't stay around here there's no work, and I can't expect Tudor to keep me. I'll tell her a couple of weeks before I'm due to leave"

"If you wanted to stay I could ask Pryce to take you back."

Iwan's face darkened. "That bastard, I wouldn't trust myself around him."

"Why, what's he done to you? I know he's an arrogant sod and bullies everyone."

"Well he can mess with who he likes, but he's not going to fuck with me."

Rhys was taken back by Iwan's colourful language, he was used to it from men at work but Iwan was his young nephew. He realized he wasn't talking to the boy who'd run away, the boy he'd seen sobbing in Porthcawl, Iwan had grown up and it was more than just physical.

"It's a job and he won't be there forever, and besides your mother is so pleased having you back home, she'll be mortified if you

118

disappear again." Rhys was mindful he was suggesting Iwan put aside his feelings in favour of his family, the way Gomer had so often advised him.

"They won't take me until after Christmas so I'll be around for a while."

"Why do you feel the need to go away? Your family is here, none of us understand why you went last time."

Iwan stopped walking and turned to face him. "Ok, let's stop pussyfooting around. I'll tell you why I went as long as it remains between us and it goes no further, not even Nerys is to know."

"I don't like keeping secrets from Nerys, she usually finds out sooner or later and then I'm in trouble."

"Better you don't know then."

"Why not tell your mother she's the one who needs to know."

"Christ she'd be the last person I'd tell." Iwan said with a derisory intonation.

Rhys was struck by the resolve portrayed in the unyielding green eyes that met his. "I promise I'll tell no one, not even Nerys."

Catrin's father shook his head. "Her mother won't go against me, but I can see the pain in her eyes when she looks at me. I'd like nothing more than to have Catrin back, but it can't be, I wish it could. I'm not like you, you stand up to Pryce while he walks over every one else, she's better off with you I'm afraid to have her home. If I do I'd lose my job and my house, and it's not only Catrin that will be homeless I got three other kids to think of. Is it too much to ask she let Pryce have his day so I can keep my family together."

Rhys feelings of contempt for this man who'd disowned his daughter were being replaced by understanding and sympathy. He wasn't a bad man he was as much a victim of Pryce as Catrin. "It's always him, whatever trouble is in the village he's part of it, he's had his own way for too long, it's about time people stood up and told him where to get off."

"Fine words, so you go and tell him because until you've watched your children crying with empty bellies, or because the stones cut their bare feet, or their cold and you've spent all day scrabbling for coal on the tip, dodging the police, and it'll mean prison if you're caught because you've no money to pay a fine, and then you can't always collect enough coal for an evenings warmth. Until you've lain awake night after night huddled together shivering, and your coat is their only blanket, then you can tell me I'm wrong but until then you know where to stick your advice."

The house shook with the force of the slammed door. Rhys couldn't have argued if he'd been given the opportunity, he'd been fortunate to have some work throughout the strike, he'd helped others as much as he could, and although it had been a struggle his family hadn't experienced the deprivation endured by the majority.

"What did he say?" Nerys already saw the answer in Rhys' expression. "I thought as much, stubborn old sod."

"Not as simple as that, he'd have her back if he could."

"Of course he could, she's his daughter that's all that matters."

"You don't understand, he's got next to nothing and he could lose that."

"Well he can't think a lot of Catrin that's all I know."

"Everything is always black and white to you, sometimes I think you wear blinkers you silly mare." He pushed passed dumbfounded Nerys, leaving the back door wide open he stormed into the back yard lashing out with his boot at an inoffensive galvanised bucket that bounced off the lavatory door and came to a buckled rest on the path.

"Feel better now?" He didn't answer but continued staring up at the stars. Nerys slipped her arm around him. "You frightened me, you're not usually so prickly."

"I'm sorry, I shouldn't take it out on you, but Catrin's father made me feel guilty."

"What you looking at?"

"Just the sky, and wondering."

"What."

"Well look how big it is, the nearest star millions of miles away makes life in Pentre seem so trivial, and us, we're about as important as the spider in the bath."

"You're important to me and the boys."

"Yes, and I love you, but we mean nothing to anyone else."

"As long as we have each other we can cope."

He lowered his eyes to hers. "That's just it we shouldn't have to cope, why should we be dictated to and told how to live? And I don't mean just by Pryce."

"That's the way it has always been."

"Well that don't make it right."

"Not much we can do to change it."

"But if we don't try what does that make us?"

"You can't take on the world; we have to make the best of what we've got."

"Perhaps, but maybe we can change it just a little bit."

"Not without a lot of pain and suffering, who's benefited from this last fiasco? No one we know."

121

Nationally the miners strike collapsed, and they returned to work for less money and worse conditions, until the only people left to man the picket lines at Pentre Bach were those considered to be the local ringleaders, and Siencyn-Pryce resolutely refused to allow them back. No exception would be made, not even for Gruff Roberts who'd been instrumental in extracting Pryce from a premature grave. In work and in chapel Pryce wielded unequivocal power, and the congregation sat in subservient silence while he stood high in his holy pulpit corrupting the sacred text to censure their foolishness.

"It is God's will that neither refuge nor nourishment should be offered to the families of the devil's collaborators, those who having tricked the poorest in this community by lies and deceit into believing the mine owners were exploiting them. If people had only taken the time to consider instead of following like gullible sheep they would have seen the opposite is the truth, that the owners should be viewed as Christian benefactors providing work and housing. Who was it that assisted in building the Gilfach Miners Hospital? Without these eminent men's patronage there'd be no employment, no hospitals, no schools for your children, no clothes to keep them warm in winter and no food on their plates. But instead of showing gratitude you were reckless enough to allow yourselves to be coerced on mass into turning against them. Luckily the ill conceived plan hasn't worked, and the calculated malicious criminal intentions born by nefarious discontents has been thwarted, and now it is time for them to learn that simple truth and honesty will always prevail on Gods earth."

Rhys doubted anyone but Pryce's most devout hangers-on would be taken in, but all would have no other option but to bite their tongues, and the first time in his life experienced real hatred. He also realised whatever misgivings he'd had Gomer had been right, if the likes of Pryce were to be brought to book it would be by stealth and cunning, not confrontation. Yet as far as he could see confrontation was unavoidable, because that's the only way he could highlight the cause of Gruff Roberts, blacklisted by the man whose life they'd saved. The other matter that bit even deeper could wait a little longer, he needed a plan that would not only curtail but redress Pryce's excesses.

On the rare occasions he found his presence underground unavoidable it wasn't unusual for Pryce to tell Rhys to wait for him on pit-bottom. Since the accident he'd only venture into the mine when absolutely necessary and then always in the company of Rhys. Rhys sat on the makeshift bench, screened by a sheet of brattice from the biting wind that whistled from the shaft. He stood up several times to aid his circulation in the hour or more he had to rehearse what he needed to say, although each time he practised his uncertainty compelled him to edit and re-edit.

"Rhys, here he is," called Islwyn the onsetter. Rhys walked to the shaft as the cage landed.

"Morning Mr Pryce," said Islwyn as he opened the safety gate, the manager walked past him without even a grunt of recognition. Formalities with Rhys were curt and they'd walked just over a hundred yards along the main when Rhys decided to broach the subject of Gruff Roberts.

"I'd like your advice Mr Pryce, it's a bit awkward."

"As colliery manager and minister of the chapel there's not much I haven't witnessed."

"It's a friend of mine, he's been told something, and he doesn't know what to do about it."

They turned into a branch tunnel leading toward the six foot seam, Pryce stopped leaning on his stick and rested his lamp on a stack of timber props.

"There's no one to overhear, so if you can't be more explicit then I don't see I can help."

It was a strong urge not to say anymore that Rhys quelled, he took a deep breath and could feel himself trembling with a combination of fear and revulsion of his companion.

"Well it concerns a well known person in the village."

"And the chapel?"

"Yes and the chapel."

"Then it's your duty to speak out, it would be unpardonable to allow disgrace to fall on God's house, no matter how fond you are of a person."

"Oh I don't like the man I detest him," blurted Rhys before he was able to check himself."

"I thought you said he was a friend?"

"The one that's suffering is."

"Then why are you so reluctant to speak?

"Because it involves others, innocent people who could be hurt through no fault of their own"

"A wound will fester until the rotten is cut out, then with time it heals and the pain is gone."

Suppressing the desire to ask him if he was a doctor as well as God's right hand, Rhys decided to try a less aggressive approach before resorting to blackmail. "There's something else that you could put right."

"So you're not going to tell me?"

"I've said too much already."

"If it involves the chapel I have a right to know." Pryce picked up his lamp and started to move on. "What's the other matter?" His tone changing from his best chapel ministers voice, to one of an impatient colliery manager.

"Gruff Roberts." Pryce turned angrily, but Rhys continued. "He helped save your life yet you deny him the means to live his." The accusation hit home and Pryce glared venomously at Rhys.

"He's also one of the most militant insolent excuses for a man besides you it's been my misfortune to come across."

"You were glad enough to come across him when he helped dig you out, and as a man of God I thought you'd show some compassion."

"Don't you dare bring God into it, the man has to learn to respect his betters."

"I thought religion was about humility, not dwelling on our own importance, isn't it said somewhere all men are born equal?" Rhys readied himself for a verbal thrashing, as Pryce viewed him disparagingly.

"You think you're educated or intelligent enough, or is it blind stupidity that makes you think you're capable of arguing the scriptures with me?"

Rhys interrupted before he could say any more. "No maybe I'm not, and maybe I can't, and maybe I don't want to twist the bible to suit my own ends. But I do know what's right, and what you've done isn't the actions of any half decent man."

A sneer spread across the manager's face. "God help me but I've bent over backwards to help you and your family. If that's how you feel you're free to go and join Roberts and his crowd and share their begging bowls. In fact I'll make it easy for you and ensure you do, then perhaps you'll learn some respect and gratitude."

125

Rhys leapt forward grabbing the other by the throat, with such ferocity Pryce's helmet flew from his head as he was propelled backwards, until he lay prostrate on the stacked timber.

"Gratitude, you fucking bastard, gratitude for shagging my sister in law while her son watched, what threats did you use to make her go with scum like you? Gratitude for having to take what ever shit you dish out, gratitude for shamelessly sending my sister to her death, here's all the fucking gratitude you deserve." He raised his fist and sent it crashing into the other's gaping mouth. The knocked over lamp highlighted the whites of Pryce's widening eyes inciting Rhys to squeeze harder on his throat as he willed them to pop free of their sockets. "Come near me or my family again and I'll fucking kill you, I'll kill you, you no good fucking bastard."

Rhys fought to maintain his grip as hands wrenched at his fingers.

"For Christ sake Rhys let go you'll kill him."

The moment of insanity slowly subsided and Rhys' grip relaxed.

"What the hells got into you Rhys you gone bloody mad?" Densil Vaughan pulled him away, shining his lamp on the unconscious manager.

Rhys tried to collect his thoughts, this wasn't what he'd planned he'd never lost control of himself like that before, his legs felt weak and he slid to the floor.

"I dunno Dens, I dunno."

Densil examined Pryce. "He's still breathing, he's going to have less teeth and a sore throat when he wakes up. What'd he do to deserve that?"

Rhys pulled himself to his feet. "None of your business, you better bugger off before he comes round and sees you, unless you want a share of the blame."

"What you going to do?"

"No idea, I didn't plan on this."

"You're not going to hit him again?"

"No."

"You sure?"

"I got it out my system, you haven't seen anything, right?"

"I don't want to see anything either, he could have you in prison for this."

"He had it coming."

"Say that when you're in gaol, Jesus, I thought you had more sense."

"I just snapped, you go back in I'll see to him."

"That's what I'm afraid of, you seeing to him."

"Go on." Rhys opened his water jack and emptied it over the manager's bloody face, who coughing and spluttering hauled himself groggily into a sitting position.

Chapter Eleven

Friday October 24th 1926

Alice dreaded him coming home, the last few days he'd hardly spoken and when he had he'd been less than civil, not that it was uncommon, quite the reverse. On Tuesday he'd come home his face and neck bruised, his mouth swollen and a mood the worst she'd ever experienced, she'd locked herself in her room as she often did to avoid being the target of his rage. He'd obviously been in a fight but insisted angrily he'd fallen in work, fallen on someone's fist more like, whoever it was deserved a medal, a gold one at that, now he knew what it was like to be on the receiving end. He hadn't always been a bully, that hadn't started until after they were married, but before they moved to Pentre. She looked at her mother's photo, the one that had escaped, when in one of his fits of pique he'd thrown all her memories onto the fire, laughing and mocking her as he found amusement in the coloured flames. "You were right mum, why couldn't I see him as you did?" The familiar squeak of un-oiled hinges caused her to hurriedly replace the picture in the small shoe box that contained her most cherished possessions, and return it to its hiding place at the back of the draw.

What could she expect today? The bruise on her arm still ached from where he'd grabbed her and propelled her across the room when she'd tried to examine his injuries. Uneasily she made her way down the stairs speculating on what flaw he'd find in her today.

"Have a good day dear?"
He stood with his back to the fire, rubbing the cheeks of his backside.

"Huh, the pretext that you care with what I have to put up with to keep a roof over our heads is almost credible."

So it was one of those days again, oh well she'd see to his dinner and escape back to her room. "Dinner will be about fifteen minutes."

"Fine I've some things to do." He moved away from the fire tugging his trousers from his overheated seat. "I'll be in my study."
She didn't have a lot to do in the kitchen as Mair Jones, a local woman who came daily and did, had as usual prepared their evening meal, leaving Alice only having to serve, the used dishes would be left for Mrs Jones to attend to the following morning. She was delayed reaching the kitchen by the jangling subpoena of the front door bell. Very rarely they had any callers apart from local tradesmen and Mrs Jones usually dealt with them around the back.

"Yes can I help you?" The hall light shone on the well dressed man whose speech betrayed his unaccustomed use of English.

"Good evening Mrs Pryce." He took of his cap. "Is Mr Pryce at home?"

She stood a side for him to enter and showed him into the sitting room. "He's in his study, who shall I say wishes to see him?" Not actually needing confirmation of his identity having had reason to be aware of the family.

"Rhys Morgan."

129

"Take a seat Mr Morgan I'll tell him you're here."

He had time to scrutinize his surroundings, not as grand as Plas Amman but quite posh, compared to what he was used to this was luxury.

A few minutes later she returned, her face flushed. "I'm sorry to keep you waiting Mr Pryce will be with you shortly. I understand you work with my husband?"

"Yes, well I used to work for him." She didn't question his answer, from Dafydd's response when she'd told him his visitor's identity she'd known instantly there was animosity between them, and the prospect of a moderately peaceful evening looked decidedly bleaker.

When Pryce entered the room Alice excused herself and Pryce closed the door behind her.

"Well, well, come to finish the job?"

Rhys got to his feet and fumbled nervously with his cap. "No Mr Pryce I came to apologise."

"I didn't think you were the type to come crawling for your job," he sneered.

Rhys put every effort into making his apology appear genuine.

"I can only say how sorry I am and thank you for not reporting the incident to the police." As Gomer had often told him politeness cost nothing and was always the best approach.

"That's alright then, I'll just forget the incident as you call it ever happened until you decide you want to try and kill me again." Rhys ignored Pryce's acerbity.

"I do want my job back Mr Pryce, I'll beg and I'll crawl if that's what you want."

Dafydd Siencyn-Pryce's eyes widened in amazement and a smirk of triumph slithered across his face. He hadn't raised his voice which Rhys had expected. In truth Rhys hadn't anticipated being invited over the doorstep; he'd imagined he'd have been lucky being admonished on the threshold before the door was slammed in his face.

Pryce's expression conveyed incredulity. "You think you can take advantage because I'm a Christian and try to live according to Christ's teaching. Yet should I turn the other cheek I fear you will punch that as well."

"I'm sorry, I lost my temper."

"Oh you lost your temper and you're sorry, and that makes it alright does it? I'll forget whatever pain or damage you inflicted or intended in your assault because you're sorry."

"No Mr Pryce, it doesn't make it alright, and I'm ashamed my anger got the better of my reason, I'm not usually a violent man."
Alice listened from behind the door wondering why Dafydd hadn't flown into a blind rage with this man who'd hit him, or did he only do that with her? She felt the icy change in her husband's voice as it became louder and harsher.

"You showed what sort of man you are Morgan, attacking me the colliery manager, the lords servant in this heathen village , trying to kill one of Gods ordained ministers is no one safe from a ruffian like you? I should have had you imprisoned and by God I just might yet if you don't get out of my house." His yelling had evolved into a high pitch scream.

Rhys made no attempt to leave and stood his ground, keeping his tone calm and level. "Shout at me all you like but what will your wife think, what will the chapel think about the way you treat the women in this village, especially Gwen?"

Pryce's colour drained from bright red to white. "Don't dare to try and threaten me, who'd believe a sacked man, a man consumed with hate and bent on revenge?"

131

"I'm full of hate for good reason, but it's not just me there's Gwen, Iwan, and the child you fathered, you want I get up and denounce you in chapel ,as you did with Moira and Catrin, find yourself loathed and despised even more than you are, if that's possible?" Rhys was counting on Pryce not realising Gwen was ignorant her secret was known.

"You can't prove a thing, and as for that whore of a sister in law she's married the father of her whelp, you haven't got a thread of evidence against me."

"I believe him." Neither of the men had noticed Alice as she'd quietly slipped into the room. "I believe every word, and so will everyone else because I'll tell them and make sure they do." Without another word she abruptly turned and left.

Rhys was sorry for Alice she shouldn't have found out like this. Pryce on the other hand continued feigning her interruption as being of little consequence.

"I don't think you'll want Gwen's name sullied, especially as she's just re-wed."

Rhys was gambling that his standing in the chapel and the wider community would be his major concern. "If you want to put it to the test go ahead, and remember Iwan watched as you violated his mother, and without the support of your own family your standing wouldn't be worth a brass farthing, you'd be finished." Pryce looked fit to burst but thanks to Alice's intervention Rhys had the upper hand sustaining his attack. "And don't think Tudor's so naive he doesn't know the child's not his, but he's yet to learn who the father is, and I pity the man if he does find out. I'll be at work in the morning, and Gruff Roberts will be there on Monday. Oh and I nearly forgot, Catrin will expect to be welcome in chapel Sunday, and what I said about you ever coming near my family again I meant every word. I'll see myself out."

Alice heard the front door slam and immediately shot the bolt on her bedroom door. Footsteps padded quickly along the landing pausing momentarily outside her door, she eyed the door handle, it remained still, the footsteps continued until silenced by his bedroom door closing with a loud thud. From her window she watched the man; in her estimation worth at least another five gold medals, she got the impression he looked up and smiled at her as he closed the gate.

Showing her into the front room Gwen was mystified, why had she come, a colliery manager's wife didn't make social calls on the likes of her and Tudor?

"Please don't look so worried Mrs Gruffydd I don't bite." She spoke softly, her manner and tone in keeping with that of a gentlewoman. "Forgive me for calling unannounced but I was passing and thought it would be fitting if I introduced myself."

"It's no trouble." Gwen felt uneasy, unsure how to respond.
Alice sat on the edge of the seat as if signifying her business wouldn't take long.

"Perhaps I could call at a more convenient time or we could arrange for you to visit me, as we have a great deal to discuss."

Discuss what? What did they have in common unless she knows, she must know, what else would they have to talk about?

Alice seeing the panic on Gwen's face placed a soothing hand on her arm. "There's no need to worry I'm not here to cause trouble."

"You know don't you?" Gwen stuttered.

"Yes I know, and you're not the first and I doubt you'll be the last, come for coffee tomorrow about eleven we can talk it through."

133

Gwen nodded, unsure of what she should do, "How did you find out?"

Alice smiled reassuringly. "You've nothing to fear from me. Tomorrow, we'll talk tomorrow, don't worry he won't be there, if you want someone to accompany you they are more than welcome, but perhaps it would be preferable for our mutual privacy if you came alone."

Alice waited until she'd placed the tray on the table, "Thank you Mair, if you've nothing urgent to take care of then you can take the rest of the day off."

"But I haven't prepared dinner."

"I'm not completely helpless, anyway if I have any problems Gwen here will sort me out, won't you Gwen?
 Gwen nodded, not sure she knew why.

"Take the opportunity while it's offered Mair, tomorrow I might not be able to be so generous."

"If you're sure Mrs Pryce I'll just finish the bedrooms then I'll get my coat."

"Don't trouble about the bedrooms an extra speck or two of dust is no great calamity." Alice poured the tea. "We'll just give Mair time to get her coat we don't want to compromise ourselves. Milk or cream, sugar?"

"Milk please, one sugar."

"Help yourself to biscuits."

"I've been trying to think why you've asked me here Mrs Siencyn-Pryce."

"Alice please, there's no need for formalities, we're just two friends having a chat over coffee"

"But we're not friends we hardly know each other, so why am I here Alice?"

"I didn't ask you here to play cat and mouse Gwen, I know about the baby."

The harder Gwen concentrated to prevent it her cheeks burned even more. "How, who told you?"

"A man came to see Dafydd the other evening and I overheard their conversation, in fact I made sure I did."

"You know who he was?"

"Your brother-in-law Rhys Morgan."

Gwen gasped. "I'd heard there'd been an argument but no one seemed to know what it was about."

"Slightly more than an argument, your brother-in- law gave Dafydd a good hiding if his bruises are anything to go by."

"No not Rhys he may lose his rag and rant but he's never been known to be violent."

"It's not unknown for the most gentle of people to be driven to extremes."

"And you think it's because of me?"

"No not because of you, because of the evil that is Dafydd. Oh! I know all about the way he blackmails women especially the married ones. You're not the first, not even when he seduced you the first time." Gwen inhaled sharply her hand covering her mouth. Alice continued. "I didn't invite you here to accuse or blame you, I'm aware who's the villain and who's the victim."

Gwen opened her mouth to speak, but Alice's hand bade her to be silent.

"Let me tell you of when I first met Dafydd, I was approaching middle age and resigned to remaining a spinster. I'd never been much to look at, too skinny and no one would ever have considered me more

135

than plain." Alice's mouth smiled but her face betrayed her sorrow. "My father owned a small mine near Derby, nowhere near as big as the one here, but he managed to make a comfortable living, and provided as well as he could for his workers. He was a good man but too trusting, unlike my mother who saw through Dafydd within five minutes of meeting him. But before to long Dafydd had ingratiated himself with my father, and was turning his attentions towards me. He could be so charming and I was flattered, no man had shown any romantic inclination towards me, and like my father I ignored my mother's fears. I fell under his spell, probably because I saw him as not my last but my only chance." Alice paused, staring dreamily past Gwen and out of the window, watching her father cutting roses for her mother at their home in Littleover. Gwen remained silent allowing Alice her moment of reflection. "More tea?"

Gwen shook her head. "No thank you, I haven't finished this." Alice poured herself another and Gwen decided to take the initiative. "If you knew about him why haven't you spoken out earlier?"

"Oh I did, I found out about his philandering long before we came to Wales, by then my feelings were of sympathy for the women, especially the impressionable young girls, be truthful what would any pretty young woman see in him?" She gazed again out of the window talking to Gwen but her mind again in tune with the past. "My father gave us such a wedding the kind a girl dreams about, a carriage drawn by four white horses, the church absolutely brimming with floral decorations, and a reception in a huge marquee in the garden attended by the most notable people in the area. Dafydd was at his best charming and witty with the guests yet still attentive to me, I felt my entire life had been in preparation for that day. We honeymooned in Paris the most romantic city in the world, a wedding gift from my father." Her focus returned to Gwen and the present. "And Dafydd played his part to perfection, because that was what he was doing acting a role. My father looked on him as a son, and not long after our return announced he was making Dafydd a partner in his business so he could take things a little easier."

"What did your mother say about that?"

"I know they had some arguments about it, but never in front of us or the servants, and my mother never said a bad word about Dafydd to me once we were married. As if she'd resigned herself to a fact she couldn't alter, though in her dealings with him she was never more than coldly polite."

"When did you begin to suspect him?"

"Dafydd had become distant, no, it was more as if I irritated him, then he began coming home late at night, or more often the early hours, when I asked him what kept him out so late I was made aware of my place and that I had no right to question him."

"How do you mean made aware?"

"My parents were taking a long holiday, a cruise something that had been a dream but out of the question until Dafydd persuaded them, we'll my father, that the business would be safe in his hands."

"So he changed while they were away."

"Yes he changed, and instead of me worrying where he was I prayed he stay out and not come home. He never hit me where it would show, always my stomach, back or chest. That's how I lost my baby, when he was delivering one of his lessons."

"The bastard, oops sorry," Gwen raised her hand to her mouth.

"Don't be sorry I couldn't have put it better myself."

"Does he still beat you?"

"Not so often now, he's afraid of what I know."

"Why do you stay with him?"

"Why, what else could I do I'd no money? My father died penniless his business floundered after paying off Dafydd's debts trying to preserve the family name. I've no relatives and no friends of my own."

"What about your mother?"

Alice looked away shamefully "She died in the workhouse."

"I'm so sorry."

"I could do nothing to help her, I pleaded with Dafydd but he just laughed and said she was getting her comeuppance for thinking she was better than him."

"Since we came to Wales I've felt even more isolated, people converse in a language I don't understand, yet their asides are easily translated."

"I understand exactly what you mean. But what do you expect of me?"

"Nothing, I expect nothing. I hoped through adversity we could be friends."

"We've had a chat over coffee so I suppose we could be called friends." Gwen wasn't responding from pity she genuinely liked this woman, and not because they both loathed her husband.

"I'd like that, you'll come and see me again?"

"Whenever you want, or you could come to me but you'll have to take me as you find me." Gwen conscious that in comparison her house was no where near as large or comfortable.

"I've love to come and visit and get away from here for a while," said Alice glancing disdainfully around the room. "We still have much to talk about."

"Then my house it is. My problem is what do I do about Rhys, and has he told my sister?"

138

"I'd wait and see if they broach the subject, you could tackle him but I'd wait, if he hasn't told her already why should he now?"

Gwen's walk home took twice the time it would normally, there was so much to mull over. So much Alice hadn't told her, so many questions she could now think of, questions that required answers, and how did Rhys find out, and how much did he know? Did he know about the other times and Mari? God what a mess, could she play innocent until he approached her, whenever she saw him she'd know what he'd be thinking. Then there were all the others, Iwan, Mari, Tudor, Nerys, and her mother how could she explain to them, especially Mari, the truth would devastate her.

"You going to tell me what happened?" Nerys' anger had dwindled to annoyance now his job was no longer threatened.

"Like I told you, I had a row with Pryce over the way he'd treated Gruff Roberts and Catrin, he's seen sense now, Catrin's gone home and Gruff is back in work, so that's the end of it."

"So why did he sack you?"

"We'll convincing him to see reason wasn't easy and the argument got a bit heated, and we both said things."

"And you hit him?"

"Who told you that?"

"Never mind who told me, his bruises speak for themselves."

"I might have given him a shove and he fell over."

Nerys shook her head in disbelief, "Why you lying to me?"

"I'm not lying," he protested, believing keeping his explanation sparse wasn't strictly being untruthful.

"You're hiding something you and Gwen, and why's she suddenly so chummy with Alice Pryce?

"We've had this squabble every day for the last week it's about time you gave it a rest. You'll have to ask Gwen about Mrs Pryce how the hell am I supposed to know?" He closed the back door behind him savouring the crisp November air. Wouldn't she ever give up? There was the plus side, Catrin and Nia were back with their family, Mari had finally forgiven him over the pig and was talking to him again, if somewhat restrained, but if he wasn't careful Nerys' grumblings would replace her. He felt humbled as he studied the night sky, hypnotised by the mysteries of the full moon suspended by gossamer threads from the stars high above the mountain peaks, and wondered where God, if there was one fitted in such vastness, his eyes drifted to where the moons soft glow emphasised the cold steel starkness of the pithead rising high above the terraced rows, and he shivered at the skeletal reminder of his mortality

Chapter Twelve
Monday July 24th 1933

Her excitement heightened as the car's headlights picked out familiar landmarks on the outskirts of Rhydamman. Geraint would be waiting to see her no matter how late she arrived. Mari had wanted to come, and she'd also wanted to stay at home to see Huw when he arrived home Friday. She'd originally tried to talk Huw out of enlisting, and had missed him enormously the first few months he'd been away, but relished the times since when she'd been able to parade him in full army uniform through the village, delighting at the envious looks from the other girls. Tudor brought the car to a halt alongside the young man standing in the shadows by the gates. Instantly Mari flung open the door, and all thoughts of Huw were forgotten as she launched herself from the running board into Geraint's waiting arms, whirling her around he pressed his lips to hers. Chuckling Tudor drove on to the house.

Enid greeted them warmly in turn, hugging Sara and Gwen and shaking Tudor's hand, she asked, "Mari not with you?"

"Guess who was waiting at the gates?"

"He's been mooning about all afternoon, his father hasn't been able to squeeze an ounce of work out of him all week," Enid joked. "I'd hoped Nerys would have come as well."

"She had intended to but mam's not been too good lately, she's getting forgetful and having dizzy spells; besides it's just a fleeting visit to drop these two off."

"What does the doctor say?"

Gwen shook her head. "She repeatedly refused to see one. When Tudor said he'd ask Doc Richards to call she was adamant it would be just a waste of half a crown and told him to mind his own business, quite nasty she was and that's not like her."

"Did you still get him?"

"Eventually, when he came she'd forgotten her objections, he sat for a while chatting about old times."

"I hope he did more than that."

Gwen's struggled to dam the flood that threatened to burst forth. "Said there wasn't a lot could be done, gave us some tablets and told us to keep an eye on her and make her comfortable." stopping briefly to regain her composure. "She'll probably slip away one night in her sleep."

Enid slipped her arm around Gwen. "I thought she looked frail last time you brought her."

"He said her heart is weak, she could last six months, six days or six hours. She's determined to come and see you next week."

"Don't bring her if it'll be too much for her, I'll get Joshua to take me to see her."

Tudor entered the room carrying Sara her head resting in the crook of his arm. "This one wanted to help me unload the car," he chortled.

142

"Somebody's had a busy day, come on let me show you her and Mari's room." Gwen relieved Tudor of slumbering Sara and followed Enid upstairs, while Tudor returned to the car and retrieved the luggage.

"Hello Mr Gruffydd."

Tudor withdrew his head from the car boot. "Ah! Geraint just in time," he said offering him a suitcase. "That is if Mari can put you down for a few minutes."

Her face reddened slightly at Tudor's teasing. "Well I haven't seen him for a long time," she laughingly defended herself.

Gwen's journey home was one of mixed emotions, she was happy Sara was having a holiday and knew Enid and Mari would look after her, yet she felt empty as if she'd left part of herself behind.

"It's only for a week we'll be fetching her before you know it." Tudor had read her thoughts.

"I know it's silly." She turned from him and looked out into the darkness, so he wouldn't see the moistening corners of her eyes.

"Is Huw coming next week?" Tudor asked in an effort to deflect her attention.

"I should think so, he's only got seven days leave and he'll certainly want to see Mari,"

"Enid has always made a fuss of those boys, especially Elis."

"Not just Elis she's been good to, we'd be in right pickle without her help."

"I know that, but she's putting Elis through grammar school and promising to see him through university. Did her stepsons go to university? Don't believe I've met anyone who's been to university,

"Of course you have, how about Doc Richards? I don't think either of her boys did; Joshua had the business to take over and the

143

other one Dewi, the way she speaks about him he was a waste of time. Neither were blood relatives and you can't feel the same when they're not yours." Gwen's words like arrows once loosed couldn't be retrieved.

"Do you think I love Sara any less because she's not mine, that I wouldn't do anything I could for her I love that child no end, and Enid must have loved her sons.

"I didn't mean that." Gwen hastily tried to make amends for the upset she'd caused.

"I know full well what you meant." Gwen opened her mouth to protest but Tudor cut her short.

"Leave it, just shut up."

It was a full thirty minutes before Gwen ventured to speak again. "It's a pity Iwan isn't as bright as Elis."

And another five before Tudor replied. "Iwan seems to be getting on well enough, leading seamen, he may even get to be petty officer before too long."

Gwen forced a smile, "I never thought he'd take to the Navy but it does seem to agree with him, and anything's better than the blooming pits"

"Not too many working there these days. I can't help feeling guilty when I see the men I've worked with just aimlessly hanging around, it's like the strike all over again, only now I think its worse. Even Rhys is struggling, Pryce gives him the odd shift and what we pay him doesn't go far."

"We pay him as much as we can, if Enid hadn't encouraged Joshua to invest in our business we'd be as bad off as anyone. The buses are only barely paying their way, and it's the funeral business that's keeping us afloat."

"Not every one sees it like that, they know only too well what they haven't got, and to them we look like we're sitting pretty."

"We're not responsible for the world and his wife, you got up off your backside and did something, we took a chance, ok it's not making a fortune especially with Joshua taking a fifth of the profits plus the repayments on his loan, but it's keeping body and soul together, if it had failed and we were in the workhouse who'd worry about us? No bugger that's who."

"Doesn't stop people turning their backs on us, or spitting as we go past."

"And nothing we do can change that, they're jealous because we're coping."

"Aye I suppose you're right." Tudor conceded. "If it's just Huw and Nerys next week we'll be ok in the car, but if Rhys and Maude come as well it'll be a bit tight especially coming back, I might have to use one of the buses."

"Or the hearse they can stretch out in the back," giggled Gwen.

"Aye, get some practice in for when the time comes." He realised he was too near the mark as far as Maude was concerned and thankfully Gwen let it pass.

Rhys left two full sacks on the tip to collect later, the third he took to the widow Delyth Thomas whose gratitude would have seemed excessive under different circumstances. "It's just a bag of coal," he repeated as she thanked him for the umpteenth time. "I'll have to get back or mine will have disappeared," he said refusing the invitation to stay for a cup of tea.

"If you've left a full sack on the tip I don't expect it'll be there long."

"Gwil Lloyd's boy said he'd keep an eye on it for me."

"Is it true the police arrested Twm Twm yesterday for picking coal?"

"Everyone else got away but Twm's as deaf as a post, didn't hear the warnings."

"Who caught him not old Davies?"

"No he was nowhere to be seen keeping his head down as usual, they sent half a dozen young coppers and a sergeant up from Bridgend in a van.

"You be careful, I don't want you being arrested because of me."

"And I don't want you hungry because you've no fire to cook on."

"Nice to have something that's not means tested."

"Aye, they even came and counted the chairs in Edna and Joseph Powell's house yesterday, and because they had four they are expected to sell the two they don't need. Who do the blooming social think got money to spend on furniture?"

"That's nothing, after Will and Hayden were killed they told me to sell my double bed and use Hayden's single in the back room."

"Hard as bloody nails don't know where they find people like that, Pryce would have been good in that job. I wish I could have saved at least one of yours instead of him."

"It's said we're all here for a purpose."

Rhys grimaced. "Maybe but I can't think of a reason for him, except making life a misery for everyone else. I best get back or it'll be dark, I'll try and drop another off tomorrow."

"Now don't you go getting caught, that won't do you or me any good."

"But you need to stock up for the winter."

146

Rhys made his way to where he'd left the other sacks, and slung one on each shoulder. He took one home first because it was nearer, then after a cup of tea with Nerys he carried the other to Gwen's. Guessing they'd probably already left for Rhydamman he emptied the bag in the shed, then opening the back door to check he called. "Anyone in?" There was no reply. As he pulled the door closed he thought he saw a movement from the front room, he re-opened the door and called again. "Hello Gwen, Tudor, you there?" Silence. There it was again a shadow passing across the doorway to the front room. "Mari that you?" Kicking the step to remove the dirt from his boots he went in.

She was trying to conceal herself by crouching beside the settee, her arms drawn around her face. "Gwen what's up?" Kneeling, he tried to raise her to her feet, and realised it wasn't Gwen or Mari. She pulled herself from him backing against the wall, regardless of her hands attempting to hide her black puffy eyes, he recognised her.

"I won't hurt you," he said calmly. "What on earths happened to you, who did it?" Edging towards her he caught her as she crumpled forward sobbing uncontrollably.

"I think I'll take a walk and see what Rhys is up to. You sure you'll be ok? Now don't go messing about with the kettle your tea is by here." Nerys placed the mug of warm tea beside her mother. "It isn't very hot so don't leave it go cold. I won't be long." Nerys escaped into the night air, God it was nice to get away for five minutes. It had been amusing at first when Maude had misplaced something and they'd all had to hunt for it, but now it wasn't just forgetfulness, how many times had she put the kettle on the hob without filling it, or made tea with cold water. Yesterday morning she'd gone out partly dressed and Nerys had to go after her and bring her back. The day before she'd piled the fire so high hot cokes were tumbling onto the hearth, saying she was cold, cold in the height of summer.

The sight of him with his arms around her made Nerys' blood run cold. He didn't try and push her away when Nerys entered, utterly stunned by her discovery she turned and fled. Rhys called after her but she continued running, and she'd already turned the corner at the bottom of the street when he caught up with her, grabbing her arm he spun her round.

"What you saw back there it's not what you think." He panted.

"I saw you and her, that's what I saw." She screamed back at him trying to wrench herself free.

"You didn't see anything come back with me and I'll show you."

"I've seen enough, you go back to your trollop whoever she is."

"She's not my anything. It's Mrs Pryce and she's hurt and frightened, I was trying to calm her down."

Nerys finally wrenched her arm free of him, and started marching angrily back towards Gwen's house. "You'd better be telling the truth."

"Gwen stirred as the car bounced unevenly when the road surface changed from tarmac to cobbles. "We home?" She asked without opening her eyes.

"Yes, and we've visitors."
She peered through the windscreen at the couple caught in the headlights.

"It's Rhys and Nerys, wonder what they want? Perhaps something's happened to mam." Before Tudor could pull the car to a

148

stand still Gwen had the door open and was hastily firing questions at Nerys

"No mam's fine, you'd better ask Rhys what's up."

Nerys didn't need much convincing to feel guilty, guilty for not believing Rhys, guilty for thinking perhaps he'd done it before, guilty for thinking maybe she'd been blind all these years and Catrin's baby had been his. How could she have been so stupid to let her imagination run riot?

"I didn't know where else to go, I forgot you were out today," said Alice wiping her eyes.

"Where does it hurt? Gwen asked as she examined Alice's swollen eyes.

"Here," Alice moved her hand onto her ribcage. "Every time I breathe," she winced.

"Nerys will you get Dr Richards on your way home?" Nerys looked slightly surprised, not because she'd been asked to get the doctor but because Gwen was trying to get rid of her.

"Rhys and I'll go and get him in the car it'll be quicker." Noticing Gwen's look of disapproval Tudor added hurriedly. "Then I'll run Rhys and Nerys home."

Nerys tried to protest but Gwen was adamant.

"There's nothing you can do here, and mam's on her own."

Rhys hadn't been able to satisfy Nerys' curiosity, and early the next morning she was questioning Gwen over a cup of tea at the latter's house.

"So what happened to her?"

"She's upstairs in Mari's room, Doc wanted her to go straight to hospital but she wouldn't."

"I didn't mean that, who hit her?"

"Said she fell down the stairs."

"Huh, I don't believe that, do you?

"It's what she says. What did she tell Rhys?"

"Not much, he'd only just calmed her down when I walked in."

"And you jumped to the wrong conclusion."

"So would you if you saw your husband with his arms around another woman."

Gwen raised her eyebrows questioningly as she poured an extra cup. "I'll take this up see how she is this morning."

Nerys listened to the muffled voices coming from upstairs. Why was Gwen being so evasive?   She'd always avoided explaining just how she and Alice had become so close, and it was unheard of for a colliery manager's wife to befriend the wives of ordinary miners.

"She seems better this morning, a bit sore, the doc didn't think anything was broken."

"Well why did she come here? Why didn't Tudor take her home? Why didn't someone go and tell Pryce where she was? And why were you so keen to get rid of me and Rhys last night?"

"What's this the Spanish inquisition? I wasn't getting rid of you I don't like mam being left alone for too long that's all."

"Don't give me that, you've never been a good liar. What you hiding Gwen?"

"What do you mean hiding?"

"Hiding, like when you're not being truthful."

Gwen held eye contact with Nerys. "I can't tell you, there's stuff Alice has told me in confidence."

"What stuff?" Gwen's mouth remained silent. "You don't trust your own sister think I'm going to blab around the village? Nerys' anger raising her voice

"No don't be silly I know you wouldn't but I promised."

"I've always been open with you Gwen, still if you think I can't keep a secret."

"If only it were as simple as that, if I told you would you tell Rhys?"

"Have you told Tudor?"

Gwen hesitated. "No but I would if it concerned him."

"So why wouldn't I be able to tell Rhys you think he's the town crier? Now we know what you think of us." She seized her bag knocking her cup over in the process and stormed out leaving the door wide open. Gwen sank onto a chair her hands clasped in front of her on the kitchen table and watched her sister disappear through the yard gate.

"No I don't but I'm afraid of what he might do," she whispered to herself.

Chapter Thirteen

Saturday July 29th 1933

So you're definitely not going?"

"No."

"Good, if your mam's going we'll have a day to ourselves."

"That's not why i'm not going."

"I know why, 'cos you've fallen out with your sister."

"I was only defending you."

"I don't think I needed defending, not from Gwen anyhow."

"That's right take her side, you weren't there but you still think it's all my fault."

"I don't think anything, all I know is you'd better make it up damn quick 'cos I can't put up with your moods."

"Moods, I wouldn't be in a mood if you stood by me."

"I'm not getting involved between you and Gwen, whatever happens I'll be the one on the receiving end. If you're not going can we have one day without mentioning Gwen, or Alice bloody Pryce?"

"You used to harp on enough about Gomer when you two had an argument."

"That was different."

"What makes you so special then?"

"There's no talking to you when you're like this, I'll be down with the ducks, their quacking don't give me a headache."

"That's right run away when you can't answer."

"There is no answer you're not talking sense woman."

He'd drawn level with the lavatory when the backdoor slammed behind him, if their arguing hadn't woken Huw that was sure to. So much for a quiet day.

Huw lingered in bed until he was sure the quarrelling had ceased, the slamming door punctuating the end of the row.

Nerys forced a smile as he entered the kitchen. "Did you sleep well?"

"I can sleep anywhere after the bunks in camp. What time is Tudor picking us up?"

"About eleven but I'm not coming."

"I know I heard." He moved closer so he could cwtch her. "I don't like to see you upset Mam."

"Oh go on," Pushing him gently away. "Me and your father got to clear the air now and again."

"When's Elis coming home?"

"End of term last week, and he has gone to stay with a friend and their family for a fortnight."

"Boy or girl?"

"What?"

"Friend?"

"Being as it's a boys school I assumed it's a boy, I never thought."

Huw laughed at the uncertainty he'd created. "You know Elis anything wouldn't surprise me." Adding mischievously. "There must be an exceptional reason for not wanting to come home."

"He's taking the opportunity to have a holiday, not many get the chance of a proper holiday, just an odd day at Barry Island if their lucky."

"Elis is not short on opportunities." Nerys' raised eyebrows told him to elaborate. "Another year or so he'll be off to university, how many get that chance?"

"That's only because Aunt Enid has offered to sponsor him."

"She's never offered to do anything for the rest of us."

"Are you jealous?"

"No of course I'm not jealous, good luck to him but, oh lets leave it."

"No say what's on your mind."

"Well I wonder if I'd had the brains if she'd have done the same for me?"

"You're not stupid you and Elis are both clever, just show it in different ways."

"No Mam I know my limitations, I'm no academic."

"Your doing well enough, not everyone makes corporal at nineteen."

"Not like going to university though is it?"

Nerys passed him a mug of tea. "We can't all be scholars, and life's about more than books."

"I can't remember Elis not having his head in one."

"I'd better go and wake my mam."

"Is she any better?"

"Some days are worse than others, but the good days are becoming less frequent."

154

"It's not fair, when I think how she used to be."

"When you look at her that's what you have to remember."

"I'll tell you Mam I've met some really horrible people in the army, real vicious sods, but getting old can be a hell of a lot crueller."

Nerys was visibly paler than when she returned from taking Maude her morning cuppa. "Huw go and get your father please." She looked past him her sight fixed rigidly on the third shelf of the dresser.

"What is it Mam?"

Unflinching she repeated. "Get your father."

Gwen and Tudor arrived as Doc Richards was leaving. Gwen's fears were confirmed by the doctor's grim countenance. As she rushed past him into the house he turned to Tudor.

"I'm sorry, she went in her sleep."

Tudor nodded. "Even when you're expecting it, it can still come as a shock, when shall I call round for the certificate."

"Anytime."

Rhys left the sisters, their discord forgotten as they consoled each other in their mutual grief. Slouching on the front wing of the car he rolled himself a cigarette; raising his boot he struck a match against the metal studs. Dragging the cool palliative smoke deep into his lungs he glanced at Tudor.

"Someone will have to let them know in Rhydamman."

Tudor motioned towards the house. "I'll just check on Gwen and then I'll go and telephone."

Rhys continued puffing on his roly, only moving from the car when Tudor engaged the gears.

"It is with deep sadness that we mourn the passing of our dear sister Maude, and our hearts are heavy with sorrow and empathy with the family. They are not alone for we and God are with them and they can find comfort knowing Maude will have been welcomed into the kingdom of heaven. Maude will be remembered with much love by this community. My personal regret is although I have, and always will regarded her with affection, as a dear, dear friend, I was never able to spend as much time in her company as I would have wished. My failing is a common human failing in that we are preoccupied with trivialities until someone is lost to us, and too late we realise they should have taken precedence. I draw consolation knowing Maude has gone to a better place where one day she will be reunited with her family, those she loved and was loved by, and on the day of resurrection and unification we will join with those that have gone ahead and together we will share in the glory of Christ. Let us pray for the soul of our dear departed sister.

> *"Our Father who art in heaven,*
> *hallowed be thy name"*

Rhys wished he hadn't come and instead had gone with Tudor to collect Sara. He felt ashamed that Pryce's influence over him remained strong enough for him to waver at the prospect of missing Sunday Chapel.

> *"Thy kingdom come, thy will be done,*
> *on earth as it is in heaven"*

The day he'd hit Pryce he'd convinced himself that he'd no longer allow himself to be intimidated, an over estimation of what he'd accomplished had lulled him into complacency, allowing Pryce's dominance to stealthily reassert itself

> *"Give us this day our Daily Bread.*
> *And forgive us our trespasses,*
> *As we forgive them who trespass against us."*

Well he wasn't going to get away with his mendacity making a mockery of a woman ten times his better.

156

"Lead us not in to temptation, but deliver us from evil."

The bastard he'd never credited her as being anything more than another low classed collier's widow, and would never have given her the time of day he was just using her death as a podium to feed his ego.

"For thine is the kingdom the power and the glory."

Rhys rose from the pew and walked purposefully toward the pulpit.

"Forever and ever. Amen."

He halted alongside the pew of Pryce's most ardent followers, the chapel deacons, a hushed nervous expectancy hung over the gathering. Raising his head to meet Pryce's piercing gaze he spoke evenly with composure, not as a person filled with hate and loathing, but as a man filled with disgust for his own failures and the self-righteous gullibility of the congregation. "If there's a God which I am seriously beginning to doubt, because I have no answer when I ask myself what God would have created the likes of you, and allow his name to be used to satisfy ambitions and desires such as yours? Without conscience you heap suffering and degradation on others as if you alone are judge, jury and executioner. I pray there is a God who'll one day soon take your soul and casts it down into darkest depths of hell where you belong."

Pryce and the stunned congregation remained silent until Rhys left the building. At first there were hushed indignant whispers which became louder until everyone was expressing an opinion, some quite heatedly. Pryce recovering from his initial shock called for order reminding them of where they were, and having regained their attention he used Rhys as an example for a short sermon. "We are only mortal, and as mortals our emotions can take control leaving us blinded by hate. We must try to understand how grief can strike at the very soul of man, a man so distraught with his judgement impaired to such a precarious degree it compelled him to strike out, and lay blame without deliberation. God and his servants are clearly the easiest of targets, we must forgive as God will forgive and accept the failings of mortal man."

Much to Pryce's annoyance the funeral service was held Thursday at noon at Bethania Chapel in Maude's home village of Gelli. Even more infuriating was Alice disobeying his instructions and going to Gwen's house to pay her respects, which he regarded as a personal affront considering the way Rhys had spoken publicly against him. It was about time Alice showed the veneration due to her husband and the Morgan family learned their place, and with God's aid he'd show them exactly where that was.

Tudor went to Rhydamman the day after Maude's death and collected Mari and Sara. Elis cut short his holiday and came home, while Huw unsuccessfully applied to extend his leave on compassionate grounds, and had to leave directly after the funeral. Joshua represented Enid who still felt ashamed to return to the village she'd left so many years before.

"Gelli people have long memories," she'd said before reasoning. "There seemed little point in her going as it was the custom for only men to actually attended the funeral, while the excluded women were expected to stay at the house from where the cortège departed, and prepare refreshments for the male mourners return.

"Are you going back to Aunt Enid's with Joshua?"

Mari shook her head, "No not for a while, not until you and mam resolve whatever's between you." Nerys looked surprised at Mari's bluntness but she didn't offer any clarification. Mari lifted the tea tray. "I'll take these through I think I heard a car, they must be back."

"I'll come in a minute, I just need a moment on my own." Nerys sat viewing Gwen's kitchen yet observing nothing, her subconscious coming to the fore as it skipped erratically through loving memories of her mother.

"I'm sorry, I liked Maude she was a kind lady."
Nerys jolted back to reality slowly surveyed the speaker but stayed silent hoping she'd go away.

"I didn't mean to come between you and Gwen."

"Not now Alice, not today." Nerys tried to discourage any further comments.

"As long as you know it was never my intention."

"Not your fault Alice, you may be the reason but the cause goes far deeper, it's between me and Gwen you're not to blame."

"I did make her swear not to tell a soul."

"It's not because I want to know your business, it's because my sister doesn't trust me, and we were not just sisters but best friends, or so I thought."

"She couldn't tell you because I specifically asked her not to." Alice touched Nerys' arm. "It was unfair of me to place her in that position."

"You had your reasons."

"That's why I've released her from her promise and left it to her to decide who she tells."

"Do you think that's fair? Seems to me you've made your position clear and are passing the buck, whatever she does now she'll think she'll upset one of us." Nerys drew away from Alice's' hand.

"Rather than see you two at odds I'd prefer Gwen to do what she thinks is right, but whatever she decides you must believe she's doing it for the best."

"It's too late we'll never be the same again."

"All I'll say is if you love your family let it be."

159

"Answer me this does it involve Rhys?"

Alice dithered uncomfortably uncertain how much she should say.

"Only indirectly."

"How can I not worry, if it involves Rhys I've a right to know."

"Knowing won't make you any richer, wiser or happier."

"Thanks, now I'm wondering what the hell Rhys has been up to, so I expect I'll fall out with him as well."

"I've made it worse and all I was doing."

Nerys cut her short. "I don't know what you're doing, all I know is every time I see you there's trouble, now please leave me alone."

Alice opened the door before leaving she turned and huskily whispered. "Sorry."

Whatever Alice's intentions all she'd achieved was creating further confusion, one thing was certain she didn't want an argument with Rhys, not today, better to wait and see if Gwen had anything to announce.

Serving endless cups of tea while being required to engage in polite conversation when really they wanted privacy to mourn took a toll on both sisters. Nerys couldn't face a parting at the railway station and said her farewells to Huw before she and Rhys made their way home.

Tudor, Elis, and Sara had took Huw to catch his train, so Gwen taking advantage of Mari and Catrin's offer to wash the dishes and tidy up, went to have a lie down. Although her body was still her mind wrestled with her problems. Alice's good intentions had made it worse, what on earth was she going to tell Nerys? Could she tell her part, but which part? There were others to consider who'd done nothing, but they'd be wounded the most. No one in the village had questioned Tudor being the father of Sara, and if she revealed too much the whole family would be torn apart, but then what right did she have to censor the truth?

"I don't think your nan would have wanted you to be so upset."

"Can't help it I'm going to miss her." Mari brushed her eye with the tea towel.

"I'll miss her as well, she was kind to me when my father disowned me."

"She wasn't one to judge."

Catrin tried to lighten the conversation asking, "Who's this Geraint then?" As she placed the last of the dishes in the sink.

"He works for my Uncle Joshua, and helps his father with the gardening."

"What's he like."

"Tall, ginger hair and nice." Mari giggled.

"That's not much of a description.

"That's all you're getting, you'll have to meet him."

"Not much chance of me going all the way to Rhydamman."

"Never know he might come here one day."

"Serious then is it?"

"Maybe."

"As long as you don't end up alone with a kid."

Mari folded the tea towel over the back of a chair. "You never said who Nia's dad was."

"No."

"Even when my Uncle Rhys was being blamed you never said."

"No, everyone who mattered knew it wasn't him."

"I remember it not being nice for Nerys with all the whisperings behind her back."

"I know I felt really awful."

"So why didn't you tell who it was, and save her all the embarrassment?"

"I had reasons that I can't say, your nan knew she coaxed it out of me."

"You told my nan, when?"

"The day Sara was born."

"She never said a word."

"She promised not to, she's the only one I've ever told, it's over now so best forgotten."

"You can't forget, Nia's a fact."

"Nia's the finest thing in my life it's how she came about I want to forget."

"I thought that you might have eventually married the father."

"Never, any way he's married, he wanted me to say it was my boyfriend's, but I'd never gone that far with him so there was no chance it was his. Anyway we were talking about you and Geraint."

"But you're more interesting," Mari laughed lightly. "Just answer me one question?"

"What?"

"Why did you go with a married man?"

"That's history let's talk about the future, your future."

"No just answer me that and I'll shut up?"

Catrin thought for a moment. "Ok, but you promise not to tell a soul."

"On my mother's life."

"You've been lucky, all through the strike and even now when there's no work and people are suffering your family is not having it as hard as most."

"You saying Tudor and Rhys are wrong in trying to provide for their family?"

"No everyone has to do what they can to survive, and that's what I did."

"I don't get you."

"I watched my mam struggling to feed my brothers, sisters and father let alone herself. I can remember her boiling an egg for my youngest brother's dinner, he had the yoke, one of my sisters the white and my father claimed the bit cut off the top. That's how bad it was."

"Maybe we didn't have it as hard as you, but you don't have to tell me how hard it was."

"Harder for some than others, don't forget I came to live with Nerys and Rhys, and I'm not saying they had it easy and I'm more than grateful to them for the kindness they showed me, but they weren't exactly on the bread line."

"So what's that got to do with you and Nia's dad?"
Catrin seemed reluctant to expand any further, but Mari having got this far wasn't going to give up easily.

"So your family had a rough time, getting pregnant must have been a great help."

"I didn't set out to have a child that was an accident." Catrin sat on the stool by the bath." My mother had run up big bills in the shops, she had no hope of paying them and Bronwen refused her any more tick."

"Go on."

"I was offered a way of paying the bills."

"By Bronwen?"

"Owain."

Mari's mouth dropped. "So he's the father."

163

"I think so, although I'd made the same deal with Mostyn, but I'm almost sure it was Owain. Neither wanted to know when I caught, I felt utterly rejected and desperate I didn't know which way to turn or what I was going to do. When the chapel set my family against me it all became too much and you know the rest."

"Rhys stopped you killing yourself."

"Yes if it wasn't for him I wouldn't be here, I thought the whole world was against me, and preacher Pryce made me feel dirty and worthless."

"I still don't understand why you didn't name one of them."

"Because they both promised my mam wouldn't go short if I stayed quiet." A faint smile crossed her face. "Both Owain and Mostyn wanted to start up again after all the fuss settled down."

"And did you?"

"Only after getting a better deal with Mostyn, Owain always made my skin crawl."

"Don't you feel like a, like a,"

"I'll say it for you, a prostitute."

"Yes but I don't mean."

Catrin butted in. "I think a prostitute goes with anyone who'll pay her, I don't do that, Mostyn looks after me and Nia like Rhys looks after Nerys, or Tudor Gwen, or any man his wife and kids, does that make all women prostitutes?

"Put like that no, but you're not his wife."

"And never will be or anyone else's, man I love is spoken for."

"Who's is he then."

"You'd be the last, no last but two I'd tell." Without further clarification Catrin slipped through the door to join the others. Nerys remained still, numbed by Catrin's answer; she could only mean one man, Rhys.

Leaving Huw and Elis chatting on the platform, Tudor took Sara onto the footbridge so she would be engulfed in the exclusive aroma as the engine passed beneath.

"You don't know when your next leave is?"

Huw shook his head. "Hopefully Christmas but don't count on it."

"It would mean a lot to mam if the family were together this year, especially now nan's gone."

"Let's hope Gwen and her have patched things up by then, or Christmas will be a non event."

"Did you ask dad if he knew what was up?" The shrill whistle of the train drowned Huw's reply as it thundered into the station.

Releasing his brother from an affectionate hug Huw slung his kit bag over his shoulder. "You make sure you study hard, I might need a lawyer one day."

Elis grinned. "A solicitor, if I'm good enough."

Tudor and Sara returned in time to say goodbye as the train pulled away, and the tear Elis wiped from the corner of his eye didn't go unnoticed.

Gwen's restlessness continued throughout the night and by morning she'd come to a decision, not her first, but being the one she now favoured she decided to act on it. Tudor was up and out as usual by half six, and leaving Mari to see to Sara's breakfast Gwen found herself opening the door to Nerys' kitchen well before eight o'clock.

"I've been expecting you." Nerys said, glancing at Rhys who immediately read the situation.

"I'll just pop down and see if there are any eggs."

"There's no need to go on my account." Gwen said more earnestly than she intended.

"No you two want to talk, better if I'm not here." Without further comment he made his escape.

"I don't know where to start."

"That's up to you, try the beginning."

"Ok. There are a lot of things I've had to keep to myself, and I know not confiding in you caused offence, but there are other people to consider, and if what I'm about to tell you should slip out, then you could do untold harm."

"Then don't tell me."

"But I thought that's what all this is about."

"No its not, it's because you didn't trust me, I thought we'd always been so close we didn't need to have any secrets, that's what's upsetting, if you'd explained I would have understood, I didn't need to know everything, only that you were prepared to tell me."

Gwen thought for a moment. "Have you ever done anything you're so ashamed of you can't bear to think about it, let alone tell anyone, something so terrible that the closer someone is the more ashamed you are to tell them?"

"No I've done plenty I regret and wouldn't do again, but nothing like that."

"Remember when Pryce wanted you to meet him?"

"Yes but I didn't, thank God you sorted him out."

"What would you have done if I hadn't, would you have done what he wanted?"

"No definitely not."

166

"How can you be so sure, what if it were the only way to keep a roof over your head, would you let your children suffer knowing a few minutes unpleasantness for you is all it would take?"

Nerys failed to see the logic of Gwen's questions. "Where's this leading?"

"I just want you to admit when your backs to the wall you don't know what you're capable of."

"I've never been and hope I won't be in that position."

"Did you tell Rhys about Pryce?"

"Good grief no."

"Why not you and him are close, no secrets?"

"Because he'd have gone berserk and made things worse."

"Then understand why I've kept things from you, Alice's revelations could really do a lot of damage."

Nerys reached across the table and took hold of her sister's hands. "I'm sorry it seemed like I was being replaced by Alice."

"Alice and I have a lot in common and I like her, but she'll never be my sister."

"You don't have to tell me, as long as you're willing to I can accept it."

"I'll tell you everything if you like, but you won't thank me."

"It can't be that bad surely?"

"You'll have to make up your own mind."

"Don't tell me then, not just now."

"Why I thought you'd be bursting to know?"

"I am, but I'm scared."

"Remember when Rhys hit Pryce?"

"He never admitted it, said he knocked him over accidentally."

"Make the tea and I'll tell you why."

Chapter Fourteen

Saturday 19th August 1933

Nine years ago today, well not today because today's a Saturday, and it happened on a Monday. Twelve thirty on Monday the nineteenth of August 1924. Usually Tudor came with them, but he was busier than normal today so it was just her and Mari. Even if Iwan were home he wouldn't have come, not once since his return had he been to the cemetery with her, he always had to be somewhere else, but he'd go on his own and spend a long time talking to his father, but never with her. She knew why because Alice had told her, yet in all the time since neither Rhys nor Iwan had tried to discuss what they knew. She couldn't approach the subject what could she say? Oh, by the way Iwan the day you saw me shagging Pryce, well it never meant anything, I was just keeping everyone happy and a roof over our heads. And if he asked, then she'd have to tell him, yes she'd done it before, that's how he got both his sisters. She'd come almost clean with Nerys, and Rhys didn't know the full story, but just how much was he aware of? She prayed he didn't know about Mari. God what a mess. If Mari found out she'd probably never speak to her again, and Sara, she worshipped Tudor,

168

what effect would it have on her to find out he wasn't her father? Then there was the part neither Nerys nor Rhys knew, but the truth seemed to have a way of wriggling to the surface. Was it time to make a clean breast of things, and hang the consequences?

Mari stooped and removed the tired flowers from the vase beneath the granite head stone, and replaced them with some new blossoms, gathering the remainder she took and placed them alongside other tributes at the base of the newly erected monument. The contrast of the names engraved in gold lettering against the polished black marble was even more prominent when highlighted by the morning sun. They stood together in respectful silence for a few minutes.

"Disgusting that's what it is." Gwen agreed but said nothing. "People who had nothing to start with went without to raise the money for this, and how much did the mine owners contribute? Twenty five measly pounds and every single penny begrudged, I'm going to write to the Leader, see if they can shame them."

"I doubt the newspapers will be interested, especially the local rag, they won't criticise anyone with a bit of clout."

"We'll see about that."

Gwen could see a lot of her old self in Mari, she had a strength that the past few years had stealthily sapped from her, where once she'd have taken control of a situation now she was ever willing to at best compromise, and more often acquiesce.

"I'll wait for you by the gate." As she always did when they went to the graveyard Mari left her to have a few moments alone.

"I've made a terrible mess of things, I can't tell you what I've done I'm too ashamed although I expect Iwan has. Forgive me Gomer what I did I did for us, for the family. The saying, *Needs must where*

169

the *devil drives.*' is apt, for there's no bigger devil than Pryce and such was our need. I can tell you the secret that I've been keeping from Nerys and Rhys, if only you were here to tell me what to do, but then if you were I couldn't tell you." She stopped speaking, disturbed by the crunching footsteps on the gravel behind her. She felt the arm around her shoulder, and instinctively knew it was Rhys before he spoke.

"Nerys is talking to Mari down by the gate she'll be up in a minute."

"I'm done here, you have a minute with him, I'll go and see Nerys." She put her arms around his broad chest hugging him for a few seconds then walked towards where Mari and Nerys were waiting.

Rhys squatted on his haunches. "So brawd you've had nine years laying here while the rest of us have had to get on with things. I told you I'd lose it with Pryce one day. No I haven't hit him again just told him what I thought of him, trouble is I did it in chapel. I know what you're thinking, and I do try, but it's hard sometimes, I wish I were more like you." Rhys shifted position so his shoulder gained support from the headstone. "Pryce wants to see me in his office Monday, now he's had time to think about what he's going to do. I expect I'll get all the shit jobs thrown at me again, he tried that before and it didn't work, so he's probably thought up a new way of getting back at me. Tudor is doing well, not making a fortune but he's a grafter he'll make it work. You must be glad Gwen's not on her own and he's good with Mari, everything he's learned about business he's passing on to her. Rhys glanced along the path, Nerys had left the other two and was making her way towards him. "I'll just go and have a word with Moira."

Nerys stopped by Gomer's grave and looked over towards Rhys, his head bowed, even with his back to her she had a pretty good idea what he was saying. The amount of times she'd watched him in one-sided conversations with his parents, Gomer and always Moira. No matter how rushed he was, or how heavy the rain he always had time for Moira, and always finished by apologising for letting her down. She waited until he turned towards her not needing to look at his face to see the burden of self imposed guilt. Slipping her arm through his they thoughtfully made their way home.

Mari placed the kettle on the hob and raked out some of the ash, she wouldn't have to do that for much longer and was looking forward to the new house with a gas stove, hot water on tap and especially being able to flick a switch and instantly banish the dark. Oil lamps, boiling water on an open fire would be a thing of the past, along with the tin tub in the kitchen not that she'd used it in a while, she usually went to Nerys' once a week to soak In a proper bath. The deciding factor on moving wasn't because the new house was larger or more modern; it was due to the large yard where Tudor's lorries, buses and the hearse could be based instead of the three different sites spread between Pentre, Gelli and Gilfach.

"What time is dad coming home?" Her question didn't register. "Mam." The sharpness of Mari's tone finally got Gwen's attention. "Are you listening?"

"I'm sorry I was day dreaming, what did you say?"

"Oh it doesn't matter."

"Go on I am listening."

"I asked what time dad is coming home?" She'd started calling him dad the day he married her mother.

"When he's ready I suppose." Her tone listless.

"Just think this time next week we'll be in the new house."

"Mmm."

"What's up Mam?"

"Nothing, it's just today, and my mother going."

"It's more than that you've been like it for weeks. Is it this stupid row you had with Nerys?"

"I'd be lying if I said it hadn't upset me."

"C'mon, Mam, cheer up, where's the interest you had in the business? I'm doing all the paper work you used to do, not that I'm complaining I enjoy it, and I feel I'm earning my keep."

"You're welcome to it, I've had enough."

"Not like you."

"It's just life love, it wears you down."

"Dad's noticed as well, he's not blind."

Gwen turned her back so Mari wouldn't see her eyes filling.

"I hope you're not forced to make choices that seem right at the time, because you've got no choice, but years later the consequences come back to haunt you."

"You sound like Catrin."

"There's another one."

"Another one what?"

"Someone else who'll have some reckoning to do. What's she been saying?"

"I can't say, Mam, I promised."

"I'm beyond being surprised at anything. I can guess, she's told you who Nia's father is."

"More or less."

"Secrets no matter how deeply they get buried have a way of biting you when your back is turned. Take my advice and don't get involved,"

172

"I'm not involved, but I do think Nia's got a right to know who her dad is."

"Half the country can't be sure of that," said Gwen while desperately thinking how to change the subject. "Perhaps Catrin will tell her when she's older when she thinks the time is right, not for us to interfere."

"If you hadn't married Tudor, would Sara have known he was her dad?"

"Don't let's get into ifs and buts, it's Catrin's business not yours." Gwen breathed a sigh of relief at the sound of a lorry pulling up outside. "Sounds like Tudor's back." Having the excuse she needed she escaped through the door.

"It's been a hard decision, and one I've not made without a lot of thought and prayer." Pryce at his most pompous viewed Rhys over the top of his gold wire spectacles. "You must believe it's nothing personal even though we've never seen eye to eye, in the past, God has given me the strength and grace to put our differences aside."

Christ why doesn't he get on with it? What's he on about personal of course its bloody personal couldn't be anything but. Rhys rolled the tobacco from one cheek to the other and back again collecting the juices in the void around his gums. "I have to consider the welfare of all the men in this colliery, I need men who can remain in control whatever situation they find themselves in, and you have shown an inability to command your emotions."

Externally Rhys was calm and controlled, but before him was the catalyst that could enrage him in an instant. "If I hadn't stayed calm you wouldn't be here today, staying in control produced the worst day's work of my life."

173

"That's the reason I'm demoting you to fireman, by all means take the opportunity to prove me wrong." A smile sneaked across Pryce's face, Rhys stopped chewing curling back his lips mirroring the others smile, their eyes momentarily locked, then a thick black gravy substance splattered over the top of Pryce's glasses into his eyes and dripped down his face.

"You're right I can't." Rhys said as he turned towards the office door, leaving Pryce frantically trying to remove the foul smelling saliva.

"Have you told Nerys yet?" Tudor continued dipping the sweeping brush into the bucket, and scrubbing the wheels of the bus.

"Yeah, last night."

"She's happy then?"

"Aye, over the bloody moon, she's not speaking to me. It's not just the money we could lose the house."

"I could find you a bit more work but I can't help with the house."

"Messed up again haven't I? Story of my life."

"Perhaps it won't come to that."

"You think Pryce won't turn the screw? He's not the type to let me off the hook."

"Then why didn't he just sack you? I could never understand why he gave you your job back after you hit him."

"I sweet talked him." Rhys said flippantly.

"Well do it again."

"I don't think it will work anymore."

"I can't understand you Rhys, you're usually pretty easy going, then you do things like that. Didn't your brother teach you anything?

174

He'd have just got on with it, we all have our off days but why have you been pushing Pryce so hard?"

"If Gomer new what I know, he'd have done the same as me. And if I'm harassing Pryce it's between me and him."

"Fair enough, but you look to me to help you out, and it's Nerys who's suffering. You're making life hard for everyone around you."

"Gwen been having her say has she?"

"She did mention it, but she took your side."

"So what time do you want me tomorrow?"

"Be here by eight the funeral is at ten, that'll give you time to wash and polish the hearse."

"Suits me I have to be in work by one."

Elis laid his head on Mari's lap twiddling the grass stem protruding from between his teeth, while listening to the water gurgling into Penny Well.

"When you going to Rhydamman next?" She gave a deep sigh, her attention drawn to the dark blue and bright red dragonflies as they meandered above the pond.

"I'd go tomorrow but I think mam needs me here just now."

Elis sat up abruptly. "Remember when we were kids we used to strip off and jump in the water."

She laughed, "Yes, you me and Huw."

Elis jumped to his feet and started removing his shirt. "Last one across is a sissy."

Mari had slipped out of her dress and was running down the grassy slope while Elis still fumbled with his boot laces.

175

"God it's cold, I don't think it used to be as cold as this." Elis waded in, the water barely lapping the legs of his pants and he was already regretting having had the idea.

Mari had nearly reached midway when Elis finally took the plunge and swam after her. They reached the opposite bank almost together and collapsed panting.

"I won," coughed Mari trying to exhale the swallowed water.

Laughing Elis rolled onto his back. "We've got to go back yet."

"Don't think I can, I've drunk so much I'll sink."

"Just like a woman, can't keep your mouth shut."

She punched him hard on his shoulder, only intensifying his laughter.

"I wish it was always that easy to go back, then you could change things."

"That sounds serious, what you done that's so terrible?"

"Mari shook her head. "Something my mam said about the past catching up with you."

"You're not old enough to have a past."

"She's worried about something from before, but she won't say what."

"Then there's not much you can do. C'mon I'll give you a start I'll count to ten."

"Twenty."

"Rhys gone to work then?"

Nerys nodded. "I hope he doesn't do anything to make things worse today."

"I've decided I'm going to come clean tell Mari everything."

"You sure that's wise Gwen? I mean it'll be one hell of a shock."

"She has a right to know, and she'd hate me if she found out."

"She might hate you anyhow, maybe you should have told her before, and maybe it's better she don't know, whatever you do don't make the same mistake with Sara."

"Something else I'm going to tell you might be an even bigger one, what you do about it is up to you."

"If it's the thing you want to keep from Rhys I don't want to know."

"Well I can't keep it to myself any longer, with that and Mari it's driving me mad."

"Who's mad?" Elis and Mari came giggling through the back door.

"We are, it's the weather we've all had too much sun." Nerys' forced joviality noted but overlooked.

Finishing detailing his orders for the afternoon shift. "And if it's not done I'll want to know why." Jimmy Whiz pulled Rhys to one side. "Don't think because this used to be your job you know better than me, because if you did you'd still have it."

"I've never thought I was better than anyone."

"Just remember who's in charge."

Pryce entered the room and glared at Rhys.

"Morgan in my office." Rhys followed him in and closed the door.

"Let's get something straight now, you've used violence, blackmail, verbally abused me in chapel, but you overplayed your hand when you spat your vile filth at me, that was the final straw." Pryce moved closer his face inches from Rhys, his beady brown eyes squinting through the thick lens of his spectacles and a globule of perspiration hung from his nose, sneeringly he went on. "The threats you made concerning Gwen, well no one would believe them now, who'd believe a man who'd lost his senses. You've made no secret of your dislike for me, anything I'm accused of will be dismissed as being part of your paranoia, and if your family back you well that's only to be expected. So don't be surprised that I intend full retribution, an eye for an eye."

Rhys moved one pace back away from the spittle spray generated by Pryce's eagerness to put him in his place. "Go and broadcast your lies, your fantasies to all and sundry, because that's all people will think they are. You're finished Morgan, after your public exhibition in chapel everyone is questioning your mental stability, anything you do now will be put down to sour grapes because you've been deservedly demoted. I'm regarded as a saint by some, for instead of penalising you when you assaulted me for no reason I gave you another chance as the good book teaches us we should. The only reason I'm not sacking you is because you helped pull me out of the fall."

"Don't remind me, we all do things we regret."

"Well you'll have more to regret because I'll have you back on your knees shovelling coal."

"Now get out of my office before I change my mind, and get to work while you still have a job." Making sure his last sentence was loud enough to be heard by those in the outer office.

"You think no one will believe your wife either."

"Leave it Morgan, if you know what's good for you."

"Or what you'll sack me, you'll bring God's wrath upon me? Your wrath, God's wrath strikes me you believe they're the same." This time it was Rhys who sneered.

"My wife knows it's her duty to support her husband so don't rely on her."

"I expect you beat it into her. When you've had enough practise hitting women and you're ready to take on a man remember I'm head of the queue."

"You don't know when to give up do you Morgan? We'll I'll make it easy for you, get out of my office, and off of my colliery and don't come back, or I'll see to it you and your family are blacklisted throughout South Wales."

The glass in the half glazed door shattered as it rebounded off the wall and bounced back to its closed position. Rhys spun around to face him again.

"Come anywhere near me or mine, and I promise Mrs Pryce will enjoy the pleasures of widowhood."

"You all heard that." Pryce motioned to the officials gaping through the space previously occupied by the obscure glass. "I've got witness's they all heard you threaten me."

"If they're needed as witness's it'll be too fucking late for you."

Tudor pulled off his cap and scratched his head viewing Rhys with disbelief. "You had to do it, get yourself bloody sacked, Jesus, everyone scrabbling to hold on to what they can and you just chuck it away, I never had you down as that bloody senseless."

"I can do without the sermon I've had enough earache from Nerys and Gwen."

"If it were anyone else I'd tell them to get lost but I can't because I know Gwen won't hear of it, but I tell you Rhys I'm going to be hard pushed to find enough work to keep you afloat."

"I'll be grateful for anything."

"You're a stupid bastard. Your brother must be turning in his grave. I can't believe anyone could be so bloody brainless."

179

"Thanks I love you to."

Nerys checked Mari wasn't in earshot. "Did you tell her?"

"Not yet I'll have to choose the right moment."

Nerys grimaced. "Gwen there can never be a right moment. Where is she?"

"Upstairs getting ready Tudor is going to take her to Rhydamman to stay for a few days, hopefully her and Geraint will set a date."

"Oh yes Elis is going as well, he's not staying though."

"Hope he's not going to see Geraint." Gwen smiled with a twinkle in her eye, something Nerys hadn't seen for a while.

"No he's going to see Aunt Enid tell her how he's getting on in school."

"I think she's got her mind set on an Easter wedding."

"Chapel?"

"Yes, Hermon in Rhydamman."

"I gathered it wouldn't be Saron."

"Once everyone's gone we can finish that chat we began the other day."

"There's no need I've enough on my plate as it is."

"There's need for me."

Chapter Fifteen

Sunday 3rd September 1939

Gwen's tension mounted with each monotonous swing of the pendulum.

"It's nearly eleven." Tudor entered the living room and joined the others gathered around the wireless waiting for an announcement to stand by for a speech by the Prime Minister. No one paid any attention to the lady presenter giving a talk on tinned food recipes. Rhys glanced out of the window, not a soul to be seen just a lone black cat stealthily slinking across the road. Was that a good or bad omen?

At eleven fifteen Neville Chamberlain his voice tired and strained began his address to the nation.

'I am speaking to you from the Cabinet Room at 10 Downing Street. This morning the British Ambassador in Berlin handed the German Government an official note stating that unless we heard from them by eleven o'clock, that they were prepared at once to withdraw their troops from Poland, a state of war would exist between us. I have

to tell you now that no such undertaking has been received, and consequently this country is at war with Germany.

You can imagine what a bitter blow it is to me that all my long struggle to win peace has failed. Yet I cannot believe that there is anything more or anything different that I could have done and that would have been more successful.

Up to the very last it would have been quite possible to arrange a peaceful and honourable settlement between Germany and Poland, but Hitler would not have it. He had evidently made up his mind to attack Poland whatever happened, and although he now says he put forward reasonable proposals which were rejected by the Poles, that is not a true statement. The proposals were never shown to the Poles nor to us, and although they were announced in the German broadcast on Thursday night, Hitler did not wait to bear comment on them, but ordered his troops to cross the Polish frontier next morning. His action shows convincingly that there is no chance of expecting that this man will ever give up his practice of using force to gain his will, and he. can only be stopped by force.

We and France are to day, in fulfilment of our obligations, going to the aid of Poland, so bravely resisting this wicked and unprovoked attack on her people. We have a clear conscience, we have done all that any country could do to establish peace. The situation in which no word given by Germany's ruler could be trusted and no people or country could feel safe has become intolerable. Now we have resolved to finish it, I know you will all play your part with calmness and courage. At such a moment as this the assurances of support that we have received from the, Empire are a source of profound encouragement to us.

When I have finished speaking certain detailed announcements will be made on behalf of the Government. Give these your closest *attention. The Government have made plans under' which It will be possible' to carry on the work of the nation in the days of stress and strain which may be ahead of us. These plans need your help you may be taking your part in the fighting Services or as a volunteer in one of the branches of civil defence. If so, you will report for duty in accordance with the instructions you have received. You may be engaged in work essential to the prosecution of war, or for the maintenance of the life of the people in factories in transport in public utility concerns, or in the supply of other necessaries of life. If so it is of vital importance that you should carry on with your job.*

Now may God bless you all, and may he defend the right. For it is evil things that we shall be fighting, against brute force, bad faith, injustice, oppression and persecution, and against them I am certain that right will prevail.'

The sentence, '*This country is at war with Germany.'* and the dread it instilled lingered long after he'd finished speaking. Nerys and Gwen fearing for their sons sought comfort in each other. Rhys didn't move, although a declaration of war had been anticipated he'd been numbed by the Prime Ministers speech. Only Tudor seemed capable of constructing a coherent sentence.

"It won't last long it's just posturing; Germany will back down before any fighting starts." His words didn't have the reassuring ring he'd sought."

"You said they wouldn't invade Poland, what makes you think you're right this time?" Gwen said accusingly.

"I was just." He halted deciding a reply was pointless.

Nerys moved away from Gwen and caught Rhys' arm, the understanding in the meeting of their eyes needed no qualification, he put his arms around her and wordlessly cursed all politicians.

In Rhydamman Mari nursed in one hand the photograph of Geraint in her other arm she cradled three month old Kathryn, Edmund played on the floor with the fire engine he'd had three days earlier on his fourth birthday.

"Look how smart your dad is in his new uniform, we should send it out to that chap Hitler and he'd soon realise your dad's not someone to mess with."

Edmund carried on trying to imitate the sound of the fire engine's bell, and Kathryn focused exclusively on trying to chew as many of her fingers she could get in her mouth. It was at times like these Mari missed her family, she got on well with Geraint's parents but it wasn't the same. While Geraint had been there it was ok, but she wasn't from this area and no matter how hard she tried not to she felt a stranger. She looked forward to the days her mother and Tudor came to visit, and she'd been tempted more than once to write and request Tudor fetch her, so she could stay with them for a week or two. Only she knew there wasn't room, not with Rhys and Nerys having moved in after he lost his job. Anyway Siân and Emlyn would miss Edmund and fussing over Kathryn. Also Enid wasn't as sprightly as she used to be, adding to Mari feeling trapped, and dwelling on being home in Pentre only intensified her sensation of isolation.

It had been the birth of Edmund that had brought about the reconciliation with her mother. It had taken Mari two years to come to terms with Gwen's disclosure, and without Tudor's persistence in facilitating opportunities to build bridges her resentment may well have lingered. At the time of her revelations Gwen balked at the idea of disclosing her youngest daughter's paternity, because she didn't want to endanger the bond between Sara and Tudor. He'd always been there and raised and loved her as his own, and would there be a benefit to anyone in the telling? She'd only known one dad and that was Tudor.

Iwan viewed his shipmates in a new light, there'd always been a few hotheads who didn't look further than the end of their noses, but it disturbed him to see so many embracing the news with such relish. Only the older hands such as Jonathan Farnham who'd seen combat in the fourteen-eighteen conflict, displayed any real understanding of the implications. Jon had been twenty at the start of those hostilities, and reckoned he'd aged another twenty years in as many months, and believed it was the cause of his grey hair and furrowed brow.

"It won't be like in books or films, with honour, glory and tales of heroism to write home about." Jon sat with his feet dangling over the edge of his hammock. "Think I'll go and get a breath of air."

The young man next to him nodded. "Aye, me to."

On deck they lit their cigarettes and looked across the harbour to Gosport. A fortnight earlier the dockyard had been bustling with sailors returning to their ships as they prepared for sea. The waterway constantly criss-crossed by tenders as supplies and armaments were ferried in all directions at all hours.

The battleships, cruisers and destroyers had sailed, their places taken by smaller trawlers and coasters being converted to anti aircraft gun platforms, while larger merchant vessels were being fitted with four or six inch armaments. The feverishness of the earlier preparations had been replaced by a mood of readiness, although this was far from the truth.

"I wonder where they all are?" Iwan said wistfully.

"Wishing you was with them taff? Well don't, you'll be there soon enough."

"No Jon I've no desire to get myself killed, not that I'm a coward mind I'll do my bit."

"Look over there." Jon pointed at the Victory's ghostly silhouette, her topgallants the joint between earth and the heavens. "The oldest ship still in commission, flagship of the navy. Half the buggers who'll be running this show still think it's eighteen ò five and the British Navy is indestructible, when in truth we ain't nowhere near what we was."

"We won last time."

"There's no winners in war, just some don't lose as much as others."

"Wonder why we weren't sent out with the rest?"

Jon smiled wryly. "This old bucket couldn't keep up, be lucky to make it past the breakwater. Rumour is she's staying here as a training ship, and will probably end up being used for target practice."

"You got family Jon?"

"No just me. Had a wife once, she ran off with a salesman years ago. I came home on leave and the house was full of strangers, they'd been living there for two months, no one knew, or if they did they didn't say where she'd buggered off to. You?"

"My parents and two sisters. Did you try and find her?"

"No point we'd only been married six months, and I'd been away for five, gave her time to have second thoughts." He gave a dry chuckle. "What does your dad do?"

"He's my step dad really, my real father got killed in the pits. He has a bus company come haulage business, and he's also an undertaker."

186

"Could be a busy time for him, undertaker," said Jon cynically.

Left, left, left right left, right turn, about turn. Huw marched the squad to the four corners of the parade ground, barking orders in the manner of experienced drill sergeant, which he wasn't. He'd only received his third stripe a couple of months ago, and now faced the test of whipping these raw recruits into a fighting force in a very short time. His preference would have been to have remained with his company, but his wishes carried no weight in the decision of where he was posted. Captain Grant had assured him it was only temporary, and he would return to his unit within two months, three at the most, but a lot could happen in thirteen weeks. Now the fighting was about to begin maybe he wouldn't be stuck in Catterick for too long, though it was proving to have compensations.

Elis returned to his office, it wasn't really an office, just a corner tucked away from the reception area, allowing him to fill in for Violet the receptionist when required. Violet came across and sat on the corner of his desk.

"I think we all knew it was coming."

"Yes, but no one wanted to believe it. Your husband's in the army isn't he?"

"Frank, he would have been home this weekend but his leave was cancelled." She pulled her hankie from her sleeve and blew her nose.

"I expect he'll have another soon," said Elis trying to cheer her up.

"What you going to do, you had your call up yet?"

187

"No but I don't suppose it will be long, in fact I think I'd better have a talk to Mr Stanley about it."

Gerald Stanley Senior, head of the firm of Stanley, Stanley and King flicked the switch on the intercom.

"Yes Violet."

"Mr Morgan would like to see you."

"Send him in."

Elis stood in front of the desk and waited. Gerald Stanley shuffled the papers in front of him, and motioned to Elis to be seated.

"I know you've been an influence in delaying my call up, and I'm grateful but it's obvious I'm going to be conscripted any day, in fact a letter might be at my lodgings as we speak."

The older man nodded in agreement but added in contradiction. "Then I would have been mistaken and my sway would have counted for nought." A smile flickered across his face at the notion.

"I thought if I volunteered I might be able to avoid being drafted into the army, I've already made enquiries with the air force, so with your permission I'd like to go lunchtime to enlist."

Gerald Stanley rose and walked around his desk.

"I don't blame you son, I was an infantry major during the last lot and I'd never wish anyone the horror of trench warfare. You've only been here a very short time and I'll be sad to lose you. I can recognise if someone has what it takes to succeed in this profession. I could use my connections to pull a few more strings and get you a commission."

Elis shook his head. "Thanks, but it wouldn't mean anything unless I obtained it through my own abilities."

"I understand I'd have been disappointed if you'd agreed. Go and enlist if you must, but come back and say goodbye."

Later that day Elis left the offices of Stanley, Stanley and King all had wished him well, and he'd been assured he could resume his position when he returned, in reality they meant if. Sorry as she was to see him go Elis knew the tears Violet shed on his shoulder were for her husband.

"How long before you have to report." Rhys wished Elis' reason for coming home had been different.

"I have to be at camp by noon on the tenth."

"That'll give your mother a chance to spend some time with you."

"I hope I get a chance to see Mari"

Rhys drew the car to a halt. "Where's the nearest big town?"

"Darlington."

"It's a bloody long way."

"Aye, and there's no trains Sunday so I'll have to go Saturday."

"How long will you be there?"

"Just for my basic training about six weeks."

"Then where?"

"I don't know, wherever it is they train navigators."

"Wouldn't fancy that."

"Navigating?"

"No bloody flying, like to keep my feet on the ground."

"Like you did when you were in the pit, underground with the world on top of you? Well I'll be on top of the world surrounded by blue sky not thick black dust."

"You'd be safer down the pit, nobody's going to shoot at you down there."

Nerys waited impatiently at the door while Rhys and Elis sat chatting in the car. Finally the eagerness to greet her son pushed her out into the yard and she tugged opened the car door.

"What you going to do." Tudor read the letter Rhys had handed him.

"Not a lot I can do, it says it's only a request in the light of the government's intention to make it compulsory."

"Can they do that then?"

"According to Elis yes, wartime gives them the power to do what they like."

Tudor wasn't happy. Since Rhys had been sacked from the colliery he had proved to have a vocation as an undertaker. Where Tudor had always felt discomfort dealing with bereavement Rhys coped easily with an inborn sympathetic manner. He'd taken over the daily running of that side of the business leaving Tudor free to concentrate on the lorries and buses.

"But you don't have to go now, you can wait until they make you or it'll leave me short handed."

"If I go now perhaps I can arrange it so I'm able to carry on here, if I wait who knows, let me find out what's what."

Tudor shrugged his shoulders resolutely. "Will you be moving back to a pit house?"

"You trying to get rid of us?"

"No I'd rather you stayed here, be easier for you to keep tabs on what's going on."

"Good, 'cos I don't think Pryce will go as far as offering me a house, and if he did it would bound to be in bottom row next to the toilets."

Rhys had anticipated his return being rewarded with Pryce making sure he was made as miserable as possible, at best he'd hoped for indifference, and was surprised when he took his letter to the colliery he was shown into the manager's office. Pryce surveyed him for what seemed like minutes, but was in truth less than a couple of seconds.

"Never thought I'd see you back here."

"Perhaps you should have informed the government I was blacklisted." Rhys enjoyed his chance at sarcasm.

"Listen Morgan since I got rid of you this pit has run smoothly, and if it wasn't for the war I'd be looking forward to my retirement."

"I feel sorry for you, I'll tell the men about to be blown to pieces they're causing you some inconvenience perhaps they'll think twice about dieing."

"Still the same troublemaker, I had hoped we could come to an understanding. I don't want you here, and you don't really want to be here, but it looks like one way or another we're going to be stuck with each other. It's true I am short of men, and would rather that than take you back on." He held the letter aloft. "We can delay the inevitable but not prevent it, and it'll be better for all of us if we make an attempt to get along."

"So we kiss and make up do we?"

"No but I'll make a deal with you."

"Go on."

"You cause me no trouble, you do your job and I'll do mine, and we'll keep our differences out of work and to ourselves, and I'll throw in a house for good measure." Rhys was completely thrown off balance by the offer and Pryce pressed home the advantage. "I've done as much as I'm able to it's your choice."

191

"The only house that's vacant is Eli Jones' place and he died a few years back, it's very run down."

"It's a good house, just needs tidying and a bit of elbow grease. Being married to you I doubt your wife's afraid of hard work."

Rhys noticed the others jibe but restrained the impulse to retaliate. "And what exactly will my job be."

"That's up to you, you can get your shovel and I'll find you a place on a hard heading, or I could find you a deputy's job entirely your decision."

Rhys waited a while before answering, to make believe he was struggling with his conscience. The idea of using a shovel wouldn't have disturbed him a few years ago but lately life had been softer, he hadn't done any hard manual work, and had no motivation to go hewing his way into a wall of solid rock, perhaps he could still do it, but why bother to find out?

"Ok, it's a deal, but me or my family are not going near your chapel, and I'll have to talk the house over with Nerys"

Pryce rose from his seat. "Chapel you can justify with God, but I doubt you'll ever have the opportunity. Just remember I'm in charge here, and no matter what your opinion of me I expect to be treated with respect in front of the other men." Rhys viewed the offered hand with suspicion.

"I don't think we need to go that far, I'd be wondering what the other hand was up to."

The train rumbled into Darlington Station, and Elis spotted the army sergeant standing at the forefront of the passengers waiting to embark. "Huw it's good to see you." Dropping his suitcase he hugged his brother, "I hoped you'd be able to get a pass, how long have you got?"

"Twenty four hours, until eighteen hundred tomorrow, I didn't get your letter till noon today, but the CO's a pretty decent chap. Let's go and find a pub."

They chatted about Huw's role in the army, of Elis' time at university and the few months as an articled clerk at Stanley, Stanley and King. Then on to his prospects in the R. A. F. and how long he'd be at Middleton St George. Huw confirming Elis' suspicion he wouldn't be allowed any leave until he'd completed his basic training. They reminisced on their childhood and times long past, they talked about home and their father going back to the colliery, about Mari feeling home sick since Geraint had been posted, about Kathryn, the niece Elis had seen but Huw hadn't, about Gwen Tudor, Sara, and Iwan who was aboard ship God knows where. Whatever they discussed the topic always returned to their mother and her concern for their father having to re-enter 'Satan's lair' as she called it, and her fears that she may never see her sons again. As easily as the words flowed from their mouths, beer flowed just as freely in the other direction, and the conversation spiralled in an endless circle.

Huw let his head drop slowly forward relieving the pain in his neck caused by the windowsill. He peered through the blur trying to remember where he was, gradually the tables and the bar became vaguely familiar, when he struggled to sit upright his head left his body and floated in a mist away from him.

"You Ok?" The voice boomed in his left ear. He nodded and wished he hadn't. "Your friends gone to the toilet, he's been a while I'll go and check he's ok." The owner of the voice returned a few minutes later supporting Elis, who apparently had lost control over his legs. "I

193

didn't know if I should have called an ambulance for you pair. I'll get you a cup of tea then you'll have to be on your way." Huw paid the penalty for making the mistake of nodding again. Elis replied with a sentence of fluent gibberish and collapsed along side his brother.

Forty five minutes and several cups of tea later the brothers eased their way out onto the pavement. Both thanking the landlord for his hospitality in allowing them to sleep it off in the bar. He laughed assuring they weren't the first or the last.

"What time is it?" Elis focused on his watch.

"Just gone half ten."

"We've time for me to show you the area and have a bite to eat and a drink."

"I can't face another drink."   Elis screwed his face at the prospect

"Well you might after you've eaten, then if I can find my car I'll run you to your camp."

"You've got a car?"

"Not mine I borrowed it."

"I haven't got to be there till tomorrow."

"What you going to do you can't sleep in the pub again tonight?"

"Whose car is it?"

"Just a friends."

"Woman friend?"

Huw's head hurt as he laughed at the others persistence. "Yes, her names Doris and she lives not far from camp in Richmond, she's thirty two, married no kids and her husband's in France, satisfied?"

"What is he squaddie?"

"Didn't ask."

"Will you have time to get back to Catterick?"

"It's only about twenty miles from your camp, sometimes your lot use our training facilities."

Sara swept the papers and fag ends along the aisle onto the steps, and finally into the bucket. "Mam."

"What love?"

"Will the government make dad go back to the pit as well?"

"I shouldn't think so, why?" Gwen carried the bucket towards the next bus to be cleaned.

"Well they're making Uncle Rhys. They won't make dad go and fight instead will they?"

"They haven't ordered Rhys yet only suggested, as for your father I can't see it, who would run the business? And anyway he's too old for the army"

"Good I'm glad he's old."

Nerys' voice sounded across the yard. "Teas made."

Gwen put down the bucket and leaned the brush against the bus. "C'mon lets go and have a cuppa."

"You go I'll finish this last one."

Nerys was pouring the tea when Gwen entered the kitchen.

"All done out there?"

"Sara's finishing off." Gwen glanced at the clock. "I hope Tudor will be back soon, he's got Dai the farms funeral at eleven."

"Rhys did his best to swap shifts, I can't see how Tudors going to do the funerals and keep the buses going, he can't be in two places at once."

Gwen didn't know either, she knew he would knock himself out trying.

"If losing Rhys wasn't enough they had to take Nant as well, anyway we haven't got enough fuel allowance to operate both the lorries and buses full time."

"Funny isn't it, Rhys worried himself sick when he got sacked, then he said it was the best thing ever happened to him and he'd do anything not to have to go back, yet all it took was one letter."

"You worried about him and Pryce?

"I wouldn't be so worried if I didn't know."

"As long as Rhys doesn't find out."

"I wish you hadn't told me."

"I can't un-tell you can I?"

"I worried about it at first, but then Rhys not working with him I thought maybe he'd never find out."

"He still sees him at the funerals."

"Not the same though they're not in each others pockets."

"I hardly think Pryce is going to tell him."

Nerys grimaced nursing her cup in both hands. "I wouldn't count on anything with that man, if he thought he could hurt Rhys he'd make a deal with the devil."

"Too late for that, he did it when he was in nappies."

Chapter Sixteen

Monday 19th May 1940

Alice Pryce was determined she wouldn't allow Adolf Hitler to interfere with her plans. The preparations she'd made over the past eleven years were not to be foiled by a jumped up popinjay, she'd suffered too long under one dictator to be thwarted by a German version. It didn't matter her being delayed she'd enjoyed sitting anonymously on the platform observing other travellers hurrying to catch their trains, none of them giving her a second glance. Despite being squashed with eleven other people in a carriage built for eight it didn't seem smoky or claustrophobic, the air felt fresh, invigorating and exciting. Her life smelt and tasted sweeter than ever, even better than when she was young, before him. Her hand crept into her handbag seeking the reassurance the savings book gave her, some of the weekly deposits had been small, others quite substantial, and she took pride in not having missed one week. So she'd left it late but seventy-one was better than never, and now she had thirty-seven wasted years of marriage to make up for.

The advert in the Telegraph, 'Mature Lady Seeks Companion,' had given her the opportunity she sought. She'd contacted Mrs Bishop a widow the same age as herself, who sought a companion to share living expenses. The pair had corresponded regularly for the past six months and though having never met they had agreed that Alice moving to the Isle of Wight would be beneficial to both. The train rumbled into the central station, and a sailor crammed on the seat opposite jumped up and reached her bag from the luggage net, and escorted her onto the platform. As she thanked him it occurred to her how familiar he looked.

"Is your ship here?"

His colour heightened slightly. "I'm sorry I'm not allowed to say, careless talk and all that."

"Forgive me I shouldn't have asked." Alice annoyed at her thoughtlessness. "I was only making polite conversation."

"I'm sure you were, I never considered you were doing anything else. Allow me to carry your bag, taxi rank is it?"

"I suppose so, I need to get to the ferry."

"I've spent some time in Pompey but I've never been across to the island."

"It'll be my first time, then I haven't been anywhere for a long while. You're Welsh aren't you?"

"Yes, born and bred."

"South Wales?"

"Yes, Glamorgan."

" I recognised the accent, you know Bridgend?"

"Yes, I was born in a village not that far from there."

"Pentre, you're Gwen's boy?"

Iwan nearly dropped her bag. "How do you know?"

"I'm Mrs Pryce."

"The manager's wife, I recognise you now.   Arglwydd mawr fancy meeting you here."

As Iwan passed through the dockyard gate the siren wound itself into full screech, some people made their way to the shelter, but most carried on as normal as they'd experienced false alarms regularly for the past few months, and no one on the mainland had sighted an enemy aircraft. Except the one occasion the Luftwaffe had attempted to lay mines in the Solent, and a couple of Spitfires had sent them packing. He wondered if Mrs Pryce would be panicked by the air raid siren. Glancing at his watch he reckoned he'd less than five minutes to get back to the ship, he didn't like cutting it this fine but the excursion to Fareham and Hilary had been a good decision, especially as her mother and father were out and they'd had the house to themselves.   He needn't have worried he wasn't the last of his ships company to return, there were half a dozen thirty minutes behind him reporting as the all clear sounded. Portsmouth hid underneath the blackout, the harbours rippling water barely visible in the moonless night. Jonathan Farnham scurried up the gangway, presenting himself to the duty officer before joining Iwan.

"One night the bastards will be here for real."

Iwan nodded. "And we'll be sitting ducks on this old tub."

"They won't waste any bombs on us we're already sinking from the weight of the rust."

Iwan grinned in agreement with Jon's disparagement as they watched the last members of the crew hurry aboard, followed by the captain Lieutenant Osborne RNR, recently summoned to resume active service from retirement as a department store manager.

Before first light the next morning Iwan with the rest of the crew were rushing about making ready to sail. HMS Virago had been a merchant vessel for ten years prior to nineteen fifteen, she was then commandeered and armed with two four inch guns, one fore and one aft. She'd only left her moorings once in the past two years, then merely to be towed to a little used corner of the dockyard where she remained after being fitted with a dubious anti aircraft gun. Shortly before noon they passed the outer breakwater, Virago's weary bow plunging once more into the open sea.

Huw dragged himself out of the ditch, and using his rifle as a crutch he hobbled along the road. "C'mon you lot no time to take a nap, the bastard might be back." Men scrambled unenthusiastically onto the road.

"That's the third today we're never going to make it' grumbled one exhausted soldier .

Seizing the dissenter by his tunic Huw shouted into the man's panic stricken face. "Make it of course we'll bloody make it, if little shits like you move their fucking arses." His legs buckling with pain he threw the man forward screaming, "Now get fucking moving."

With each step the searing pain in his calf were a reminder of the metal fragments he carried with him, fuelled by pain, and anger at his stupidity in his eagerness to leave Catterick, he cursed his men step by step nearer to the coast. "C'mon you bastards the navy won't wait forever."

Each yard he trod, and each mile they conquered was that much closer to home, to beautiful Pentre's looming spoil tips and coal black river.

Dismayed he sank to his knees in the sand, he'd struggled, each step being more painful than the last, he'd shouted and cajoled his men even threatened one he'd shoot him himself, and what had it all been for?   A bayonet couldn't be placed between the bodies that filled the beach, a shooting gallery for the aeroplanes that came at their leisure. Men queued up to their necks in the rolling breakers, while the sea mated with the distant horizon, without the faintest hint of a ship.   There was nowhere else to go, if the British Navy didn't come the German Luftwaffe would.

Rhys ran his fingers over the equine relief etched in the lid of the box, then picked up the framed photograph standing next to it. She was still as beautiful as the day they'd married, only one thing had changed, he loved her even more, if only Moira were here to share his family. The raucous blast of the colliery hooter jolted him from his melancholy; over the past few years he'd taught himself to ignore it.   Now daily it beckoned him to a place he'd gladly never have wished to see again, but then there were thousands dieing in worse places than Pentre Bach Colliery. Siencyn-Pryce had been true to his word taking Rhys back on as a junior official, and the house had been in slightly better condition than he or Nerys had anticipated.

Nerys had insisted they take it stating. "No matter how well they all got on she liked having her own front door."

Rhys had laughed to himself when after the first few weeks he'd been put permanently on the night shift.   Pryce hadn't considered he was doing him a favour, enabling him to continue with the majority of his undertaking commitments. It had the added benefit of him having the minimum contact with the manager, who had been even less amenable since his wife had upped and left. Rhys often overheard other officials complaining of Pryce's petty tantrums, and rebuked them for the triviality of their concerns when scores of young men were dieing in France. Huw was in France.

"You going or you spending the day dreaming?" Nerys placed a hand on his shoulder.

"I was just thinking."

"He'll be alright, they'll both be alright."

Nodding he stood up and drew her to him, the colliery could wait, they both needed the comfort of each other for a while.

The pilot's request for an accurate position went unanswered as Elis studied his plot finally the instructor beside him intervened.

"You're taking too long Morgan the pilot needs to know now."

"I was rechecking the strength and effect of the crosswind I didn't want to make the same mistake again." Elis knew there was no mitigation he'd cocked up, he'd have one more attempt tomorrow to get it right and if he didn't then there was little chance of him becoming a navigator. He couldn't fathom why it was he made such fundamental errors, plotting courses and positions in the classroom was fine but as soon as he was airborne he seemed to always be wrong, and if he took the time to double check that got him into hot water. However certain he was he'd fixed their position and plotted the correct course the instructor invariably proved him wrong, humiliating him in front of the other trainees who'd successfully accomplished their tasks. Once again he'd be the source of their amusement, which he considered unmerited because they'd received twice the amount of training, as he'd joined the course midway through. The plane came to a halt and making sure he was first to alight he hastily put some distance between himself and the others hilarity. The next morning he prepared himself for what he anticipated would in all probability be his final flight, and made his way to the operations room where the briefing for today's exercise would commence at 0730 hours. Flight Sergeant Harris called him to one side,

"You're not flying today you've to report to Wing Commander Barstow at 0900 hours."

So this was it, he wasn't good enough, and he'd probably end up as an infantryman in the RAF Regiment.

"I wish these bones wouldn't keep reminding me i'm getting old," complained Enid as Mari helped her on with her coat and passed her walking stick which she carried more as an accessory than an aid.

"You can expect a little stiffness at eighty three." Mari wondered if Maude's lifestyle had been as balanced as Enid's would she still be alive.

"Now don't stay out too long."

"Don't fuss over me girl I'm not a child." That's it, that's exactly what it was like, she had three children one a twelve month old, one five this year, and the other one eighty three going on two. To be fair Lowri, who was no spring chicken herself, did the majority of caring for Enid, not that she needed too much looking after in a physical sense, just someone to keep an eye so she didn't over estimate her limitations. Enid left the door for Mari to close and shuffled along the garden path in the manner of a woman of her years, stopping occasionally to look at the new shoots that appeared almost daily.

"I'll be with you in a minute Emlyn, just want to check on the children." A few minutes later Mari reappeared in the kitchen as Emlyn helped himself to another cup of tea. "Kathryn's fast asleep and Edmund's helping your mother."

"She'll enjoy that."

"She'd have him with her all day, as would you and Siân."

"It's funny how to some people family is everything, and to others." He pulled a face."

203

"I miss my family; don't get me wrong without you and Sián I don't think I could stay.

"I know what you mean Enid's kind and full of good intentions, but she doesn't allow anyone to get too close, though she's better with you. All the years I've worked here she's never acknowledged me as her grandson. I know strictly we're not blood relatives, but I was the child of her stepson." He laughed. "Still am, can't change that. She's just as distant with Joshua's children, and Geraint wasn't treated any differently, seems like she just goes through the motions."

"That's unfair some people aren't as tactile as others, she just finds it hard to show her feelings."

"She's doesn't have a problem with your family, with you or your mother and Nerys."

"Perhaps she's more at ease with women." Mari was making excuses to make him feel better, not to excuse Enid.

"Yet she dotes on your children, blood relations see. I don't let her get to me like she used to when Geraint was small, she seems to have more time for him since he married you. Perhaps he should have met you sooner and maybe she'd have done more for him." Mari looked at him quizzically so he added. "Well it's not him she's put through university or set up in business."

Not wanting to accuse him of jealousy because there was truth in what he said she replied, "I can't answer for her, except she's been good to me, especially since Geraint's been away."

Emlyn changed tack. "Have you heard from him?"

"Nothing in the post this morning."

"I expect it's hard to get letters home from France." He was sorry he'd asked again, if she'd heard she'd have told him, all he'd achieved was to set her worrying even more.

"You and Sián will probably get a letter the same time as I do."

"I'll just go and have a quick word with my mother and see my grandson." He disappeared through the doorway and Mari could hear him chanting as he stamped along the hallway. "Fi-fi-fo-fum I smell the blood of a little welsh man."

Mari peered out into the garden, replacing the old lady nestled on the bench amongst the Rhododendrons with a young man. Her heart skipped a beat at the sight of his bright red hair and cheeky boyish features acknowledging her with a loving smile, then raising one hand to his lips he blew kiss as the image slowly merged with foliage.

Wing Commander Barstow told him to stand easy. Elis wondered who the pin stripped suited civilian was sitting at the end of the wing commander's desk. Fingering the papers in front of him Barstow made a few grunts of disapproval. "Not exactly lived up to our expectations have you Morgan?"

"No Sir."

"You think you are capable of guiding a bomber to an enemy target delivering the payload and then find your way back."

"Yes sir."

"We'll you have more confidence in your ability to do so than the RAF, and I'm not prepared to risk men's lives and equipment unnecessarily."

"No sir. Permission to speak sir?"

"Go ahead."

"Thank you sir. I think you'll see from the reports that I can plot a course as good as anyone sir, it's only when I'm actually airborne I seem to mess up sir."

"You have an explanation?"

"No sir, but I think an explanation from the instructor might be of interest."

"You think you're being unfairly treated?"

"No sir I wouldn't go as far as to say that." Elis sensed he'd nearly over stepped the mark.

"So how far would you go?"

"I thought the flying officer's opinion might be of value sir."

"I've read his report and taken it into account and if you've nothing constructive to add I don't see any value in pursuing that direction."

"Yes sir, thank you sir."

"This is Mr Wallace from the Foreign Office," Barstow gestured to the man beside him, "He'd like a word with you and I'd like you to consider carefully what he has to say."

Wallace a fair-haired man in his early thirties leaned back in his chair tilting it on its rear legs. Elis had a vision of it toppling and knew he'd be unable to contain his laughter if it did.

"University, first in law, read politics and languages, correct."

"Yes sir."

"Joined the communist party in thirty-six?"

"No sir I never joined or intended to, out of sheer curiosity I attended a few meetings and discussion groups."

"Hmm," The chair resumed its natural position, "That fits in with what I was told."

"By whom sir?"

"I see you are fluent in two foreign languages."

"Three sir, and I can get by in Italian."

"Three, French, German and?" Wallace raised his eyebrows.

"And English sir, my first language is of my country."

Wallace smiled amused at being corrected. "You consider England a foreign country?"

"I'm Welsh sir and proud of it."

"Good I'm glad to hear it, though I'd prefer if you thought of yourself as a British patriot wanting to serve his country."

"That's why I volunteered sir."

"Perhaps you're wasted here."

"Sir?"

Barstow interjected, "It was suggested when you enlisted that your talents might be put to better use."

"I wanted to fly sir."

"In this war Morgan we don't all get what we want."

For the past five days Virago had shepherded the small civilian craft, it seemed that everything remotely seaworthy along with its crew was being requisitioned and herded in to every available port on the south coast. Tugs, small fishing boats, pleasure craft, yachts, even riverboats many from the Thames and Norfolk Broads had answered the call. Iwan wondered how many of Virago's flock would survive Operation Dynamo, and Virago's prospects as she led her flotilla across the channel.

The air stank with the petrol and diesel fumes from the engines of the little boats as they scurried back and forth to the larger waiting ships. Like bees visiting the flower then returning to the hive with its precious cargo, the boats worked relentlessly ferrying the remnants of the British Army from the beach. Men scrambled up the nets onto the deck, some lay exhausted where they fell and had to be carried by Iwan and other crew members, while others found the strength to crawl and find a space to rest. Iwan wished his ship could get closer to the bulk of the fleeing soldiers. Although she was a small ship compared to the other navy vessels her draught was too deep, and the sandbanks to treacherous. The beach was a mass of heaving khaki seeking any meagre shelter from the enemy aircraft as they swooped, their guns raking the unfortunates below. Dive bombers and fighters harassed the armada, the boats weaving erratically to avoid the high explosive charges aimed at them. Hundreds of men filled every available space aboard the Virago, and while the uninjured attempted to aid their stricken comrades the Luftwaffe continued to rain death upon them. Beneath him Iwan felt the increasing throb of the engines as the Virago turned for home to deliver its load, they'd run the gauntlet of death until every available space was crammed to bursting point His senses became oblivious to the mixed smell of cordite and blood, exhaustion was over riding all emotions bar one, an intense terror pulsed within him as bullets tore apart the men compressed together on the red carpeted deck. The plane circled and came again low from the stern, spitting bolts of death from both wings. He curled himself into as small a target as he could, his bullet-proof hands wrapped tightly around his head. Behind the plane came others with larger and more potent weapons, the first explosion missed the bow by inches, sending a huge wall of water over the foredeck, the second along side the vessel caused it to roll wildly in the water. Luckily the third bomb failed to explode when it demolished the stern deck, leaving a large hole exposing the ballast laden hold, now decorated with bloody human remnants. Iwan tried desperately to free himself from the crushing weight of several bodies on top of him squeezing the air from his lungs.

On the cliff top Alice Pryce and Freda Bishop observed the activity in the Solent, a continuous stream of boats heading to and from

Portsmouth many of the smaller craft not entering the harbour but discharging their cargo on Southsea beach.

Alice passed the binoculars to Freda. "See that boat over there." She pointed to the larger boat, which from amongst a constant plume of smoke fluttered the remnants of a White Ensign. "It looks like she's' sinking."

Freda removed her spectacles replacing them with the binoculars.

"It's certainly leaning a lot to one side." The boat limped on unsteadily. "I think she's going to make it."

Chapter Seventeen

Friday 31st May 1940

The newspapers still headlined the story of the great naval success, some success, did the government believe the public were that stupid? The army had been close to annihilation, and the navy unable to stage an evacuation of the beach at Dunkirk without the aid of every Tom Dick and Harry who owned a small boat. Elis tossed the newspaper aside, he hadn't been reading anymore than the headlines, simply using it as a blind so he could study the two wrens sat chatting opposite. They paid little attention to anyone else in the carriage, and Elis' attempts to establish eye contact if noticed went ignored. He'd had a long journey, and ample time to reflect on Wallace's proposition. Of course there'd be a commission, a junior rank, a short period of further training and then he'd be on his own, probably in France collecting and sending back information on enemy movements, certain death if he were caught. If he refused then the very thing he'd sought to avoid had been alluded to. He'd been given a rail warrant and an extended weekend pass to think it over. It hadn't taken a great deal of consideration to reach the conclusion that in the S.O.E. he stood only a minute chance of survival, while as an R.A.F. Regiment infantryman he was offered the same chance as every other serviceman.

The delay in the rail connection from Cardiff to Bridgend gave him the opportunity to call at the offices of his old boss Gerald Stanley. An unfamiliar middle aged woman at Violet's desk told him he couldn't see Mr Stanley without an appointment.

"Just tell him Elis Morgan is here please."

"Ok but he's very busy."

Flicking the switch closed on the intercom she curtly bade him, "This way."

Gerald Stanley rose to greet him and shook his hand warmly. "Celia I don't want to be disturbed while Mr Morgan is here, except with two coffees." Giving Elis a final look of disapproval she left the room.

"I'm so glad you called, tell me how is the R.A.F treating you?"

"Fine sir, but I'd rather be back here." Elis made himself comfortable in one of the deep buttoned leather chairs facing the desk.

"Not what you expected?"

"More of not what I hoped for."

The older man opened the lower draw of his desk and withdrew a bottle and two glasses, "You'll have one?" He asked,

Elis nodded, "Please, just a small one"

A loud knock on the door preceded Celia entering with a tray which she placed on the desk.

"Thank you that'll be all."

"Where's Violet?" Gerald Stanley winced at Elis' question.

"Her husband was killed during the Dunkirk evacuation.

"Oh dear, poor Violet." Was all Elis could find to say.

"I fear there'll be many more Violets before this is over. You off home to see your family?"

"Yes I need time to sort some things out."

"I assume they are all well?"

"As far as I know, though my brother would have been at Dunkirk."

"The majority got home safely."

"All I can do is pray he's ok."

"And you, you going to be ok?" Elis looked puzzled by the question. Gerald Stanley continued. "I know more than you think young man, i'm aware this isn't a social visit, I told you I had connections and people have been enquiring of you."

"You're right, I'm here because I need your advice. What people, and to know what exactly?"

"They didn't officially announce themselves, but I suspect they were from the Special Operations Executive. Enquiring of your political affiliations, your background, an assessment of your character and temperament, how you react under pressure, your likes and dislikes that sort of thing. I could only confirm what they knew already."

"So you know what they want of me."

"They didn't declare their intentions but it doesn't take a great deal of thought to make a pretty accurate guess."

Elis gulped back the whiskey. "You must know I flunked my course?"

"Yes that puzzled me slightly. I wouldn't have expected you to have a problem."

"Navigation and bomb aiming I could master as long as I wasn't flying, at first I thought it was my nerves and I'd overcome them, then I had doubts about the impartiality of my instructor."

212

"You think you were victim of discrimination."

Elis nodded. "But I couldn't understand why until yesterday."

"Did you confront your instructor?"

"No perhaps I should have, but at first I had to accept the fault might lie with me, and now I don't think it was down to him anyway, he was just doing as he was told."

"Even when you thought you were at fault it didn't occur to you perhaps you weren't cut out for flying."

"That would have been admitting to being a failure."

"The failures in life are the people who when knocked down stay down, there's no failure in trying. We all have limitations on what we can achieve, some waltz through life and are lucky they never have to put themselves to the test. I confronted my greatest fears at the Somme." Gerald raised the bottle. "Another?"

"No thanks I'll stick with the coffee, what I don't understand is how the ministry knew I didn't relish the R.A.F. Regiment, there were plenty of ground jobs I could have transferred to but they seemed to know which stick to beat me with."

"Gerald's face reddened. "I suppose that probably may have been my fault, sorry."

"Doesn't matter they'd have found out anyhow."

"Have you decided what you're going to do?"

"First I'm going to pay my respects to Violet, and then see my family, as for anything else the regiment is winning at the moment."

"My advice, and you can take it or leave it as it's your life that will be at risk, and I've no right or intention of influencing your decision one way or the other." Gerald Stanley looked him square in the eye. "Whatever you decide, do it because you think it's the right choice, not because it's your duty or you'll be letting anyone down. You do what ever your conscience dictates, because you only have to answer to yourself, no one else."

The flat was small and sparsely furnished, little untidy but spotlessly clean as he would have expected. On every flat surface stood a photo of Violet and a soldier or the soldier alone in full uniform. Violet had been both surprised and pleased to see him, and he was amazed by her bravery as she told him without shedding a tear that Frank had been aboard a ship fleeing Dunkirk. The bomb landed directly where he'd been sitting, fortunately for the others it didn't explode but made a hole right through the deck to the bottom of the ship. If Frank had been a few feet away he might have survived, she wasn't sure of the boats name "Virgo or something like that." He felt awkwardness at having to leave to catch his train, apologising for not being able to stay longer and promising to call to see her on his return journey, and promised he'd write to her as when circumstances allowed.

By the time the train trundled alongside the platform at Bridgend daylight was fading. He crossed the road from the station and boarded the only waiting bus.

The driver smiled and got up to greet him. "If the train had been any later I think this lot would have lynched me." Tudor nodded towards the half dozen passengers on board.

"About bloody time to." Called an irate voice.

"Aye, he wouldn't have waited for any of us, but we're supposed to just sit here for an hour, happy like." Offered another

Tudor stood at the head of the aisle facing the passengers. "This is my bus. My bus." He added emphasis by stabbing his chest with his index finger. "And I say where, when and if it goes, and who travels on it. Now if any of you don't like it, you can get off. "

There were no further mutterings just glares at Elis as the passengers alighted at their stops.

Rhys arrived at the pit and was passed a sealed envelope by the overman going off shift. "Mr Pryce asked me to give you this personally." Rhys placed the envelope in his inside pocket to read later, amid jibes from other officials.

"Getting backhanders are you?"

"Pryce sending you love letters now is he?"

"Sending you on a special mission to find his wife?" The last remark brought a loud hoot of laughter.

Smiling he tapped his pocket. "I can't say, secret orders and walls might have ears." Inwardly he was as inquisitive as the others only his curiosity would be satisfied in privacy. It was several hours later and when he was sure that the night's tasks were well in hand that he sat down and took the envelope from his pocket.

'Morgan

It seems that my attempts at putting aside our past differences, and not allowing them to influence any decisions concerning you are being severely jeopardised by members of your family. I understood our agreement included your family not undermining my standing. This has not been adhered to and our agreement cannot continue under the present circumstances, it is your responsibility to rectify the matter or reconcile yourself to the consequences. As this is not yet a Colliery concern you are obliged to call on me at my home Saturday afternoon at three pm.

Dafydd Siencyn-Pryce

Colliery General Manager'

Rhys was even more perplexed, family members undermining his position? What on earth was he on about? Man must be cracking up since his wife buggered off. He replaced the note in his pocket, there were more important issues than Pryce's standing. In the light of Elis' disclosure and the message from Iwan to worry about, Pryce could wait his turn.

Gwen held the letter for Nerys to read. "Alice has settled in ok. Says the first person she met in Portsmouth was Iwan, there's funny they were both on the same train."

Nery's took hold of the letter. "She also says she saw the boats landing the troops from Dunkirk, some barely afloat. When you write ask her to go and see Huw."

"You're not going?"

"Of course I am. Can you come with me Gwen then perhaps you could see Iwan, I've never been further than Ponty?" Nerys' uneasiness at travelling alone conflicted with her desire to see her son. "If only it wasn't so far."

"It's easy, go to the station and get on a train, if it were Iwan nothing would stop me."

"It's alright for you, I've never been on a train."

"People do it everyday, why don't you and Rhys go?"

Nerys had already asked him earlier that morning, he hadn't said no, neither had he shown any enthusiasm and had seemed preoccupied since Elis' arrival home last night. He and Rhys had spent over an hour in the darkness of the allotments. She'd asked Rhys what they'd found so interesting but he'd just laughed and said men's talk. Sensing something was bothering him she persisted and he'd told her it was nothing just Pryce wanted to see him Saturday. She hadn't believed

216

him, he hardly gave Pryce a second thought these days. Then Iwan had rung.

Mari bounced Kathryn on her knee, while Edmund sat triumphantly astride the redheaded soldier he'd wrestled to the ground. "Get up Geraint the grass is damp."

He stood up, the child under his arm wildly flailing his limbs in an effort to regain control. "There have been times when I never thought I'd ever do this again, so a little bit of dew's not going to stop me now." He dumped Edmund flat on his back, his foot hovering above his son's stomach. "Winner," he cried bending down to tickle his victim.

"Ger did you see Iwan or Huw?" He stopped tickling Edmund and sat on the seat beside her,

"Mar there were so many of us crammed on those boats." He looked down at the ground to avoid her seeing the contempt he felt for himself. "Some were injured, some were dieing, all I could think of was you and the children and if I'd ever see any of you again. This may sound cowardly and selfish but I didn't care about anyone else. I didn't care who died as long as I was safe as long as I'd get home to my family, I didn't look for anyone, I didn't want to see anyone, I closed my eyes and I prayed. I prayed that the next bullet would have someone else's name on it, the chap beside me or the one in front, anyone but me. Those days we spent on the beach with the Jerry planes using us as target practice I'd have trampled on anyone to get away. I haven't got words to describe the horror and the fear." His voice faltered his hands hiding his face.

"Mum why is dad crying?"

"He's just tired love." With her free arm she pressed Geraint's head to her shoulder. "I prayed as well, for you to be safe and come back to us."

"Where's Elis?" Rhys was annoyed he'd had spent longer in bed than he'd intended, that was the drawback with nightshift, come Saturday if you weren't careful you could miss it.

"Gone over to Gwen's he's off somewhere with Tudor, they'll be back about tea time." Nerys sensed his disappointment. "You might as well go and see what Pryce wants."

"Aye, I'd forgotten about that, it's not till three though. I was going to ask Elis if he fancied going down the Bell."

The bowl almost slipped from her grasp. "You down the Bell? How many years since you were last in there?"

"Don't sound so surprised a man can go for a drink with his son."

"But you don't drink."

"Maybe it's about time I started."

"Pity you don't feel the same about your other son."

"What do you mean?"

"The one in hospital, the one Iwan phoned about, the one you won't take me to see, or is your meeting with Pryce so important that it's just slipped your mind?"

"I never said I wouldn't." Of course it hadn't slipped his mind but Elis was on it as well.

"You never said you would either."

"Monday morning is the earliest we can go, when I see Pryce this afternoon I'll tell him I won't be in work for a few days."

The gate was wide open and he automatically closed it behind him, a lesson he'd quickly learned after his allotment being the victim of Pugh's scavenging sheep. He'd expected his knock to be answered by the housekeeper and was mildly surprised when Pryce greeted him.

"Come in Morgan you're late, and in future use the back door." Rhys followed him into the sitting room and Pryce motioned him to be seated, while he stood by the fireplace resting one arm on the mantel along side an ornate ormolu clock. "All I expect to hear from you is an apology and you've taken steps to remedy the situation"

"I would if I knew what the situation was."

"Don't try and play the innocent with me, you know full well what I mean."

Rhys wasn't sure whether to laugh or be angry. "I've one son in hospital in Portsmouth and a second who'll be off to God knows where next week, I'm not interested in guessing games so say what's on your mind."

Pryce nodded, "Alright, my wife has, well she's gone away for a while, for a holiday."

"Yes I know."

"It appears your wife and sister in law are spreading a rumour telling all and sundry that she's run away."

"I think it's more truth than rumour."

Pryce's face reddened, "That's just the sort of remark that I'd expect from you Morgan. Well these rumours have to be spiked and pretty damn quick."

"You want me to tell Gwen and Nerys, well my whole family to put it about your wife's gone on an extended holiday." The sarcastic edge was unmistakable. "Where's she gone then on this err, holiday?"

"You know full well where she is, and I wouldn't be surprised if you didn't have something to do with her going." Pryce was on the verge of losing control and Rhys was happy to keep pushing.

"I couldn't advise anyone where to go on holiday never having been myself."

"I didn't ask you here to mock me, just tell your women to stop their gossiping, and you tell me where Mrs Pryce is."

"If I knew and I don't know exactly where she is, but if I did you'd be the last person I'd tell."

Pryce looked as if he were about to burst. "Damn you Morgan you've held a grudge against me since your whore of a sister killed herself."

Pryce knew where to aim and Rhys felt his blood rising.

"Mention my sister again and I'll make you eat your words."

"Why because it turned out she wasn't as pure as you thought, some women can't wait to sell themselves to the highest bidder."

Rhys was too quick for Pryce and leapt from his seat, grabbing Pryce by the lapels as he tried to move away.

"I told you once keep away from my family, you're not fit to mention them living or dead."

Pryce held Rhys' stare. "What was her name now? That's it Moira, well I'll tell you Moira didn't mind raising her skirts, as long as she got something in return."

"You lying bastard I'll shut your mouth for good." Rhys raised his fist but held from landing the blow.

"Go ahead but I wasn't the only one, she'd go with anybody just like your brother's wife, two of a kind they were both eager to trade themselves for what's on offer." Pulling backwards Pryce wrenched himself free his foot striking the brass fender causing him to lose his balance, swaying momentarily and grasping thin air he toppled, the back of his head crashing with a dull thud against the fire basket.

Rhys stared down at him shaking his head. "It was you, Moira died because of you." Pryce lay staring blankly at underside of the mantelpiece, his head resting on red coals out of which yellow flames darted licking his hair.

Rhys lifted the clock, not for the time or to admire it, but because it was heavy, clasping it in both hands he raised it above his head and threw it forcefully as he was able at the hated face.

"Dad, not here?"

"No he went to see Pryce ages ago he should be back by now."

Elis made for the door, "I'll go and meet him."

"Stay here love you've been gone all day and I want to spend some time with you to."

"Sorry, Mam," he said circling her with his arms.

"I know there's something bothering you and you would tell me if you were in trouble?

"Of course I would, Mam, I should have joined the navy like Iwan, I'm not cut out for flying so I'm going to have to do a ground job."

"Disappointed are you? I'm not I'm glad, you'll be safer."

"I've never been afraid of heights and it's not that I'm scared, but I just seem to freeze once we take off." It wasn't a complete lie he did feel a little queasy on take off.

"If it keeps you safe I don't care if you turn into an icicle."

"I'll be ok honest."

"Your father and I are going to see Huw on Monday."

221

"Say hello for me and tell him I'll try and wangle some leave so I can go and see him. I'll phone Auntie Gwen Wednesday to find out how he is."

"If you phone in the evening I can let Gwen know."

"I'll phone about nine'ish."

"What time is your train tomorrow?"

"There's a late one, I can travel overnight so you'll have to put up with me for most of the day."

"Think I can manage that." She squeezed him fondly

"C'mon, let's go and see if we can find dad?"

"He won't have been at Pryce's all this time he's probably down the allotment shutting the chickens up for the night."

The image he saw wasn't through his eyes, and it wasn't Pryce laying with his head in the fire, it was Moira and what Pryce did to her. What pressures did he put on her to make her do that? Even when he found out about Gwen it never entered his head that Pryce had somehow forced himself on Moira. For years he'd blamed Mostyn, but it wasn't him, it was Pryce the man whose life he'd saved. He'd stood up in chapel and called her a harlot while he'd been her seducer and the father of the child she carried.

"What you hiding down here for love?" He didn't look up a choking sensation in his throat prevented an answer.

"I told you he'd be here, look the birds are all roosting yet the doors wide open." Elis closed the door and clicked the padlock.

"So what did old Pryce want?"

Rhys collected his thoughts cleared his throat. "Wanted to know where Alice was," he croaked clearing his throat once more. "And he wants you and Gwen to stop spreading gossip."

"You didn't tell him?"

"Of course not." Wouldn't have mattered if he had, not a lot he could do to Alice now.

Chapter Eighteen
Sunday 2nd June 1940

"Gwen I need to speak to you."

"Where's the blessed fire Rhys? I've hardly opened my eyes."

He pushed past her into the kitchen. "Where's Tudor?"

"Still in bed where I should be. Has something happened to Nerys or Elis?

"No they're fine it's something else."

"Sit down I'll make some tea."

"Who is it Gwen?" Tudor's voice boomed from upstairs.

"Only Rhys."

"Bloody hell, do he think we all work nights? I'll be down in a minute."

"You stay there no need for us all to be up."

Gwen poured the tea and one for Tudor, before she could take it to him the door opened and Tudor in his vest with his braces hanging loosely from his waist, sauntered yawning into the kitchen.

"Bloody hell Rhys you could have come when we was up, daytime would be ok."

"Sorry Tudor, I didn't think."

"Oh well you're here now, what so important?"

"Nothing I just wanted a word with Gwen."

"Jesus Rhys you pick strange times for a chat."

"I've got a lot on my mind and Gwen's a good listener."

"You go back to bed love, me and Rhys will have a natter." Her eyes flicked between Tudor and the door.

"I can tell when I'm not wanted, I'll leave you to it." Taking his mug from the table he retraced his steps.

Rhys waited until he heard Tudor's footsteps padding on the stairs. "Does Tudor know who Sara's father is?"

"No and he doesn't want to, as far as we're concerned he's her father, I hope you're not here to dig up skeletons long buried. We have a good marriage so we don't need you raking up the past?"

"I went to see Pryce yesterday."

Gwen's face remained expressionless. "And."

"He told me."

"He told you what, that Sara was his child? You knew that when you thumped him that time. I've known you knew for ages, been waiting for you to bring it up but why now all of a sudden?"

"Yes I knew and I should have thumped him harder, but he wasn't just Sara's father was he?"

"So he told you about Mari?"

Rhys jumped up from his seat. "Jesus bloody Christ that bloody man, no I didn't know about Mari. Was Gomer the father to any of your bloody kids?"

"I think you'd better go home Rhys we'll talk about this some other time."

Rhys ignored her. "Alice knew didn't she?"

225

"Yes Alice knew, and Iwan is Gomer's believe it or not."

"Did Gomer know about Mari?"

"No and I don't think he suspected anything."

"Why Gwen, why did you bother with Pryce?"

She pulled a chair from the table and sat cradling her mug.

"Does it matter why? It's all history now, I've told Mari the truth, and Sara will know if and when I think she needs to."

"You can't tell Sara without telling Tudor."

"I know that."

"And what about my sister, did you know about her?" Her hesitation confirmed the question. "How long have you known?" His voice hardening into an accusation.

"Alice told me a few years ago."

"Why didn't you tell me?"

"I was afraid what you might do, look how you reacted when you found out about Sara, if I'd told you about Moira what then. Pryce deserves all he gets and one day he'll get his comeuppance. I didn't want you getting into any more trouble."

"You thought I'd harm him?"

"You threatened to kill him often enough."

"I think I have Gwen, I think he's dead."

The service went ahead, Emyr Iorweth who for a long time had harboured ambitions, considering himself a more proficient preacher than Pryce, and at last he found himself presented with the opportunity to exhibit his repressed oratory aptitude. His persuasive rhetoric convinced his fellow deacons there was no need to investigate Pryce's absence, secretly he hoped whatever the cause it would continue for at least the rest of the day.

"Dyma gariad fel y moroedd,
Tosturiaethau fel y lli:
Twysog Bywyd pur yn marw—
Marw i brynu'n bywyd ni.
Pwy all beidio â chofio amdano?
Pwy all beidio â thraethu'I glod?
Dyma gariad nad â'n angof
Tra fo nefoedd wen yn bod.

Ar Galfaria yr ymrwygodd
Holl ffynhonnau'r dyfnder mawr;
Torrodd holl argaeau'r nefoedd
Oedd yn gyfain hyd yn awr:
Gras â chariad megis dilyw
Yn ymdywallt ymâ 'nghyd,
A chyfiawnder pur â heddwch
Yn cusanu euog fyd."

The hymn sounded sweeter and more reverent because he'd chosen it, even the organist confused by the change of service and failing to join in until midway through the first verse, didn't detract from Emyr's enjoyment. He took for his sermon the first commandment.

'*Thou shalt have no other God before me*'.

A less than subtle inference, much to the embarrassment of Pryce's followers, of how some members of the congregation set their preacher on a pedestal, and the dangers in the misconception that piety and humility were the province of the voice that preached hell fire and damnation the loudest. Before he'd reached where God was a God of love and forgiveness half the congregation had departed in disgust.

"You were out early this morning."

"Aye I couldn't sleep this nightshift knocks you for six at weekends."

"You haven't had trouble before."

Rhys sought an excuse not to tell her, perhaps it would be better to wait until Pryce was found, maybe he wasn't dead after all. If he didn't tell her Gwen was bound to. She'd wanted to send Tudor to check just in case he'd panicked and been mistaken. One thing he hadn't done was panic, he'd closed the door and garden gate when he'd left and he was sure he hadn't been seen. "Elis still in bed?"

Nerys nodded, "Making the most of his last day."

"Sit down I need to tell you something."

"It's about Elis isn't it? I knew there was something up."

"No nothing to do with Elis."

Nerys breathed a sigh of relief as she sat across the table from him.

"Something happened yesterday at Pryce's."

`"Oh Duw, Rhys, you haven't thumped him again?"

He leaned forward and cupped both her hands in his. "No I didn't punch him, now please don't interrupt until I've finished."

She could feel her colour draining as he related his meeting with Pryce, and couldn't help interrupting when he revealed Pryce's involvement with Moira.

"He put a lot of pressure on her. You know your father was full of dust and couldn't work the coal anymore, he told her he'd find him an easier job without cutting his money, or he could leave the pit and find work elsewhere."

Pulling his hands away his expression turned to one of incredulity.

228

"You knew and didn't tell me," he shouted leaving the table and shaking his head repeating. "I don't believe it," several times.

A tear crept from the corner of Nerys' eye. "I wanted to as soon as Gwen told me, and I wished she hadn't."
She tried to put her arm around him but he shrugged her off and went out into the yard. He paused behind the lavatory and leaned against the wall, his mind racing, out of step with his trembling body.

"You don't think any one would go with him out of choice." She'd followed him.

"I don't know what to think. Of course Moira had a choice and so did Gwen."

"So easy for you to judge, never having been in that position and never likely to. When's the last time a woman blackmailed you into having sex?"

"They both could have told Gomer or me, not just given in."

"That's exactly why Gwen didn't tell you, he was trying it on with me going to chuck us out of the house."

Horrified he stepped away from her. "Not you as well Nerys please tell me not you?"

She became angry that such a consideration has crossed his mind. "Of course I didn't, you don't honestly think I could?"

"I've heard so much the last couple of days I don't know anymore Things that would never have entered my head, I don't know what to believe, but I'm beyond being surprised, and I'm beginning to understand why I was offered the job of overman. What price was paid and by whom if not you? I'm glad I killed the bastard." Not waiting for a reply he turned and ran out of the gate to the sanctuary of his allotment.

Nerys stood frozen to the path his words 'I killed the bastard,' pulsating in her skull

Now he knew though she'd never admit it, at the time he'd surmised he'd been given the job because Pryce owed him his life. Well what a sucker they'd taken him for. The one thing he regretted was Pryce was dead, and he couldn't kill him again.

"Hey, Dad, what you sitting down here for?" Elis ignored the tearstains that Rhys tried to casually wipe away.

"Needed somewhere to think son." Trying to eliminate the quiver in his voice.

"I dunno what it is but mam's in a hell of a state."

"Never hide the truth son it'll catch you out in the end."

"Aunty Gwen was with her when I left."

"Then I'd better go back to the house, there's a lot of dirty washing to be aired." Elis was unsure whether he should go with him, but decided to remain where he was, for the time being anyhow.

.   Elis returned to camp ignorant of Pryce's death. Both his parents had waved him off, his father with one arm around his mother's waist, but that hadn't fooled him something was between them and it wasn't trivial. He'd tried but found his efforts at reconciliation embarrassing, and part of him was glad to be away to concentrate on his own predicament.

The rhythm of the train soon had him nodding, Nerys was already asleep her head resting on his shoulder. Neither had slept at all the previous night. Her worrying the police would come and arrest him any minute, and he desperately wanting to believe she hadn't betrayed him. Gwen had backed up her story, but then she would wouldn't she?

Rhys drifted in and out of sleep, his dreams and consciousness intermingling; when he woke he was unsure which was reality.

Gwen had despatched Tudor to check if Pryce was dead as Rhys had claimed, he'd returned unable to get a reply to his knocking and not wishing to be observed he'd quickly retreated none the wiser. Rhys knew there was little chance of the body being found until today, as the daily from the village usually finished around noon on Saturday and didn't return until mid morning on the following Monday. He ran his fingers along the chain and pulled the hunter from his pocket, flipped open the cover and studied the dial. Nine fifty, wouldn't be long now, Mrs Jones would soon be making her macabre discovery, he closed the watch and returned it to his pocket.

Iwan stood amongst the swirling steam and smoke, as the carriage doors opened and the first of the passengers disembarked. He saw them before they noticed him, and he moved swiftly across the platform to greet them. "Welcome to England," he said embracing Nerys and firmly shaking Rhys' hand, "My mam not with you?" He feigned disappointed.

"No, something to do with the business came up and Tudor needed her there." Nerys knew he didn't care and wasn't bothered by her feeble excuse.

"She's ok though?"

"Yes everyone is fine."

"I've a car outside," he said ushering them toward the exit.

"How did you manage this?" Rhys made himself comfortable on the rear seat alongside Nerys.

231

Iwan laughed. "I'm joining a brand new ship in October until then I've been seconded to the transport section. I'm a driver for some of the big wigs, and what's good for the goose."

"You won't get into trouble?"

"Only if I'm caught." He laughed again, "Don't worry it's not a hanging offence." If he'd looked in the rear view mirror he might have noticed the disquiet his remark had caused.

He parked close to the hospital entrance, and turned around to face them.

"Before we go in there's something you should know, Huw is in slightly worse shape than I knew when I rang."

Nerys leapt forward in her seat, "What do you mean? C'mon Iwan tell me."

"He's ok but he's lost one of his legs."

"But you said he was only wounded?"

"That's all I could find out at the time."

"But Gwen phoned you yesterday and you didn't say." Whether she meant it or not it sounded like an accusation.

"I'm sorry, I still didn't know not until today."

Rhys squeezed her hand. "It's not Iwan's fault we should be grateful that he did what he could."

She ignored him. "So how do you know he's had his leg off?"

"I'm friendly with one of the nurses."

Every available space in the ward was occupied with as many makeshift beds as proper ones, and the place stank of a mixture of disinfectant and body fluids. A nurse escorted them along the ward, the sight of so many wounded men sickened Rhys, most of them were boys each one somebody's son, and if all the reports were true this hospital and others were full to bursting.

"There he is." Nerys pushed past the nurse to where lay a grey gaunt young man, his eyes staring vacantly into the space above him.

As usual the table was full of unwashed dishes, strangely the beef joint she cooked on Saturday morning was untouched, and he did like his meat. What a waste there's us having to make do with scrag end when we can get it, and he leaves prime beef, oh well if he doesn't want it I know who does. Mair Jones set about tidying the kitchen and preparing his evening meal, cutting the joint in two she wrapped the larger portion in paper and placed it in her bag. Her routine meant she'd do upstairs next, the bedroom and bathroom were normally in a mess since Alice had left, the dining room and sitting room would be seen to while his meal was cooking.

Owain and Bronwen were occupied spreading the daily tittle-tattle among the usual clique, when the door burst open, and to everyone's astonishment a hysterical Mair Jones screamed her way into the shop. It was several minutes before she could string together a rational sentence. "Oh my God it was horrible he's dead, dead, he's dead on the floor, dead, just laying there dead, burnt dead."

"Yes serg dead, his head or what's left of it's in the fire. Yes of course it's out now, but it was alight when he fell. No serg only the daily no one else." PC Charles Davies replaced the receiver and walked back across the hall to the dining room. The C.I.D and a doctor will be along in a while, not much we can do until they arrive. Do you feel up to making a statement?"
Mair nodded. He placed his notebook on the table and licked the tip of his pencil.

233

"Now then tell me everything from the time you arrived."

Nerys talked about anything, every day life in Pentre Bach, Huw's adventures as a child, the more she rambled the more desperate she became. Oblivious to her and all around him, Huw's unobservant gaze stayed fixed on the ceiling. Rhys turned from Nerys and beckoned the nurse, the tear creeping from his eye was as much for his wife as Huw,

The nurse tried to instil a little positivity. "He's been like that since he came in, it's not uncommon it's a reaction to what he's been through, but he should mend given time, The doctor will be along shortly he will be able to tell you more."
Rhys nodded automatically, his attention returning to Nerys and Huw.

Elis waited in the outer office, Corporal Wishart with whom Elis had become friendly, probably because they both had been articled clerks in civvy street, busily sorted a bundle of papers into alphabetical order and added them to the bulging drawers of the filing cabinet. Opening another drawer he plucked a file and laid it on the desk. "I have to go to the lav, I can trust you not to look at anything you shouldn't before I shred it." He glanced down at the file then winked at Elis.
Elis picked up the file, his name and service number written in bold letters on the cover. He leafed through the dossier, one page crossed with two heavy red lines caught his attention

'His navigation skills are exemplary, and he would make an excellent navigator/bombardier. Even though it has been deemed necessary for him to achieve a higher standard than his contemporaries he has excelled in every area. The in flight problem of disorientation is

typical of that experienced by many during their initial flights, and those having a much longer training period to accomplish proficiency invariably do so. I disagree with implementing a condition limiting his actual flights placing an unfair restriction on his ability to adjust and prove his suitability. I also feel it unwise to criticise and degrade his progress when he is actually out performing comparable trainees. I feel that given the aptitude Morgan has exhibited it would be a great loss to the service if he were not afforded the same consideration and honest assessment of his capabilities as the others in his section.

Flying Officer

James Forester (Training Instructor)

Underneath an addition read.

Delete with immediate effect.

K Barstow (Wing Commander)

Flicking over the page he read of his academic qualifications, with a highlighted report recommending use be made of, his natural linguistic aptitude, and his suitability for transfer to the Special Operations Executive. Elis placed the file back on the table as Colin Wishart returned from his toilet excursion, glancing at the file he turned to Elis.

"Ok?"

"Yes and thanks."

"For what? I've done nothing." The buzzer rasped its summons. "You can go in now."

Confrontation would get him nowhere he'd been singled out and trying to expose a conspiracy wouldn't gain him any sympathy. He closed the door and stood to attention.

"Stand easy. Well Morgan are you of a mind?"

"Yes sir."

"And."

"I think sir if I refused then where ever I was posted I would find myself relegated to the second division sir." Barstow stayed stone faced, unmoved by the obvious connotation. "So I don't believe I have an option sir."

"Good man, it's our duty to serve where we are best suited to fulfil our potential."
A wry smile traversed Elis' face as he considered the low risk factor of Barstow's potential, flying a desk.

The wing commander rose from his seat and held out his hand. "Wishart has your orders. Good luck."

Anxious to find out if the police were investigating Pryce's death Rhys went straight to Gwen and Tudor's house, and was relieved to hear that apart from making some general inquiries they hadn't exhibited a great deal of interest.

"So how long is Nerys staying?"

"I'm not sure, Iwan helped us find lodgings for the night and Nerys is staying on at least until the end of the week."

"Perhaps I should go down and keep her company." Gwen waited for Tudor to agree.

"Don't look at me you always do what you want anyway."

"And I'd have the chance to see Iwan." Tudor didn't reply but Rhys swayed any lingering doubts.

"I wish you would Gwen, Nerys is like a fish out of water in the city, and I have to be here just in case."

"Doesn't look like you're going to have anything to worry about here." She suggested

"I Hope not."

236

Tudor held out his crossed fingers. "They took a statement from Mrs Jones the housekeeper woman, and they had a word with the chapel deacons so with a bit of luck that'll be the end of it. An unfortunate accident."

"That's what it was he fell." He knew they didn't believe him by the glance that passed between them. "It's true."

"And Iwan he's ok." Gwen had already asked, but needed to change the subject before it became awkward.

Rhys related again how the victims of an unexploded bomb had pinned down Iwan, and had he been a few feet nearer he wouldn't have survived. That he was a driver in the motor pool until joining his new ship, which was due to be commissioned in September and that he expected to be home on leave before then.

"You staying here tonight?"

"No I'm off home to change I reckon I can just make it to work if I hurry."

"You can't work tonight you must be shattered."

"That's the best thing about train's Gwen, they put you to sleep." In truth he hadn't slept since seeing Huw, each time he closed his eyes the image of Huw staring blindly at the ceiling transformed into one of Pryce circled in a ring of fire. "And anyway I'll be able to catch up on the latest developments."

Chapter Nineteen

Wednesday 5th June 1940

The house felt cold and empty, even through summer Nerys always kept the fire alight so his bath water would be piping hot well before he got home. He placed the untouched sandwiches Gwen had made on the table. He hadn't felt like eating and was saving them for later, rationing had made certain good food wasn't wasted. Stripping off his work clothes and forced to wash with cold water he half wished they'd stayed at Gwen's instead of moving back to Gaffer's Row. He dressed in his clean clothes and set the fire, then settled down in an armchair encouraging the feeble flame not to abandon its flickering ballet. Content no one in work had thought Pryce's death suspicious; he pulled his coat around him and closed his eyes.

At first he was uncertain where he was, another bang on the door fully aroused him to the familiarity of his surroundings. Rubbing his eyes and yawning he staggered to the door.

"Mr Morgan, Mr Rhys Morgan?" Two men, each wearing the obligatory trilby, and suits with shiny trousers waited for his reply."

"Yes."

"I'm Sergeant Barrelle, this is Constable Moyle." He briefly held up his identification. He needn't have bothered; Rhys recognised what they were as soon as he'd opened the door.

"I think we should come in." Without waiting for consent they stepped forward forcing Rhys to give way.

"Can you tell us where you were between the hours of noon Saturday June the first, and nine a.m. Monday June the third?"

"Why?"

"We're investigating the death of a Mr Dafydd Siencyn-Pryce."

"What's that got to do with me?"

"That's what we're here to determine."

"Then you're wasting your time."

"I'll be the judge of that Mr Morgan, we can either do it here or down at the police station, either way you'll answer my questions."

"You arresting me?"

"That wasn't our intention, but if we have to."

"Let me put the kettle on and come around I've been up all night."

"Why's that, got something on your mind?"

"Yes I've a wounded son in hospital in Portsmouth, and I've been in bloody work all night, so I'm not ecstatic about you coming here interrogating me."

"Just routine sir."

"Everyone said it was an accident."

"Are you suggesting it wasn't?"

"No, how would I know."

"Well tell me what you do know Rhys?"

"That's easy bugger all, and it's Mr Morgan to you."

Nerys was thankful to see Iwan if it was only for a few minutes.

"I can't stop I'm supposed to be elsewhere. How is he?"

Nerys shook her head. "No change."

"My mother is coming today and I've told her where you're staying, her train comes into Fratton Station around six but I can't meet her can you? Oh, and she said there's nothing to worry about, and you'd know what she meant."

Nerys nodded. "Ok thanks." Relief on two counts she wouldn't be alone, and Rhys was ok, so far.

"I'll be in later, one of my shipmates is in here somewhere. Sorry I better dash."

"What's his name?"

"Jon. Jonathan Farnham."

"From this moment all conversations and I mean all will be conducted in French or German, the use of English, Welsh, Chinese, Serbo-Croat, or any other mumbo jumbo is strictly forbidden, from now on you think, live and breathe as frogs or Jerries. Tomorrow you'll meet Captain Ludlow, he's in charge of your section," barked the sergeant major. "Corporal show them to their quarters." The accommodation was far better than expected, the hut consisted of a well-furnished communal area, with a corridor leading off from the furthest corner to six small rooms, of which they were allocated one each. Through the door at the end of the corridor were the ablutions, which consisted of two showers along one wall, two Belfast sinks on another and opposite a pair of toilet bowls without seats.

"You have the rest of the day to familiarise yourselves with the camp, the Officers' Mess is on the corner of the main block, by the main entrance. I have to point out your strictly prohibited from using it." The corporal's manner seemed more slightly relaxed than regular army NCOs. "Just one other detail, you can ditch those uniforms and get into civvies as soon as you like. Induction's in here tomorrow at 10-00 hours." A wry smile flicked across Flying Officer Elis Morgan's face, he'd been an officer for only a few hours and he was forbidden to sport his rank or enjoy the benefits.

"Bonjour." He strode into the room erect, shoulders back, as you would expect of a British Officer, except he wore beige linen slacks, a white cotton shirt and a Fair Isle sleeveless pullover, gesturing them to be seated he dumped a paper file on the table. "Je m'appelle Capitaine Robert Ludlow, mais nous have little use for formal rank here, or little use for whom we were prior to today. One day you may become that person again but from today you'll take on a new identity." He pulled a chair to the centre of the room and sat astride it his arms resting on the back. "You've come here six strangers and I want you to leave as six strangers, make no friends, because to have friends means you're vulnerable, and in this business make no mistake if you're a vulnerable you're dead, and if you're dead you've wasted my time. You have to learn to live a life of a chameleon and blend into the background, draw attention to yourself and you'll have a life expectancy of a mayfly, probably less. You're all new to this and I expect you to make mistakes, my job is to make sure all the mistakes are made here and not when you leave. I have information here telling me about each and every one of you." He slapped the file then reached under the table and dragged out a large tin bucket. "There's an envelope for each one of you on the table containing a name badge, wear it at all times, because that's who you are until I tell you differently. Also in the envelope you'll find details of your past, learn it, believe it as if you've lived it." He picked up the file and drew a lighter from his pocket and set the file alight, before dropping it into the bucket, the flames leaping above the rim. "Now you've no past only who you are here, who I tell you to be, and your future if you are to have one depends on one thing, your ability to learn the art of secrecy and deception."

Rhys poured himself another cup, why had they come to see him and what did they know? They certainly gave nothing away but seemed keen to know when he'd last seen Pryce. Well they hadn't accused him of anything just wanted him to go to the station and sign a statement and God willing that would be the end of it. There being no point in trying to sleep with all the possible scenarios rampaging through his head he decided to go over and see if Gwen had gone.

"She caught the six thirty train, has to change in Bristol." Tudor's cap disappeared into the bus's engine compartment once more. "Can't understand it, it was ok last night, this morning won't bloody start."

"Temperamental?"

"Aye, like a sodding woman."

"You and Gwen fell out or shouldn't I ask."

"It's because of you anyway." His oil streaked face emerged again.

"Me! What have I done?"

"That's the whole point Rhys what have you done? Whatever it is we're accessories."

"I never touched him."

"You got to say that, you're not likely to say you did are you. Why did you just leave him?"

"I panicked." He lied

242

"That I don't buy not you, not the only bloody man to keep his head when all those men were killed. I heard that everyone was running round like bloody headless chickens until you took charge. So don't tell me you bloody panicked."

"Ok so I didn't panic, but I didn't kill him, he was laying his head in the fire and I thought good burn in hell you bastard, and I left him."

"Shit Rhys let's hope no one saw you."

"If they had I think the police would have arrested me this morning."

"They been to see you?"

"Came about half nine." Rhys related the interview in detail. "I just carry on as normal and stick to my story that I was over here helping you all Saturday afternoon."

"How long we known each other?"

"As long as I can remember."

"Well friend or not I'm doing this for Gwen, I wouldn't lie to the police for you Rhys. I'm doing it only because Gwen asked me, I don't believe he just fell, I think you're a liar and you're hiding something."

"Nice to know who your friends are." Seeing little point in continuing a conversation destined to descend into an argument Rhys left Tudor to his bus.

"Hello I'm Nerys."
Behind his bandages the sailor's attempt to smile ended in a painful grimace.

"My luck must be changing."

"I'm Iwan's Aunt."

"Thought it was too good to be true. Call me Jon."

"You and Iwan were on the same ship then?"

"Yes, we were two of the lucky ones."

"You don't look all that lucky to me."

"I was in the wrong place that's all, got a few burns but I'm alive."

"Is it painful?" Nerys realising how ridiculous her question sounded added. "I just called by to tell you Iwan will be in to see you later."

"You're not going so soon?"

"Yes I have a son in another ward."

"Surely he can spare you for a little longer?"

"He doesn't even know I'm here. I should go they're very strict on visiting times, and they have made a concession for me to be with Huw."

"Matron's bark is worse than her bite. Your son is he in the navy?

"No army, one of the soldiers you went to Dunkirk to rescue."

"I'm glad he made it."

"So am I, but it was at a cost to so many others. Thank you."

"Just following orders as I expect he was. You will come and see me again?"

Nerys nodded, "If I can." Not entirely sure she'd be able, but having promised she'd make the effort.

"Call by anytime I'm always in."

The phoned call she'd received from her mother yesterday had a greater impact than she would have expected. So her father was dead. Her initial reaction had been, so what, he's nothing to do with me, he was never my father, Gomer was my father. Tudor and Rhys had both been more of a father than him. At last he'd done one decent thing in

244

his life, and died. A day later she'd had time to reflect and surely nobody could be totally bad? Nobody deserved to die like that whatever they'd done, and the realisation that no matter how much she'd disliked him she never really knew him, and now never would.

The police car swept up the drive to the front door, at any other time Mari would have worried it heralded more bad news, thank God Geraint was one of the fortunate who'd made it home safely. A few minutes ago he'd left and taken their son to help Emlyn in the vegetable garden. Securing Kathryn in her shawl she wandered round the back of the house, she'd know soon enough what the police wanted. Lowri knew everything that went on.

Nerys had found her way to Fratton Station, and with the help of an obliging W.V.S lady found out at which platform the train would arrive.

"How is Rhys, have the police seen him?"

Gwen shook her head, "I don't know they weren't waiting for him and he went to work last night."

"Thank God I've been on pins all day."

"Can't see why the police will want to see him there's nothing to connect him to Pryce."

"He was there."

"No one knows that except us. Any change in Huw, and have you seen Iwan?"

"No Huw's the same, and of course I've seen Iwan how else do you think I knew you were coming? He'll be at the hospital tonight visiting a friend of his."

The lodgings were adequate if austere, a twin bedded room, with a large oak wardrobe and matching dressing table without chair or stool. The toilet at the end of the landing was shared with three other rooms; baths were available at extra cost and had to be booked a day in advance.

"Bit of a dump." Gwen noticed the flowered paper wilting from the wall above the window.

"Not the Ritz I know but I couldn't afford any better."

"How's the food?"

"Like it is everywhere, short. Did you bring your ration book?"

"I've been warned about that, not to hand it over, you only spend a couple of days and you end up losing a whole week's rations."

He noticed the man waiting outside the office door as he drove the bus into the yard.

"Good morning, i'm looking for Mr Tudor Gruffydd."

"Then you've found him, what do you want him for?" Tudor climbed down from the cab.

"My name is Barrelle, Detective Sergeant Barrelle." And this is Constable Moyle." Tudor hadn't noticed the other man now walking across from the workshop to join them.

"Hope you found what you were looking for." Moyle gave no heed to Tudor's sarcasm.

"We'd like to ask you a few questions." It seemed Barrelle was to do the talking.

"'Bout what?"

"Can we go inside?"

Tudor led them into the office and took up position in the chair behind his desk. "What do you want I'm a busy man?"

"Aren't we all Mr Gruffydd? You knew Mr Siencyn-Pryce I believe?"

246

"Yes, be hard not to in this village."

"Know him well?"

"He wasn't a family friend."

"Did you like him?"

"Put it this way, no, I'd cross the road to avoid him, and I had very little to do with him, especially since I finished in the pit, and as I've never had much truck with chapel, or any other religion for that matter, our paths rarely crossed."

"Can you think of anyone who would want to harm him?"

"I should think more than half the village wished him ill."

"Anyone in particular?"

"Not that I can think of. He was generally feared because of his position."

"Your brother in law, how about him?"

"What about him?"

"He says he was with you all Saturday afternoon."   Barrelle raised his eyebrows questioningly.

"If he says so, he was."

"Is there anyone who can corroborate that?

"If my words not good enough then ask my wife she saw him."

"Hardly impartial. Is she around?"

"Gone to Portsmouth for a few days."

"Why would that be?"

"None of your damn business."

"Did Rhys Morgan have a grudge against Siencyn-Pryce?"

"You'd better ask him that. Now if you don't mind I've work to do."

"One more question. "A few years back it seems Mr Morgan attacked Mr Pryce, why was that?"

247

"Like I said, ask him."

"Are you positive Mr Morgan was with you all Saturday afternoon, he didn't slip off anywhere for a little while?"

"Positive, we were changing the springs on the Max over there." He pointed to the Maxwell outside the workshop. "Now if that's all." He added more assertively.

"All for the moment but I'm sure we'll need to talk again."

"I can't wait." Tudor lingered by the office door as they turned out of the gate and headed towards the village. They obviously didn't believe Pryce's death was an accident, and were trying to implicate Rhys. If he hadn't killed him why on earth had he lied?

Iwan wished she hadn't come, whenever he looked at her he was sickened by the vision of Pryce pounding away between her legs, and despite the time lapse the graphic image remained. "So how's things back in Pentre?"

"Same as ever take more than a war to change it."

"Nerys told me Pryce is dead."

Gwen coloured at Pryce's name, conscious of what Iwan knew but never mentioned. "Yes, an accident by all accounts."
Iwan resisted the temptation to say how pleasing Nerys' news had been.

"How are Mari and Geraint?"

"Mari is happy enough now Geraint's back, she was feeling a little homesick."

"He home on leave?"

"Yes, he was evacuated from Dunkirk, physically he's ok but it shook him up a bit."

"I bet, I think everyone there was affected in some way, it was terrible but it could have been far worse. Thank God the Jerries didn't throw everything at us."

"They threw enough. You seemed to have landed on your feet this time, driving for the bigwigs."

"Not just them, anyone with any rank, won't be for long though I'm joining my new ship in September."

"Brand new one?"

"Yes I'm not supposed to say." He looked around to check no one was within earshot. "She's a light cruiser HMS Dido."

"What will you be doing?"

He pointed proudly to a recently acquired badge on his uniform. "I'll be firing the guns, well not actually pulling the trigger."
Gwen's preference would be for him to continue as a driver.

The black bakelite telephone commanded to be answered, Tudor picked up the receiver, "Hello Rhys I was expecting Gwen. No Nerys hasn't rung. Arrested! Solicitor, ok I'll get onto one straightaway. Don't admit to anything." Tudor replaced the receiver, then opening the hall table's drawer he took out the address book and flicked through until he found what he wanted. Before he could dial the number the phone rang again. "Hello Mari how are you? No your mother won't be home until Saturday, what's so important? No I haven't a phone number for her, she'll ring me either tonight or tomorrow. What's up? Don't give me that, I know you better than you think, something's upset you what is it? Why can't you tell me? Saying you just can't isn't a reason. Ok I'll get her to ring you."

Chapter Twenty
Saturday 8th June 1940

A stony faced policeman stood inside the door of the sparsely furnished interview room, when Rhys had attempted to initiate a conversation he'd been subject to a cold stare and compassionless silence.

"How long they gone for this time? If they've gone off duty we got a problem, 'cos I'm busting for a piss."

The constable finally nodded and pressed a push button at the side of the door.

"Thank Christ I thought I'd have to piss myself to get you to move." He really wasn't desperate but felt he had to get away from this room for five minutes, having already counted the mucus green painted bricks, or as many as he could see in the shadows cast by single low wattage bulb that hung above the table and the three other unoccupied chairs. Another uniformed bobby opened the door and Rhys found himself with his joint escort on his way to the toilet.

"Might as well have a crap while I'm here." He went into a cubicle, one of the policemen held the door.

"Keep it open if you don't mind."

"And if I do?"

"Just leave it fucking open. Sir."

"Bloody hell you think I'm hiding something in my shit? Don't think I want to go now."

The exercise had if nothing else cured the cramp in his legs. "I want to see Barrelle," he said as he was marched back to the green room to restart his brick count.

Thirty minutes later Barrelle and Moyle took their seats opposite him.

"Am I to take it you wish to continue this interview without legal representation?"

"No, I just wanted to check you were still here. If I got to stay here don't see why you should go home."

"Clever bugger eh."

"No, just bored and pissed off."

"You'll stay until we have the right answers."

"Well perhaps you're not asking the right bloody questions."

"Ok we'll give it another try, I must advise you your still under caution and anything you say may be used in evidence. Do you want your solicitor?"

Rhys shook his head. "Just get on with it, according to Mr Protheroe I don't have to answer."

"Ok, why did you go to Pryce's house on the Saturday?"

"I didn't, how many more times I got to tell you?"

"We have evidence you did." Barrelle unfolded apiece of dirty paper that Rhys recognised

"Where did you get that?"

"Where you left it, in the inside pocket of your work jacket." Barrelle waited for an explanation.

251

"Means nothing, I didn't go, I'd forgot all about it."

Barrelle laid the paper on the table. "Now then it says here, *'putting aside our past differences.'* What differences would they be?"

Rhys shrugged his shoulders. "Most people in the village had a difference of opinion with him, he could turn a worm cast into Snowdon."

"And then he refers to, an *'agreement'* between you."

"We made an agreement when I was more or less conscripted back to the pit, I'd do my job, and he'd do his, and we wouldn't interfere with each other."

"Strange a colliery manager would require such an assurance don't you think?"

"We'd had a few minor run-ins when I worked there before, this time we seemed to be getting along just fine."

"Fine, like the time you assaulted him?"

"Assaulted is a bit strong, I knocked into him and he fell over, it was an accident."

"Not according to a statement by Mr Densil Vaughan, who witnessed the attack."

"There was no attack, he didn't arrive until I was helping Pryce up."

"You usually put your hands around some ones throat to pull them to their feet?"

"It was dark, ever been down a mine? You can spit further than you can see, Densil was mistaken."

"So why did Pryce sack you the first time?"

"He was annoyed that I'd knocked him over, but he changed his mind when he calmed down, he was like that up in the air one minute then rationale the next. Act first and think later that was the way of him."

"Took a few days to think about it, and then only after you went to see him."

"I went to apologise for being careless and he said he regretted over reacting. If we were at logger heads all the time why did he take me back on and give me a house?"

"You tell us."

"Mr Vaughan says you threatened to kill Pryce, or was that accidental as well?"

"This is going nowhere. I've got nothing more to say until my solicitor is present."

"Tell me why you abused him in front of the congregation, over a hundred witnesses, or were they mistaken as well?

"It wasn't abuse just told him what I thought of him."

"Fond of that were you, it wasn't the first time was it?

"No comment without my solicitor."

Constable Moyle looked up from the notes he'd been taking.

"Something else for you to think about while your waiting, a man fitting your description was seen near Mr Pryce's house at the time suggested on the note."

Elis woke to the sound of boots stamping along the corridor's bare boards, the door burst open and he held his hand in front of his face shielding his eyes from the blinding torch.

"Get up, you're wanted." Two pair of hands roughly dragged him from his bed and bundled him out of the building.

In the torch light before a foul smelling sack was placed over his head, Elis identified his abductors as two burly redcaps he'd seen on duty at the camp gate.

"What the hells going on, can't I even get dressed?" Offering little resistance he was frogmarched across the parade ground to a hut away from the main camp. Once inside he was seated his legs tied to those of a wooden chair and his wrists lashed to the arms. The door slammed closed. He listened for a sound, any sound that would tell him he was not alone. There was none.

The train left the darkness of the Severn Tunnel, and sped towards Newport, hardly a word had passed between the two women each cogitating in their personal black void.

Nerys had one consoling thought, Huw had finally recognised her, he hadn't spoken but his smile had rallied her. The news that Rhys had been arrested had blighted any joy she'd felt.

The law was also Gwen's concern, the day following her conversation with Mari she'd sought the advice of a solicitor and explained the problem, his verdict had not been what she'd hoped. Then aside from the legal aspect there was also a moral dilemma.

"How much longer before we reach Bridgend?"

Gwen turned from the window. "Depends if we catch our connection in Cardiff, if we're late who knows? We're supposed to arrive there at five past two, but we were half hour behind leaving Bristol."

This did nothing to calm Nerys' nerves, her pounding heart hammered against the walls of her chest trying to break free from her increasing anxiety. She fought, and eventually lost the overwhelming urge to jump up and scream before she exploded. Then Gwen's arms were around her, holding her as her body entered into a series of convulsions. The other travellers hastened out into the corridor to be away from the mad woman who was having a turn in their compartment. The release of tension brought on a flood of tears along with the guard to see what was going on. He muttered something about lack of self-discipline and pulling yourself together, then disappeared to mollify the other passengers.

Tudor paced the platform, they hadn't been on the last train all he could do was wait the two hours for the next one. He crossed the footbridge to the downside platform where he could sample a cup of railway buffet tea. He immediately regretted the decision, the one mouthful he tasted he spat back into the cup and used his sleeve to wipe the disgusting residue from his lips. He went back over the footbridge and out of the station handing his platform ticket to the waiting ticket collector; a stroll around town might help pass the time. Unintentionally his course led past the police station and he was tempted to go inside and ask to see Rhys, but thinking there was little chance of the police granting consent he walked on. He'd seen enough of the police that morning when they'd questioned him again on Rhys' movements, and having repeatedly confirmed Rhys' alibi Sergeant Barrelle had warned if he continued to lie he'd be liable to prosecution when the truth was revealed. At a quarter to five he placed a penny in the ticket machine and resumed pacing the platform. Half an hour later the train finally crawled into the station, and the two women stepped down from the carriage.

Lowri had sat alone in her room since Enid told her the news, she'd long given up hope he'd come back for her, now it was definite she'd never see him again, Emlyn would never know his father nor

255

Geraint his grandfather. If only she could have seen him one more time and cast off the ghost that had haunted her for decades, now she was condemned to love a memory, a memory that hadn't faded with time. He'd been her first and only lover, and she could recall with crystal clarity when she'd given herself to him, recapturing his every facial feature and every word he'd spoken, and how could she forget him when she still heard his voice daily through Emlyn?

It seemed an eternity since he'd heard the door slam how long had he been sitting here an hour, two, three, more, was it daylight outside the hood? He presumed he'd been there quite a while, and what had been a draft across his uncovered body now felt like an icy wind, you needed more than underpants to keep warm even in early June. The sound of the door opening and several footsteps passing him heightened his senses, he could smell fresh coffee and tea and heard cups being set down. Then silence once more.

"For Christ sake this jokes gone far enough." The only reply was a loud click of a light switch, and footsteps approaching him. His head was pushed forward as the knot securing the sack was untied, and in one swift movement it was yanked from his head. Blinded by the sudden glare of the single spotlight beamed directly at him Elis screwed his eyes tightly shut.

"Name?" Commanded a voice from behind the light. "Name?"

"Anton Laval."

"Who are you Monsieur Anton Laval, where do you live, where do you work?"

"I live at 14 Rue Sablê Cháteaubriant."

"Are you married, have you children?"

"No I'm not married "

"Then who do you live with, your parents?"

"No they're both dead, I live alone."

What were their names, when did they die, what was your fathers work?"

The questioning about his family continued relentlessly until all avenues were exhausted, then it would start over again, and again. To his relief the sack was replaced over his head, leaving him in silence once more, his head slumped forward and mental fatigue overcame him.

His face stung from the slap that had brought him back to the blinding light and incessant questions. "I need a drink my tongue is welded to my mouth," he croaked.

Someone from behind the light said, "Ok." And a shadow appeared before him.

"This should quench your thirst." Elis spluttered through a torrent of water that poured over his head. "One bucket enough? I'm getting a little tired of your games Monsieur Laval I will have the truth one way or another." The shadow appeared once more and clipped something to both of Elis' index finger. "I ask you again, who are you?"

"I've told you Anton Laval, 14 Rue Sablê Cháteaubriant, I live alone and I work as an odd job man, I pick up work where I can get it how many more times?" The short burst of electric current felt like a horse had kicked him.

"This is your final chance, that was only a taster next time will be full power." Elis capitulated.

They had refused Rhys the use of a phone telling him he could use the public box on the corner outside the post office. His protests of not having the necessary pennies went unheeded; thankfully the operator had put a reverse charge call through to Tudor,

"I've been out of my mind." Nerys collapsed on the back seat beside him.

"Aye they tried to say I murdered Pryce but they got no evidence and can't prove I was even there."

Tudor interrupted, "They came to see me three times tried to get me to change my story."

"As long as the family sticks together there's nothing they can do."

"You know what still bothers me Rhys, if you didn't do it why do you need us to lie?"

"You saying you don't believe him, you think he's a murderer? Some friend you are." Nerys said angrily.

"Don't shout at me, I'm only saying it don't make sense that's all."

"Because if they find out I was there no one will believe I didn't do it, just like you."

Tudor drove this rest of the way in silence while Nerys told Rhys of Huw's first steps towards recovery.

"Does he know about his leg?"

Nerys shook her head. "No I don't think so. The only thing he seemed aware of was me."

"Then you'd better get back there as soon as possible."

"I can't leave you, they might arrest you again."

"And they may not, if they do it's up to Protheroe to get me out. Huw needs you more than me." Nerys knew he was right and had been thinking along similar lines.

Tudor had hoped he'd be able to spend Sunday servicing at least one of the buses, but Gwen had other plans.

"Do we have to go? I won't be able to run the town service the way I'm using up the fuel."

"So people will have to walk."

"But I have to answer to where the fuel has gone, and if I can't account for it I could end up in chokey."

"One little trip to Rhydamman is not going to make a great deal of difference, and Mari wouldn't have phoned if it weren't urgent."

"It's not just one trip though is it? The past couple of weeks I've been nothing but a taxi service for your family.

"They're your family too or had you forgot."

"So what's the emergency then?"

"She wouldn't say on the phone."

Tudor knew Gwen well enough to know when she was keeping something back, but didn't challenge her.

Geraint took Tudor on a tour of the garden to show him how much had been given over to the growing of vegetables. Tudor feigned interest but they both knew they were killing time while Mari and her mother had a woman to woman chat.

"How much does Aunt Enid know?" Gwen's first thought was to restrict the people with the full facts.

"The police came and told her they were investigating the death of Dafydd Siencyn-Pryce, which they believed was an alias adopted by her stepson Dewi Jenkins, Pryce was his mother's maiden name."

"You never told her about him being your father?"

"No, but she did ask me if I knew him."

"Does Geraint know?"

"Only that his grandfathers dead, to be honest neither he nor his father are the least bit bothered. Lowri's the only one who's shown any concern."

"She's carried the torch for a long time poor dab. All those years loving a waster like him."

"She must have seen some good in him."

"Poor memory more like. What are you going to tell Geraint?"

"That's what I wanted to see you for I don't know what to do. What can i do mam? This makes Geraint my I'm not sure what, and I could lose him." Mari felt confused, Pryce was everything her mother called him but he was also her father, and her husband was also her nephew or maybe something even closer.

"Geraint is only one step beyond being your brother, it's a right mess."

"I know that Mam just tell me what to do." The tears streamed down Mari's face as she pleaded for her mother to reveal a magic solution.

"I don't know love, I don't know." Gwen had no comforting answer. "It means I'll have to come clean with Tudor tell him the truth about you and Sara, he's always known Sara wasn't his but not her father's identity."

"And you don't want to tell him?"

"I should have done it a long time ago, he's never pushed to know and it's neither here or there now, there's nothing Tudor can do to Pryce. No it's you and Geraint I'm worried about, and how will it affect the children if it gets out? Rhys, Nerys and Alice are the only ones that know and they won't say anything."

"And Catrin she knows."

"Arglwydd Mari, if we could have kept it in the family we'd have had a chance."

"She only knows that Pryce was my father nothing more."

"If she finds out you're married to your nephew, that Geraint's dad is your half brother and she lets on, then your marriage will be well and truly over. The solicitor I saw in Portsmouth confirmed your marriage is definitely not legal, said in the eyes of the law it was incestuous,. You're going to have to tell Geraint he's a right to know."

Mari wished she'd kept her mouth shut, Catrin wasn't stupid, if she thought about it long enough had she sufficient information to figure it out? "But we didn't break any law, we didn't know."

"That doesn't matter, ignorance doesn't make it right, you know now and if you want to stay together you're going to have to keep quiet, that's if you think you should."

"Not you as well, Mam, you're not against us as well?"

"Of course not love. "She put her arms about Mari and cwtched her. "I just want you both to be sure you can live a lie."

"I love him, Mam, why is it wrong to love someone?" She snuggled closer into the safety of her mothers caress.

"Enid and Lowri, or Emlyn and Sián must never find out."

"I'm worried about Geraint's reaction, perhaps he won't want me anymore, the notion may disgust him."

"It's a chance you have to take, but it's going to be a hell of a shock for him. Why don't you Geraint and the children come back home with us for a while then you can tell him when you're in Pentre. Away from his mother and father and any inkling he may have of confiding in them."

Mari eased herself out of her mother's arms. "There's something else, they asked Aunt Enid if she knew a Rhys Morgan, and when she said she'd met him they kept asking her questions about him."

"Did they speak to anyone else."

"No, but they told her they might want to come back."

"Enid will tell us what they wanted. Dry your eyes, we'd better go and have a chat with her, and mind what you say."

"One other thing, Mam, is Sara finally going to find out who her father was, 'cos you'll have a job hiding it from her any longer, she's fourteen remember, and not stupid she's bound to pick up on things."

"I've been thinking about that and wondering if she really needs to know?"

"You know she does."

The comfort of the bed held him fast, glancing at his watch he blinked and shook his head, had he really slept that long? Heavy footsteps thumping along the corridor brought a feeling of déjà vu. Immediately he leapt out of bed and was half dressed when Captain Ludlow poked his head around the door.

"Ah, Laval good, my office 1700 hrs."

Elis relaxed back on his bed as Ludlow's footsteps faded and the outer door slammed.

Five o' clock prompt Elis was offered a seat in the captain's office.

"Well Laval how do you think you faired in last nights little test?"

"Not very well sir, I cracked."

"More importantly what did you learn, because if you learned nothing it was a complete failure?"

"To be honest sir my main concern is how I caved in so quickly."

262

"Ok we'll go over the events as they happened. Your first mistake was when you spoke to your abductors; do you remember what you said?"

"I asked what was going on, why was that a mistake?"

"You spoke in English immediately giving yourself away. Under interrogation you spoke only French and maintained your story in spite of intensive questioning, but you'd already blown your cover".

"I failed at the first hurdle."

"The electric shock you were given was small, twelve volt and very low amps. If we had been the Gestapo then you'd have been subject to a far greater voltage and amperage with the wires probably attached to your genitals." Ludlow's experience enabled him to know precisely the shame Elis was feeling. "You think you should have held out refused to talk, let me tell you once your caught, and they have the slightest suspicion your lying it's only a matter of time, you'll talk at some point, and when you do it will never be sufficient they'll keep on until they kill you."

It didn't make Elis feel any better, he'd broken to save himself from discomfort not even real pain.

"You told us everything you knew about the five others, which was quite a lot in view of the short time you've been together, and considering you'd been advised not talk about your pasts. The exercise was purely to show the importance of anonymity. I'm sorry you drew the short straw and were chosen as the guinea pig, but take it from me you faired no worse than any of your predecessors and none of your contemporaries would have faired any better."

Elis wasn't at all convinced of that.

"Try to examine the whole episode and tomorrow the group will scrutinise in detail last nights events. What particularly distressed me

263

was how you were able to glean so much information from them after my emphasising not to talk about yourselves."

Elis clarified the point "We did a lot of talking the night we arrived before we received any instructions."

Ludlow nodded. "I'll have to remedy that in the future. There'll be more tests during the coming weeks, obviously not the same but equally as stressful, and you can rest assured one of the others will be chosen next time. That's not to say you won't be selected in the future."

The police hadn't been around during the four days since they'd released Rhys late on Saturday evening, so Nerys felt reasonably comfortable during her journey. Huw had been transferred to the city's general hospital St Mary's, which she hoped would make visiting more convenient. Iwan not being able to meet her, and as it was within walking distance of the railway station had given directions on how she should get there. Two things helped to confuse Nerys when she arrived, firstly it was dark, and secondly her sense of direction was extremely poor. Iwan had found her a room close to the hospital, but after wandering in numerous directions for over an hour she had to admit she was lost. Wherever she'd gotten herself the streets were empty with no one she could ask the way. Then for the first time Nerys and Portsmouth simultaneously experienced the realities of war. Startled by the siren as it wailed into life, and unsure where to seek shelter Nerys hurried in the direction she'd been going. Behind her she could hear the booming of anti aircraft batteries and the terrifying detonation of the bombs. They seemed to be getting closer, when a blast sent her hurtling into a brick wall.

Someone pulled her too her feet. "C'mon quickly," they said partially dragging her along the pavement.

"My case," she protested.

"Leave it."

The shelter was full and they squeezed themselves alongside a woman and her three crying children.

"Wish i'd had them evacuated now," the woman said regretfully. "But there didn't seem much point as we hadn't seen a sign of the blooming Jerries."

For the first time Nerys was able to see her rescuer, a sailor no older than Elis with blood flowing profusely from a gash on his right cheek.

"Let me have a look at that." She said pulling a hanky from her pocket. Wiping away the blood Nerys was relieved the wound was not as serious as she'd first feared. "Think you'll need a stitch or two in that."

"I'll call in the hospital when this lot is over, it's just around the corner, if they're not too busy that is."

"I'm sorry I forgot to thank you."

"No need Mrs I was on me way here anyway."

"You didn't have to stop and help me."

"We got to pull together ain't we?"

Nerys produced the address she'd been seeking. "Have you any idea where this is?"

"Blimey, me girlfriend lives in that road, as soon as it's all clear we'll go find yer case and I'll take yer."

"I think you should go to the hospital first and get your face seen to."

"It's only a scratch, and that street's on the way."

Chapter Twenty One

Thursday 29th May 1941

Four hours on watch four hours off seven days a week, Iwan easily slipped back into the Naval routine that had replaced the more normal hours he'd enjoyed during his stint in the motor pool. He'd been with the ship since her commission the previous September. After her working up was completed in November, the light cruiser Dido had joined the fifteenth cruiser squadron patrolling the approaches to the Bay of Biscay, instead of screening Atlantic convoys, as many of the crew had speculated they'd soon be doing. April found the ship relocated to the Mediterranean escorting convoys from Alexandria to Malta. Iwan's watch was due to begin at 0800 hours but as usual they were at battle stations soon after dawn, not from any threat by the Italian Navy, who assiduously avoided contact with the British Fleet, but from the greater menace, aircraft. High level bombing had a minor impact on the ships as they constantly changed course, swerving and weaving able to confound the aim of the majority of bombers, but by the law of averages the planes occasionally got lucky. H.M.S Dido in the company of HMS Orion were evacuating troops from Sphakia and

Heraklian when they came under attack from their deadliest foe, the Stuka dive-bomber.

Iwan was at his station supervising the armaments in B turret, he was aware of the sudden changes of course as the captain turned the ship toward the attacking plane, a standard tactic as it forced the pilot to steepen his dive thus causing him to pull up sooner, at the same time the ship would also zigzag erratically hampering the pilots aim. The ship rolled as the first bomb exploded extremely close, quickly followed by another, the planes were attacking in rapid succession, and each time the captain manoeuvred his ship safely through. Iwan counted the sixth, seventh and eighth detonations adjacent to Dido, his sea legs barely able to compensate as the ship bucked like a wild stallion, the ninth he didn't hear.

Aboard the accompanying destroyer H.M.S Hotspur two cables to the port of Dido anti aircraft gunner Jon Farnham marvelled at the seamanship and good fortune of the Dido's commander, his admiration didn't interfere with his own aim as guns spat a torrent of shells at Dido's assailants. An immense sphere of black smoke burst out in front of the Dido's bridge, and a long cylindrical object hurtled up through the air and dropped smoking into the sea. Through the sooty blackness and now a mere cable's distance she emerged still engaging the aircraft with her remaining guns. The forward B turret was minus one gun with its twin bent almost double. Jon's eyes streamed as he squinted through the smoke for a better view, unconsciously he ran his hand over his nose attempting to mask the smell of cordite, and he knew unless he'd witnessed a miracle he'd lost at least one friend.

"What we queuing for?" Gwen asked as she and Nerys joined the line stretching from the Gwalia Stores past Mostyn the butchers as far as Rhodri's bakery

"I don't know but whatever it is it'll be worth having." They shuffled forward as Ruth Thomas moved a couple of steps maintaining the distance between her and the woman in front.

"Probably be all gone time we get there," added Nerys

Margaret Williams three women further on turned and said, "Owain's supposed to have had butter and cheese in this morning."

"Rhys was with Owain yesterday evening they were patrolling the road to Gelli, think Owain would have mentioned he was having a delivery."

"Out playing toy soldiers again, do they think the Germans are going to invade Pentre?" Ruth said derisively.

"It's easy to mock, what's your Gethin doing for the war effort, didn't see him rushing to join the LDV?" Nerys still used the term Local Defence Volunteers although they'd been known for some time as the Home Guard.

"You know he can't, he'd have been the first to volunteer if he didn't have his back problem."

"That would have been a sight worth seeing." Gwen joined in the fray.

"What d'you mean?" Ruth glared at Gwen daring her to say anything detrimental about her husband. A wasted effort as Gwen had never been prone to giving sway to intimidation.

"I can picture it now, all the men marching smartly along the main road in their smart new uniforms, and your Gethin staggering along behind in his pyjamas with his bed glued to his back, not a pretty sight."

The other chuckling women in the queue voiced their agreement. Fearing further humiliation crimson faced Ruth Thomas stormed off.

"Oh well Nerys, that's one less in front of us."

He'd been there two weeks now and no one had contacted him apart from Michelle a young woman of around thirty, she'd been waiting on the beach when he'd come ashore and taken him to a farm close to the village of Offranville. His equipment he concealed in a barn in a field behind the house.

"I'm not a lot of use hanging around here, I'm supposed to be reporting what Jerrie's up to and all I've seen is two bloody cows and a couple of sheep."

Michelle saw little humour in his restlessness and tersely rebuked him.

"You're so impatient, tomorrow or maybe the next day it will be safe to take you to Dieppe, it is difficult for me also, the longer you are here is more dangerous for me. I'd like to be rid of you very soon."

Elis toyed with the idea of fetching his equipment from the barn, if he didn't radio in soon they'd assume he'd been caught or even deserted, but he knew it was pointless risking a transmission just to say he'd arrived. This was his second excursion as Ludlow liked to call them, having spent the previous Christmas on Jersey gathering information on the strength of German troops deployed there. His cover of being a handyman come builder travelling the island as work demanded enabled him to get quite close to the invader's camps. He hadn't realised at the time, important as the information he obtained was it was also a training run for his present excursion.

Huw swung on his crutches to the door, and waited for one of the men to speak.

"I'd like to see Mr Gruffydd if he's at home, we've been around to the yard but there wasn't a soul insight."

Huw eyed the men with suspicion he'd learned to recognise authority.

"And who wants him?"

"Sergeant Barrelle, Bridgend CID." The speaker flashed his warrant card."

"Sorry can I see that again, you were a bit quick?"

"Of course take as long as you like." Barrelle produced the identification once more. "And you are?"

Huw deliberately ignored the question as he made a detailed examination of the policeman's warrant, then looking at Barrelle with unmistakable contempt said, "Sorry he's not in you'll have to come back later." Then slammed the door.

"Who was at the door? Asked Gwen as she entered the living room."

"Police."

"Not again, don't they ever give up?"

"Didn't ask, they wanted Tudor."

"It's a year since Pryce died, and just when we think it's finished, they pop up to remind us they don't believe a word we said. Well they'll be lucky to catch Tudor this week he's got a lot on."

"I haven't seen them before."

"They seem to harass Tudor more than your father, keep trying to persuade him to change his story."

"I wish I could be of more help about the place, I feel so useless."

"You're doing your best."

"All I do is hang around here, and then go back home."

"You do what you can to help Tudor with the buses, you keep the hearse sparkling, and you've been a tonic for Mari, and little Edmund worships you."

"Oh don't mind me, I'm just feeling sorry for myself having one of those days. Where is Mari anyhow?"

"Took the kids and gone to see Catrin."

"We haven't heard from our Elis for a while, think he's ok?" Nerys sounded worried.

Rhys nodded saying. "He'll be fine probably got nothing to write about." While thinking, could it be because he'd be doing what he's been trained for? And prayed he was trained well. "I got to go and get the hearse ready the funerals at two."

"You can have a minute Huw has gone over there, said he'd give it the once over for you to get some sleep."

"I could do with some, been a busy couple of weeks. What with the funerals and having to fill in on the buses."

"Is the new manager keeping you on nights?"

"Yeah, says he's not going to change anything just for the sake of it."

"They were a long time replacing Pryce shows he wasn't needed."

"Pit more or less runs itself, good seams and everyone knows his job." Rhys yawned and stretched his arms. "Pity about Alice, a short taste of freedom and then she snuffs it."

"At least she got away from him for a while, and outlived him."

"Story is when the police told her he was dead, she burst out laughing."

"No she didn't, she shouted hallelujah first."

271

"Rhys chuckled. "You'll be the same when it's my turn."

"Don't say that, I never would."

He laughed even more.

"Seriously I would have liked to have gone to her funeral." Rhys disapproving grimace made her more indignant. "They do that in England don't they, allow women?" "I can't understand why it's not the custom in Wales."

"I expect it's to stop distraught women throwing themselves on top of the coffin."

"Oh I'm sorry we can't conceal our emotions like men, or perhaps we care and they don't," she said haughtily.

"I didn't make the rules."

"No but you prevented me going to my own mother's funeral."
Rhys wondered how they'd got into this argument.

Tudor and Rhys arrived simultaneously at the yard. Huw hurried to meet them, the crutches a poor replacement for the lower portion of his leg. Releasing his grip on one crutch he used the hand to restrain his father, he grimly addressed Tudor.

"I think you'd better go in alone, It's Iwan."
Gwen sat at the table staring at the tear stained telegram laid out in front of her, alongside her sobbed Sara, her face buried in her mother's breast. Tudor stooped and encircled them both.

Rhys turned away from Huw. "Damn this fucking war." Not wanting to be seen shedding a tear he hastily made towards the workshop. Huw gave him a few moments before he followed, and found him sat on the steps of the old Maxwell.

"You Ok?" Huw asked as he pushed some bolts from the top of a small oil drum and sat.

272

"Yes son, I just."

"I know Dad, I've never spoken about it but I saw four of my mates die on the beach at Dunkirk, and they were only a few of so many killed there. Each night when I close my eyes I relive every second, I hear the bullets the bombs and above them the screams. I see the mangled bodies without limbs or heads, I see men's insides spread over the ground around them. I see it, I hear it and even worse I smell it. I remember wading out to the boat pushing aside the bodies floating around me in a mixture of blood and oil, there's nothing you can tell me about death."

Rhys nodded. "I'm no stranger to death but not on that scale. Only when you said it was Iwan my first thoughts weren't for him, or Gwen, I thought thank God it's not Elis. What does that make me?"

"Human. A natural reaction, if it was the other way round Gwen would have felt the same."

"Maybe, but I'm not proud of it."

"Bugger all we can do about our feelings. Someone will have to tell Mari."

"We'll do it together."

"So what did Barrelle want with you?" Puzzled Mari. "Edmund stop teasing your sister, Kathryn come here to mam love." She gathered her daughter and sat her on her lap.

"Hard to believe she's two already."

"Two years and one week, she's tall like her father."

"How is Geraint?"

"Hoping for leave soon, but then we're always hoping. What about the police?"

"Oh them, said new information had come to light and could I confirm any of it?"

"What new information?

Catrin shrugged her shoulders. "Nothing really just said they'd heard rumours that Sara wasn't Tudor's."

"Where did they get that from? No one else knew."

"Well it wasn't me. Anyway I can't see what difference it makes Sara didn't kill him."

Mari shook her head in dismay. "But maybe it's a motive for someone else, you didn't tell them?"

"We'll they knew already didn't they."

"Thanks Cat. C'mon Edmund we got to go home."

"I'm sorry Mar I didn't think."

"Just hope no one asks me about Nia, 'cos I'll do the same for you."

"Don't be like that Mar."

"I'm not being like nothing, it's a process of elimination Gwen and Tudor or Rhys and Nerys, which of them do you think told them?" Catrin couldn't answer.

"Exactly, so that leaves you, after all Rhys and Nerys did for you, you rotten cow." Mari slammed the front door behind her to be confronted by the sombre faces of Huw and Rhys.

Dieppe was a hive of activity and the closer they'd got to the town the greater the troop movements. Elis had worried that the transmitter concealed in a secret compartment in the floor of the farm truck, and shielded by several bales of hay would be discovered at any one of the checkpoints they'd encountered. Nervously he'd handed over his forged papers, aware he was more likely to be exposed by his anxiety than the non-validity of his documents. Finally they'd reached their destination, a run down house a few minutes walk from the docks. There they were met by Pierre, a skinny parrot featured man in his mid sixties who showed him to a first floor room. Elis studied the room where he'd setup his radio, for a while anyway. How long he could stay would be determined by the frequency and the duration of his radio transmissions, once he started transmitting the krauts would be trying to fix his position, the skill was judging when to move before they found him. Pierre opened a cupboard and placed the equipment on a shelf.

"No point in going to great lengths to hide it, if Jerry suspects he'll rip the place apart. Once we've done here we'll go on round to my house. Is there anything else you need?"
Elis looked around the drab walls, the top half painted pale blue the lower portion a mediocre brown, from the flaking whitewashed ceiling hung a single light bulb.

"As long as there's electric otherwise my radio will be useless." He stretched his arm and flicked the brass wall switch, the bulb instantly emitted a subdued glow. "About fifteen watts," he grinned.
 Michelle bade them goodbye, giving Elis an out of character good luck hug before disappearing with the truck, leaving them with a comfortable walk to Pierre's house in a much more salubrious district.

"Don't go out without one of us you'll stick out like a sore thumb until you've familiarised yourself with the town."

"What do you mean one of us?"

"Me then, don't go anywhere without me."
Elis was introduced to Pierre's wife Madeline as René Montfort and given a room on the fourth floor, overlooking the town towards the harbour. Pierre pointed out over the rooftops the building that housed his radio.

"I chose that house because of its location to the docks and because each room is an individual let, so you coming and going shouldn't arouse any suspicion."

"I thought you owned it."

"I do, along with a few other houses, but they're rented to families. Tomorrow morning you come with me to the boulangerie, I'll introduce you as my nephew from Lille, come to learn the business ready for when I retire."

"I know nothing about baking."

"That's why you're here, to learn."

Downstairs Madeleine prepared the evening meal, and René was about to discover the culinary delights of horse flesh.

Gwen held up the letter. "Written two days before she died, Mrs Bishop only found it a few days ago."

"What did Alice say?" Nerys stirring her tea complained, "Can't get used to it without sugar."

"Typical of Alice, she was worried because she let on to the police that Pryce was Sara's father. I bet she worried herself sick, she'd never have done it intentionally."

"That Barrelle he's a tricky bugger."

"Can't see it makes any difference, Rhys wouldn't have killed him because of me."

"It's obvious why he's come round looking for Tudor again." Nerys continued stirring her tea.

"Not to me it isn't." Gwen looked openly mystified.

"They haven't been able to pin it on Rhys, and now they've got a motive for Tudor

"Tudor was here all day, they know that."

"Aye, but now Rhys and Tudor could both be suspects, and they're alibiing each other."

"He'll not find anything to pin on Tudor."

"Meaning?"

"Meaning Tudor's got nothing to worry about."

"And Rhys has?"

"If he'd told the truth in the beginning he'd be in the clear now, and we wouldn't have to worry."

"And maybe he'd be in gaol with his head in a noose."

"Sorry Nerys, I can't think straight."

"You don't have to explain I know."

"No you don't, and I pray you never have to find out. The worst thing is." She sighed holding back the tears. "No it's not the worst thing, the worse thing is he's dead, but when Gomer went I had the grave somewhere to focus on, I could go there and talk to him I felt he was there listening. But with Iwan there's nothing, no grave, no goodbyes, no nothing."

Sunday for Pierre was as any other day, with the exception of the need to complete baking extra early, enabling him to change his clothes and be in church on time. René his newly acquired nephew even at this early stage was demonstrating a natural talent as boulanger. René hoped that they'd be able to check on the radio equipment either on the way to or from church. The church being in the opposite direction afforded him no opportunity, but it did supply him with information he knew he must relay as soon as possible. Pierre, Madeline and René rounded the corner into the square that housed both church and German headquarters. Pierre nodded in the direction of the car, its pennant fluttering atop the radiator grill as it drew alongside the headquarters granite steps. René tried to act with disinterest, while from beneath the peak cap drawn down above his eyes he observed the figure that got out as the driver smartly opened the rear door. A glance at Pierre told him he was unsure, but René recognised him he'd studied photographs of all the senior Nazis, a shiver ran down his spine as Ernst Kaltenbrunner marched up the steps into the building. Now he'd have something to report, the major- general of police was in Dieppe.

Chapter Twenty Two
Friday 22nd October 1943

He didn't think he'd ever get accustomed to the idea, as he walked in the door it had become normal for Nerys to rush past him in the opposite direction. Not that he'd have admitted it to anyone outside the immediate family but with Nerys working they'd never been so financially well off.

The Arsenal as it was known locally had become one of the major employers in the area, soaking up all the available labour. Along with hundreds of other women Nerys had welcomed the opportunity to be involved in the war effort, and spent her working hours cooped up in an armaments factory handling explosives. A job which definitely would not have been her first choice, never the less she felt she was helping to make a difference. Huw convinced it was his duty to assist the war effort in any capacity possible, joined her a week later.

Rhys would make sure the water was piping hot ready for her bath, as she had always done for him. It concerned him that while he could rub the soap over his skin and the coal black would surrender to the water, when Nerys bathed no amount of scrubbing would remove the jaundice tinge that coloured her face and unprotected skin. Knowledge of the damage coal dust could do made him worry about the effects of whatever Nerys was exposed to.

Today he'd have the first opportunity this week for some solid sleep, no funerals and unusually Tudor wasn't short of drivers, that didn't mean he wouldn't be hammering on the door because someone had let him down.

Tudor pretended he hadn't seen them approaching. "Afternoon Mr Gruffydd."

He lowered his newspaper as Barrelle mounted the steps of the coach leaving Moyle leaning against the opened door. Barrelle glanced along the seats only one passenger a middle aged woman seated near the rear.

"Business slow?

Tudor shrugged unconcerned. "Usually is this time of day, busiest times are early morning and tea time."

"Workers for the Arsenal is it?"

"Aye, but what's it to you who I take and where?"

"Just making conversation."

"Go and make it with someone else."

"Not very friendly Mr Gruffydd."

"Because we're not friends, if you got something to say then spit it out, I have to be going in a couple of minutes." Tudor glanced at his watch. "In fact I think I'll go now."

"In that case I need to know when you can come in for a chat.

"I heard you'd been around looking for me, took you long enough to find me"

"No rush you weren't going anywhere, and I didn't want to intrude unnecessarily." Tudor almost believed he cared. "And as we know what happened to Mr Pryce, there's just a few loose ends we need to tie up."

"So you finally discovered he had an accident, the only crime I can see is yours and the tax payer's money you've wasted persecuting an innocent man."

"It's taken a while I'll admit, mainly because of the truculence of witness's, but that's police work for you, slow but sure that's my motto. Just a few more minor details and I'll be able to close the file to every ones satisfaction."

"I've been pretty busy lately, I don't know when I'll have time. How about you pick a day, anyone in nineteen fifty six won't be too soon?"

"I'd prefer a little earlier say Sunday at two pm. Don't be late, I don't think your wife would be too pleased if we had to come looking for you."

"I'll worry about what pleases my wife, and Sunday is out of the question, unless you come to the memorial service and arrest me."

"Sorry I forgot, I'm attending the service as well, how about tomorrow then same time."

Tudor nodded and pressed the starter. "Be a bloody waste of my time, and yours."

A sequence of long and short bleeps confirmed his message had been received. He unplugged the connection from the light socket, rolled up the aerial wire, and placed it in the suitcase along with the rest of the kit. He looked out the window and viewed the length and breadth of the street, always half expecting to see the building surrounded by German troops. Instead he saw an elderly man leaning his bicycle against the house opposite and examining his front wheel as if he were locating a puncture. People passed by neither looking at the man or towards René's house. As inconspicuously as he could he descended the stairs and left the building, the old man saw him and beckoned, reluctantly he went over.

"You need some help?"

The old man carried on his examination. "Tell them Goering is meeting Hitler when he arrives in Calais tomorrow. We surmise their meeting is because Hitler's furious with Goering's inability to suppress the RAF. Hitler's flying into Lille sometime tonight and is expected to be in Calais by midday." The man casually pushed his bike onto the road swung his leg over the bar and was peddling away before René had absorbed the situation. He walked back toward the house, what was he to do? He'd been given strict times for making contact, and his next slot was a few minutes less than twenty four hours away, and that would be too late if an attempt on Hitler's life was in the offing. In defiance of his instructions and for the second time that day he set up the transmitter and broadcast his call sign.

The nearest any of the Morgan or Gruffydd families had for a long time come to setting foot in the chapel was when visiting the graveyard, in Rhys' view Pryce's death hadn't change the duplicity of the bulk of deacons or congregation. Today was different this morning's service was a memorial to Iwan and three other young men from the village who'd recently lost their lives. As had been his custom in past years after a service he went to visit the family graves. He hadn't admitted to Moira that he knew the identity of the father of the child she'd carried, it wasn't significant to him any longer but he didn't want to embarrass her. It was her secret, she'd taken it to the grave to conceal her shame, and she was entitled to be free of any further ignominy. Of

282

course he'd told Gomer and asked him not to make any reference of it to Moira, but he hadn't mentioned Gwen's infidelities. He'd told them both of Pryce and knew they'd both individually find solace in his demise, he hoped they wouldn't have the misfortune to meet him in the next world.

"You done?" Nerys slipped her arm through his, while Huw approached on his other side.

"Yeah, It's a pity Iwan couldn't have been buried along side his father." He said as they turned away from the graves.

"He's another one of many who'll never be found," said Huw solemnly

"You two go on home," suggested Nerys, "I want to call in Gwen's see if she's ok. Tudor and Mari had to practically carry her to the car."

Rhys shook his head, "I want to have a word with Tudor if he's up to it, he thought a lot of Iwan."

"How is she?"

"She's having a lay down, wants to be alone I'll take her up a cup of tea in a minute."

Tudor hung his jacket over the back of chair and kicked off his shoes. "What time you fetching the kids?"

Mari shook her head. "Doesn't matter Catrin said they can sleep there tonight."

"You two made it up then?"

"Not really. I know she didn't tell the police about Sara and I apologised for accusing her, but she didn't have to be so eager to back up what Mrs Pryce said."

"That's how the law works, a little bit here a bit more there until they got you tied in knots." The kettle on the gas stove whistled enthusiastically as the back door opened.

"That's what I call timing." Mari poured the water onto the tea, as Rhys and Nerys took seats by the table.

"Huw not with you?" Tudor asked, seemingly slightly disappointed. The two had struck a firm friendship, over the past few months, and while Gwen had required more of his attention Tudor had relied increasingly on Huw.

"No I think he was more upset than he showed and he went on home." Nerys got the cups from the dresser as Mari slipped the cosy over the pot.

"How's Gwen?"

"Having a lay down, I'll take her a cup before I go," said Mari

"Let me. You go on."

"Either of you feel like a walk to Catrin's with me? I might as well collect the children."

Rhys shook his head.

"Not me I want to have a chat with Tudor."

"Ok I won't be long." Mari had concerns about being alone with Catrin. Nerys had been with her when she'd taken the children, and Nerys hadn't heard Catrin tell Mari that she was only looking after Edmund and Kathryn for Gwen's sake. Mari had been on the verge of marching the children back home, but common sense had prevailed allowing Catrin her moment of spite.

"Let's go out into the yard." They exchanged their kitchen chairs for a wooden box and a damaged seat from one of the buses.

"What's on your mind?" Tudor produced a packet of Players Weights and tossed them to Rhys. "Here I found them on the bus the other day."

"Thanks." Rhys opened the packet to count its contents. "Try and find Woodbine next time," he said cheekily. "You haven't mentioned seeing Barrelle, what did he want?" Rhys lit one of the cigarettes.

"The usual, tried to get me to change my story."

"Must have been more than that or they wouldn't have had you in the station"

"That's all it was."

"Can't be, there's got to be more."

"All you need to know is I haven't changed it, yet."

"What do you mean by yet?"

"Leave it be will you?"

"Leave it be buggered, their twisting your bloody arm."

"Who said they are?"

"I did it's written all over you."

"Look Rhys I'm bloody sick of it, I've been in that police station so many times the copper on the desk thinks I'm one of them, so I don't need the third degree from you." He strode back towards the house leaving Rhys to ponder the reliability of his alibi.

"You didn't have to rush to fetch them."

"I didn't want to put you out any more than I already have." Mari answered caustically.

"I'm sure Gwen could do with a bit of quiet today."

"And I'm sure she wouldn't want to inconvenience you either."

Catrin shrugged her shoulders. "Your choice."

"I'm going to ask Tudor to take me and the children back to

Rhydamman later this week, so you needn't worry about my mother."

"Geraint due home is he?"

"I wish."

"Make the most of him while you can." Catrin's expressive smirk unsettled Mari.

"What you mean?"

"Nothing, what do you think I mean, there is a war on or hadn't you noticed?"

Unsettled by Catrin's cold stare and realising she wasn't going to get her to elucidate, Mari gathered her children and left. Was she worrying about nothing, or did Catrin know too much?

With a flourish illustrating his satisfaction on the completion of his report, Sergeant Barrelle yanked the paper from the typewriter, and tossed it across the desk to his subordinate. "That's another one wrapped up, check it through see if I've missed anything."

Moyle studied the document. "Looks fine to me serg," he said passing it back. "If we could sort out the Pryce business we'd have a clean desk."

"That'll be in the bag before too long, our little chat with Tudor Gruffydd is going to pay dividends we just have to be patient. Some times a breakthrough is a while coming, and now thanks to Miss Catrin Thomas it's arrived. " Barrelle gloated. "All we have to do is keep the pressure on and Gruffydd will deliver what we need. Give him time and we'll have our man behind bars before Christmas."

Pierre listened intently to René's tale of the man with the bicycle. "And you're sure you've never seen him before? Describe him again."

René repeated his description and Pierre shook his head. "He's definitely not one of ours."

"Well he can't be Vichy or I'd be entertaining the Gestapo."

"Don't go near the radio until I find out more, better still," Pierre donned his jacket. "If I'm not back in an hour get as far away from here as possible." Without any further explanation he opened the door and vanished into the night. Madeline's outward appearance was surprisingly nonchalant at her husbands concern and subsequent disappearance. René wondered if similar occurrences had been normal for this household before he'd came.

"Don't look so worried, Pierre is just being cautious, when he comes back he'll know who that old fellow was, probably his family history as well." Her carefree tone suiting her demeanour. The clock on the mantle struck nine and René began gathering his things and squeezing them into an old carpet bag.

"Give him another ten minutes," advised Madeline

"He said to leave if he wasn't back in an hour, and he's been gone two."

"He'll be back any minute now, I know where he's gone and he's never been there and back in less than two hours." René considered she may well be correct, but his training told him he'd stayed too long and should have done as Pierre had said.

The front door opening was almost inaudible, more pronounced was the whispering in the hallway. René's attempted escape by the rear entrance was halted by a familiar voice.

"Thank God I was afraid you'd have left." The three men and Madeline made them selves comfortable around the dining table.

"René this is André, he's responsible for putting us on our guard." Pierre eyed the man dispassionately. "He should have had more bloody sense and come himself."

The newcomer nodded in agreement and said apologetically, "We were unsure of you and needed to be cautious."

"Doesn't the resistance know what it's doing?" René asked tersely

Pierre smiled. "We're both on the same side but with different agendas, André is a communist, anti fascist and anti democracy."

"There's no greater democracy than communism, all men are equal," protested André.

René anticipating an argument that would achieve nothing intervened.

"There's only two sides in this war, your either a Jerry sympathiser or your not, nothing else matters at the moment so you can both quit posturing."

"Ok, I'll lay my cards on the table." André held his hands palms upwards. "We need help, London is unconvinced we're trustworthy and is reluctant to supply us with the arms we need."

"Wait up." René interrupted again. "How did you know who I was, and that I had a radio?"

"We've been watching you since you came here, we have our spies."

"But if you found out about me so easily so could Jerry." René turned to Pierre. "I think I'd better find somewhere else."

André shook his head. "The Germans they know nothing."

"How can you be sure?"

"If they were at all suspicious you'd be dead by now, I told you we have spies and they could be of use to London, in return we want guns and explosives."

288

"And why do you think they'd listen to me?"

"They wouldn't have sent you if you didn't have good judgement."

"Perhaps my inclination is not in your favour."

"We'd be disappointed if you weren't apprehensive, but I'm convinced we can allay any fears you may entertain."

Huw continued hosing the bus, letting the jet of water squirt in the direction of the approaching men. "Oops! Sorry, I didn't see you," he lied switching off the hosepipe as Moyle stopped in his tracks and tried to brush off the water soaking into his trousers.

"I'm sure you didn't," Barrelle said equally unconvincingly. "Is Mr Gruffydd about?"

"No won't be back till late, any message?"

"No, just tell him we called by."

"Just a social call was it? Why don't you stop harassing innocent people and go and do something useful, like fighting the Jerries, see how tough you'd be on the front line?"

Barrelle moved in closely to Huw and glowered menacingly. "Think you're bloody smart do you? Any more of your shit and I'll shove that tin leg where you keep your brains."

"That supposed to be a threat? Piss off and join the Nazis you bloody fascist." He raised his arm mockingly in a Nazis salute.
It took Huw longer to regain his feet than Barrelle to leave the yard.

Plas Amman was a lot busier than when she'd left, the four evacuees three sisters aged eight to eleven and their thirteen year old brother, had become the focus of attention for Enid, and extra work for Lowri. Emlyn had been busy turning the large garden, and three

289

additional acres, that had until two years ago been rented to a local farmer for grazing, over to successful food production. He welcomed the willing but limited assistance of young Trevor who had no idea of how or where vegetables originated. Until now Trevor had never given it much thought and had accepted they came from a stall in the market.

Enid had ordered that English would now become the everyday language in the house so the four Londoners wouldn't feel excluded, which was unfortunate for Kathryn and Edmund who were monoglot Welsh. Joan, Barbara and Elizabeth soon adopted Kathryn while Edmund fell into neither camps, dismissed by the girls for being a boy and two young to be of any consequence to Trevor. Emlyn was happy as Edmund shadowed him even more than usual, and suggested hopefully Edmund should spend a few nights with him and Sián.

"I'm not sure; he's never been away from me."

"We're only down the road, if he gets home sick I'll bring him straight back, anyway he'll be here in the day with me, and it would mean so much to Sián."

"Can I, Mam? Please." Edmund jumped up and down excitedly in front of his mother. He liked going to visit his grandmother and the treats she always had ready or him.

Tudor waited at the desk while the constable reported his presence to Sergeant Barrelle, this was the second time in as many weeks he'd visited the police station. Today he'd have to earn his forty pieces of silver and the thought disgusted him. It had occurred to him to warn Rhys of what he was about to do, but he wouldn't have understood, whatever the reason. Gwen may have, but he wanted to spare her being in the same position as himself. Barrelle sat behind his desk with Moyle perched along side him notebook in hand and pen at the ready.

"As I understand it Mr Gruffydd you've come here to change your statement of your own free will."

"Yes," Tudor lied, he wouldn't be here if Barrelle hadn't blackmailed him, there was no other word, blackmail.

"The day in question Saturday the first of June 1940, you originally stated that Rhys Morgan was with you at your premises the whole of the afternoon, do you still maintain this?"

"No"

"When did you see him?"

"Sunday morning, early."

"Was it usual for him to call around early on a Sunday?"

"No."

"Did he tell you why he'd come?"

"No."

"If you expect me to keep our bargain you'll have to do better than just no."

"I've given you what you wanted, I didn't see him Saturday and I don't know where he was."

"Why did he suddenly turn up unannounced, he must have had a reason?"

"He didn't tell me."

"Why do you think that was?"

"I don't know, I went back to bed."

"So it was very early, and you just left him on his own and went back to bed?"

"No I left him with Gwen."

"Then perhaps we should arrange to bring Mrs Gruffydd in for questioning."

"You said you'd leave her out of it."

"How can I do that when you're being so uncooperative?"

Tudor felt uncomfortable, his shirt clung to his back and he wiped the sweat from his forehead with his sleeve.

"Ok, it was like this."

Chapter Twenty Three

Saturday 3rd June 1944

It had taken Elis four and a half days to reach the outskirts of Calais, why he'd been ordered here was unclear, and he'd rather have been back in Dieppe, doing what he did best. More than likely someone in London was playing silly buggers again. Like the time a few weeks after arriving in Dieppe he'd been sent to Le Havre to check a report of troops embarking on a fleet of landing craft, only to find the harbour empty apart from a handful of barges and the town manned by a medium size garrison. The last month had been spent planning a series of raids due to take place yesterday on targets specified by London, and now he'd miss the nerve tingling stimulation of sabotage, it wasn't the rush of adrenalin experienced by the actual destruction that really excited him, but extra exhilaration brought on by the times they were nearly caught. Throughout the past year his role had altered from just being the eyes of Britain to being the central figure in the resistance, uniting the different factions into one effective cell.

His latest orders were to report any armoured convoys heading along the coast from Calais where the German fifteenth army were stationed. Ideally he would have opted for a position where he could have watched both the Calais to St Omer and Calais to Boulogne routes, as this wasn't possible he'd concentrate on the latter.

He rested the bicycle against the wall of the house with a sign that said rooms, unfastened the case that contained the radio, thinly disguised beneath a change of clothes, a token camouflage that would have been immediately discovered by the most cursory of searches. The major reason his journey had taken so long was having had to avoid any contact with the German patrols and checkpoints, while at the same time being close enough to the main highway to monitor any redeployment. With a quick scan of the immediate area he climbed the steps to the front door. The room was sparse, a single bed which had seen better days, and sounded like a rusty anchor chain being raised when he sat on it, a chair and table with a jug and basin, and two hooks on the back of the door to hang his clothes. The most important item was present, and he flicked the light switch to make sure it worked.

The bus driver avoided eye contact with either of the women, he knew them both quite well, the boss's wife and her sister and it wasn't his place to get involved in family feuds he had his own problems.

"Feeling better now?" Gwen tucked her arm through her sisters.

Nerys nodded. "I can't stand seeing him locked up in that place."

"At least he's ok and you can go to see him often."

"If they'd just get the trial started, it's eight months since he was arrested, all this waiting and not knowing, it's driving me mad. One minute I want them to get on with it and the next I don't just in case." She wiped her eyes with a hanky with a pink embroidered N in the corner.

Gwen didn't know how to sound positive, the solicitor hadn't sounded over confident. "The evidence is purely circumstantial, but cases have been lost on the flimsiest of evidence and we can't take anything for granted. " He'd said, optimism not in attendance in his tone.

Nerys had then asked, "If they haven't any hard evidence why are they prosecuting?"

"Because the circumstantial evidence is very strong and juries have been known to be swayed by it."

Gwen had been barely able to contain her anger and argued with him, "As there was no positive proof either way Rhys had no case to answer."

Damn Catrin and damn Tudor, if only he'd told her what he was doing and why, she'd have insisted Mari and Geraint take they're chances, at least neither of them would have been in jeopardy of an appointment with Albert Pierrepoint.

Tudor pushed the cat off the chair and slumped in the seat. Mari had said the house was like a pigsty and complained about the smell last time she visited, it wasn't that he hadn't the time, he didn't have the inclination to clean, or work for that matter. Since Gwen and Sara's departure the funeral business had declined and was virtually defunct, and the buses only kept going because Carwyn Jones and his pushy wife were making a good living out of his misfortune. Without Gwen he'd ceased to function, damn Rhys Morgan, damn Siencyn-Pryce, damn Barrelle, damn Catrin Thomas, damn everyone, but most of all he cursed himself.

The sailor knocked sharply on the door waited a few moments and knocked again. He turned, and about to walk away he spotted the two approaching women.

"Can we help?"

"I'm looking for Mrs Gwen Morgan, though I believe her name may have changed."

"Well I'm Mrs Morgan as is, and this is Mrs Morgan that was," Nerys said with an unfamiliar cheerfulness.

"Yes Nerys i remember you, we've met several times, it's a pleasure to see you again"
Both women glanced at each other questioningly.

"I should have let you know I was coming, my names Jonathan Farnham, I was Iwan's friend."

"I'm sorry I didn't recognise you, though when you spoke your voice was familiar." Nerys coloured slightly.

"No reason you should, a couple of brief conversations in hospital with someone cloaked in bandages is not always the most memorable, especially if you have others on your mind." The warmth in his voice left no doubt he had fond memories of her.
Nerys closed the front room door and went to the kitchen, she'd make the tea and give them a chance to talk.

"Iwan spoke of you often Mr Farnham."

"Jon please."

"Were you with him when it happened?"

"No I was on another ship close by, we were evacuating troops from Crete when we were attacked. It was as if they had singled out Dido, probably because she was a light cruiser."

"All I know is the telegram said killed in action, and later a letter from the captain saying how he regretted the loss of a fine man such as

Iwan, and that he'd died serving his country. A standard letter I suppose."

"The captain had a lot of those letters to write, and I'm sure he found each one equally stressful."

"What happened, how did he die?"

"We came under attack from dive bombers; Dido dodged quite a number how many I couldn't count." His air became distant as he relived the events. "She seemed untouchable as if she were protected by an invisible cloak as she snaked her way through the bombs, her guns blazing at her attackers." He paused, his voice softening to almost a whisper. "Then," raising a hand he dabbed his eye, "One of her gun turrets took a direct hit, Iwan's turret. He wouldn't have known a thing, death would have been instantaneous, I can assure you he wouldn't have suffered." He lied omitting the fact that the majority of the forty six killed had agonisingly burned to death before they could be reached.

Gwen stretched forward and caught his hand. "Thank you."
He stood up as Nerys entered with a tray, no one ever having stood up before when she entered a room, it made her a little self conscious.

"Please sit down Mr Farnham we don't stand on ceremony here."

"Jon, call me Jon." Gwen perceptively detected a change in his manner, his eyes lingering on Nerys, and wondered if she were another reason he called.

"I'm glad you called Jon, now I can see the face behind the bandages." Nerys poured the tea from the best china service.

Unconsciously his hand brushed a large facial scar. "I came out better than even the doctors expected. It meant a lot to me your visits, you and Iwan. If ever I can do anything for either of you I'd welcome the opportunity."
Nerys flushed, while Gwen knew the offer was intended more for Nerys.

"I'm not doing anything for him, my fathers in gaol because of him or had you forgot?"

"No Huw I haven't forgotten, but he had reasons."

"I know he was protecting you and Geraint but my father could hang, whatever the reason it don't justify what he's done."

Mari couldn't argue because Tudor hadn't thought it through, just as she hadn't when she'd confided in Catrin that Pryce was her father. Then she hadn't known Geraint was his grandson, that little gem was revealed to the public in the newspapers, courtesy of Catrin. Without her additional information the police would have been none the wiser.

"It's not just him, my mothers torn apart by what he's done, that's why she walked out."

Huw grabbed a handful of corn and threw it at the chickens. "I can't do anything about that."

"But you can, if she sees you and Nerys understand the position he was in, perhaps she'll think again and go back, they're both suffering."

"Never, whatever he gets he deserves."

Huw left Mari with the chickens and marched furiously from the allotment back to the house.

"Who's that chap I saw leaving another flaming copper?" Huw's disdain intensified by his row with Mari.

"No a shipmate of Iwan's come to see Gwen."

"Oh I'm sorry I missed him."

"I expect he'll call again." Nerys was certain he would, and as sure it would be better if he didn't.

"How was dad?" his question answered before she spoke.

"He's" she faltered, he grabbed her before she toppled and eased her onto a chair.

"He's putting on an act for me, pretending he's ok, but you could see yourself last week how much weight he's lost, if the trial don't start soon there may be no need."

"You got to be strong, Mam, if he sees you cracking up it'll finish him."

"Think I don't know that." She straightened up angrily. "Think I'm a bloody fool, of course I'm strong when I visit, it's when I get home my insides feel like they've been dragged across the cobbles." She slouched burying her face in the palm of her hand.

"Sorry, Mam, I know, I know." His stoop to embrace her hampered by his tin leg.

Jon's visit had eased her mind, while at the same time resuscitating memories that both warmed and tormented, she needed some air some time alone so she sought solitude in the allotment.

"You looking for me?" She'd failed to notice Mari sitting beside the hen house.

"No love I needed somewhere quiet to think."

"I'll go if you like," Mari rose to her feet.

"No love you sit back down. Where are the children?" Gwen sat on the makeshift bench alongside her."

"Sara took them to see dad."

"It's a mess isn't it?" sighed Gwen, "We just had a visitor, a mate of Iwans." She related what Jonathan Farnham had told her.

"I'm sorry I missed him I would like to have met him."

"I asked him to stay the night but he said he had to be back on his ship by midnight, I don't think he'll make it. I'll write to him and thank him."

"What you going to do about dad he's a wreck? He needs you, Mam."

Resolutely Gwen shook her head. "If only it was that simple, I understand his motives and the pressure he was under, but every time I look at him I see the spectre of Rhys hanging from the gallows."

He removed the headphone, disconnected the set and closed the case. His revised instructions were to watch and report any activity around the base of the fifteenth army's four panzer divisions based outside Calais. It would be a welcome break from the monotony of the last two days spent watching the inactivity on the same stretch of road, tomorrow he'd pedal in the direction of German's camp, how close he'd get was questionable. A baker from Dieppe cycling around military camps near Calais, would be subject to close scrutiny if stopped.

Determined to get an early start René was up well before dawn, hoping he could mingle with the civilian labour force reporting for work. Obviously he wouldn't gain access to even the outer confines of the base, but he might get close enough to observe through the perimeter fence, or even pick up some information from the workers. Daybreak was late again, as it had been for the past few days, the low cloud and drizzle more consistent with November than summer.

He mounted his cycle and hadn't travelled more than half a mile when the air raid warning sent him in search of cover in a disused warehouse. The first wave of aircraft passed over their pay loads reserved for more essential targets. The second wave shed their quota over a wide area, but these weren't bombs unless the R.A.F were using parachutes so they'd land softly. This had to be what he and France had been waiting for, the allied invasion. Quickly he set off in the direction of where one of the parachutes had landed which happened to be on his original course. Three miles of frantic cycling and he reached his objective. The parachutist was dangling from one of the trees on the edge of a thicket. René tossed aside his bike and ran to assist, ten yards from the tree he slowed to a walk, it wasn't a man at all but a caricature of Hitler crudely drawn on a stuffed sack.

Adolf Fawkes, he thought slightly disappointed and bemused. Unluckily for him he wasn't the only person investigating the landing and became aware of another's presence when the barrel of a gun was jabbed in the small of his back.

"My Name is Vernon Howe I've been instructed to represent you, as Mr Protheroe has been taken ill." Rhys' new solicitor introduced himself then sat on Rhys' bed his briefcase resting on his lap, and waited Rhys' reply.

"What's the matter with him?"

"A slight stroke, I believe he'll recover in time."

"Tell him I'm sorry and wish him well."

 "I will do so, now if you're agreed we'll proceed."

"Carry on."

I've some good news Mr Morgan a trial date has been set for November the twenty third and I have with me details of the prosecutions case, which we need to go through now." Opening his briefcase he pulled out a folder. "It's alleged that you murdered the man you knew as Dafydd Siencyn-Pryce, that Tudor Gruffydd went to Pryce's house the following day to check he was dead on your sister-in-law's request, and also at her request he provided you with an alibi which he later retracted. There is also a statement from a Mrs Mair Jones that she saw a man fitting your description in the vicinity of the house, and she later confirmed you as that man in an identification parade."

He raised his hand as Rhys attempted to interrupt. "Let me finish. They also have witnesses that you threatened Pryce's life and were violent towards him causing him bodily harm. Added to which there is a note discovered in your jacket, written in Pryce's hand arranging to meet you at his house on the afternoon of his death. Fingerprint analysis of a heavy clock found alongside the body has not revealed any distinguishable prints, but they claim you attacked Pryce knocking him down and he sustained severe head injuries from the assault. They also insist you then used the large clock as a weapon to ensure he was dead, and you left him with his head resting in an open fire. I've instructed the very eminent barrister Quentin Rothsey and he has agreed to act for you, he'll be coming to see you once I've completed the preliminaries."

"I've no money to pay you let alone a top barrister," Rhys scoffed. "I'm a miner not a mine owner."

"You are fortunate to have a benefactor, who has retained my services, but wishes to remain anonymous."

Rhys looked bewildered. "Benefactor?"

"I suggest you accept in good grace, and not deliberate too deeply on who or why."

The solicitor took of his glasses and wiped them with his hanky, more to give Rhys time to consider his options than any real need for cleaning.

"Now Mr Morgan lets go back to the day of Dewi Jenkins alias Dafydd Siencyn-Pryce's demise."

Pierre closed the shop and headed home, if René didn't arrive back today he'd somehow have to get word to London. The fighting hadn't slackened with the allied troops making inroads in the form of large arc that advanced well beyond the coast. The resistance had played its part, sustaining heavy casualties performing the essential sabotage requested by London. By the time he reached home Pierre had made up his mind it was far too dangerous to try and reach Calais and search for René.

Chapter Twenty Four
Monday 29th January 1945

Rhys felt he hadn't slept, not because of sounds made by the other prisoners, coughing, snoring, shouting and sometimes crying in their sleep, or the noises made by the warders as they patrolled the landing, and the clattering of metal peep holes as they were opened and closed. But he must have slept, or how could he have had that dream? He could hear the orders barked at the inmates on the landing below, and the foul stench of their nights bodily functions as they shuffled with their buckets to slop out, he'd had over a year to become use to that but it still turned his stomach. Fourteen months in prison dulls all senses and passions, apart from hope and he still had that, he hoped today would be the beginning of the end of his ordeal, and not be a repeat of the farce of last November. Then two weeks into the trial the judge had dismissed the jury on a technicality that he still didn't fully understand. Fourteen months was as long as some convicts served for burglary or suchlike, but not for murder, for murder there was only one sentence. He shivered at the thought and wondered how Nerys would be coping. She'd always displayed an inner strength when she'd visited, but he knew it was ninety percent bravado for his benefit. Undoubtedly she broke down when out of his sight, and he was thankful that she had the support of Huw and Gwen. Last Friday she'd visited with Huw, and her normal pleased to see him smile was more obviously forced, alerting him that something was wrong. Huw had brought the telegram confirming Elis had been reported as missing. He tried to assure them that soldiers often got detached from their units in war time, especially when there was a big push on, only to turn up later with some lame excuse, but it held little comfort. Today Rhys had hope, not for his own sake but hope for Nerys, she'd done nothing to deserve the burden he and Hitler had placed upon her, today he hoped would soon bring about a time when part of that load would be lifted, when he could be home with her and be her emotional rock, to hold her and share her fears for Elis. His thoughts were interrupted by the warder unlocking the cell door.

"Jump to it Morgan, the hour of reckoning is nigh." Rhys collected his soap towel and bucket and joined the procession.

Gwen helped Nerys on with her coat, they hadn't spoken since Nerys had snapped at her. Aware of her edginess Gwen had decided prudence dictated it should be Nerys who initiated any further conversation. Huw took Nerys' arm and smiled reassuringly as he looked into her eyes, her nod indicated her understanding and readiness. With Huw and Gwen on either side, and her insides filled with trepidation Nerys stared fixatedly ahead ignoring the attentions of the gloaters and well wishers alike as they walked to the bus stop.

Mari's gaze lingered for a few seconds after they'd turned the corner wishing she was going with them, instead of having to wait to see if Sara was able to come home lunch time to mind the children, then God and the railways willing she'd be able to be in court for the afternoon

305

session. Mari glanced along the street in the opposite direction and was surprised to see him, especially today of all days.

"Aren't you supposed to be in court?" She queried as Tudor drew within earshot.

"I'm not needed today, but have to be there tomorrow." He drew level with her. "Nerys gone has she?"

"And Huw and Gwen. I'd ask you in but it don't seem right."

"Good, I hoped I'd miss them."

"Only just."

"I came to tell you Emlyn's been on the phone wants you to ring him back."

"Did he say why?"

"Yes, but better you hear it from him."

"It's Geraint, something's happened to Geraint," she tried to push past him but he caught her arms.

He felt her tautness lessen as he said. "Nothing to do with Geraint calm down."

The day went as Rhys had expected, and just like the first trial he'd spent most of the day in the cells beneath the court, as the Judge deliberated on submissions by the defence on whether prosecution evidence particularly that of Mrs Mair Jones, Pryce's daily, was admissible. Barrister Quentin Rothsey had contended that Rhys Morgan was known to Mrs Jones yet she had only identified him as being the man seen going to Pryce's house after she'd recognised him in an identity parade. Him being the only man in the line up she was acquainted with, no matter however vaguely and because of it the impartiality of the parade was compromised. Claiming she selected Rhys because he was familiar to her, and not because he was the man she

306

saw near Pryce's house. If she was certain it was Rhys a man she knew by sight, why hadn't she identified him in her original statement?

While the lawyers argued the legalities Rhys was taken to the cells beneath the court where he had time to ponder a puzzle of his own. It must have been a dream there was no other explanation, but it had been so vivid and even now every detail could be recalled. He'd woken to see the man with dark glasses sitting on the end of his bed. Strangely he hadn't been surprised to see him, and found himself questioning why anyone would need to wear sunglasses at night? There was no initial communication and as Rhys' eyes focused in the darkness he scrutinised the man more closely. His clothes were normal in as much as they were identical to the suit Rhys had worn in his official capacity as undertaker, but minus the hat. His hair was dark and shoulder length, he held in his hand a plaited white bone shepherds crook, draped around his neck a gold cross and chain sparkled with unusual clarity, the cross must have become entangled because it hung upside down.

Finally he'd spoken. "I've come to help you Rhys."

"Help how?" Rhys felt no fear, but believed he should.

"Your son he is in mortal danger and only you can save him."

"Locked up in here, I don't think so."

The man stood up and held out his hand. "Come."

As he uneasily took the offered hand the cells small window grew larger and the bars vanished. Rhys lunged forward but the hand held him fast.

"You cannot pass through, but observe well."

A picture of two lorries travelling along narrow wooded track formed where the window had been, pulling into an open space between the trees the vehicles drew to an abrupt halt. Uniformed men with bayonets fixed to their rifles leapt from the backs of the trucks and ushered a dozen men from one of the lorries into a line in the middle of the

307

clearing. The tail sheet of the other lorry was raised accompanied by the rat-tat-tat of a machine gun spitting death along the defenceless column. The window zoomed in on the face of one victim as he keeled over backward and lay motionless on the floor. The officer in charge drew his pistol and began walking along the prostrate line firing one shot into the head of each man Rhys felt sickened and wrenched his hand from the others.

"Elis, that was Elis." The words hung on his lips.

"It hasn't happened yet Rhys, and you can stop it, watch." Again the man raised his hand, and the window grew again. This time Rhys saw Nerys in their kitchen, wailing hysterically a piece of paper clasped in one hand the other clawing at her face in despair as the window closed. "Your decision Rhys, for your son's life all you have to do is swear allegiance to my lord."

"When, when is it going to happen?"

"I will return tomorrow night, then I must have your answer or it will be too late. By next evening death will have brushed against you, and you'll know I speak the truth." He raised his stick from the floor and motioned as if he were going to loop the curve around Rhys' neck, then he was gone.

The viewing hole in the door slid open and shut, he heard the keys turn the lock and the door swung open. Dinner time. The warder placed the tray on the table and pulled up a chair.

"They've all gone for lunch and the jury's been sent home for the day while the judge considers the arguments. You'll be going back to prison after dinner."

"Won't make a lot of difference, the last judge was prepared to allow the prosecution to enter whatever they wanted."

"You never know it's a different judge he may not have the same views."

"They use the same law."

"Not going to eat it?" The warder hungrily eyed the food.

"Nah, you have it if you want."

"Ta I'm starving, they don't feed us as well as they do you."
A wry smile crossed Rhys' face, as the warder tucked in to his lunch.

"Your wife and sister in law have asked to see you." Rhys waited for him to finish chewing so he could continue. "Ok for your missus but her sister can't 'cos she's a witness for the prosecution."
Rhys knew Gwen was likely to be called as a hostile witness, he was less sure if her conscience would permit her to perjure herself.

"Your son's here as well."

Rhys thought about his other son and his nightmare. "Do you believe in the devil?"
The warder looked hard at him, his training had taught him to avoid dark or thought provoking discussions with prisoners, and his experience told him to keep conversations light and cheery.

"If you believe in God you have to believe in the other I suppose, never given it much thought."

"Nor me until now. That's the trouble with prison gives you too much time to think."

"I'll take this tray back up and see if your wife is ready to come down." He said arranging the empty dishes.

"Nerys, her names Nerys."
The studs in Huw's boots echoed in the austere narrow stairway, they were unable to walk abreast and the stone stairs worn in the middle from centuries of use caused Nerys to misjudge her footing, and she would have tumbled to the bottom had Huw not been in front of her.

She smoothed her clothes and tidied her hair, took a deep breath and tried to enter the cell with a positive attitude to match her simulated expression. Rhys sprung forward to greet her and hugged her passionately. Huw stood with his back to the door and scoured the dirty mustard walls as he waited to acknowledge his father. The guard to his credit stayed as far from the three as was possible in a room measuring seven feet square, and although he was probably listening to every word he gave the appearance of either being totally disinterested or profoundly deaf.

"No point in you coming every day, it'll only wear you out." Rhys looked past her attempts to hide the worry lines on her forehead and the dark circles under her eyes, in the last two years she'd aged ten.

"Nothing will stop me" Then turning to Huw she added. "So don't you even think about trying."

"I wouldn't dare."

Leaving Tudor to wait on the doorstep Mari hurriedly dressed the children, it must be serious something must have happened to Geraint why else would Emlyn ring? Hampered by the children they walked as briskly as possible with hardly a word passing between them, Tudor took the children into another room while Mari made the call.

"Hello Emlyn how are you, how's Siân?" She remained silent as he solemnly related his news.

"Oh no," she gasped steadying herself against the hall table.

The Crown Court being so close to Cardiff Prison meant Rhys was back in his cell within fifteen minutes of Nerys and Huw leaving. As he'd anticipated the defence's submissions had been refused, so tomorrow the prosecution would start setting out its case. He laid on his bed his consciousness flitting from Nerys to Elis, and reliving the vision of the night. He'd be brushed by death before evening, that's what had been said. It was Vernon Howe his solicitor who'd brought the news, the details were sketchy but sadly his benefactor had died during the night but provision had been made in their will to settle all his defence costs. Their death had made it possible for him to reveal their identity as their wish to remain anonymous was only relevant while they lived.

"She was a kind hearted woman," Rhys felt genuinely saddened by her death. "Why didn't she want me to know?"

"Although the brothers hadn't had contact for years she thought helping you might possibly present conflict between her and the other stepson, and by keeping quiet it was a risk she didn't have to take."

"I don't know Joshua that well, but from what I've heard he can be an awkward bugger."

He still wasn't hungry and didn't bother about supper preferring to remain in his cell. The fact that the prediction had come true had shaken him, was it a sign or coincidence. He'd been agnostic veering towards atheist in his beliefs saying many times to anyone who'd mentioned an after life, "Once you're dead you're bloody dead and that's an end to it." Yet wasn't it he who sat by his brother and sisters graves and asked their forgiveness, wasn't it he who'd sought his dead brothers advice, and spent hours relating events to a patch of earth, if he didn't believe he wouldn't have done that would he? Had it been the rejection of hypocrites like Pryce that had triggered his repudiation of religion and ultimately the denial of God? And did that make him an inverted hypocrite?

At lights out he was determined not to sleep, and he rose from his bed and repeatedly counted the steps, as he paced from cell door to the opposite wall. Only when through the tiny window night gave way to the sun rising behind the clouds, turning a cheerless hostile night sky to light affable blue grey and the prospect of a bright day did he allow himself to sit down

The man standing before him waited for his reply.

"Go away your not real your just a dream." Rhys shook his head and closed his eyes convinced the gaunt man with hollow cheeks and skin the texture of frogs spawn would be gone when he reopened them.

"Why do you not accept the truth, that I am here and I can save your son."

"Because you're not real."

"Are you so sure that you'd gamble you're son's life?"

"Take off those glasses let me see what's in your eyes."

"My eyes will reveal nothing," he said raising a long bony hand removing the dark lenses. "See I hide nothing." The result was not what Rhys had expected, his eyes were as black as his suit.

"If it were true I wouldn't hesitate no father would."

"You'd be surprised how many parents put themselves before their children."

"Not me."

"Then you agree?"

"How can I make a bargain with an invention of my mind?"

"Time is slipping by, it will soon be too late, didn't I prophesise a death would call close by."

"Enid was old and her time was up, just a coincidence."

"Then what is to be I shall not alter."

"Wait, your lord or whatever you call him, who is he and what does he want of me?"

"Names are of this world not of his; he gathers the souls of sinners, some he buys, others are his by right.

"By the nature of my crime am I not his by right?"

"His entitlement is for those unable to repent by the nature of their sin."

"Such as?"

"Those who terminate their mortal being."

"Moira?"

"She is one of many who also brought the soul of an unborn child."

"And why me, because I'm about to die, to be hung?"

"That is yet to be determined, all he requires is you pledge your fealty, and if you fear for yourself then I can ensure the jury verdict be in your favour."

"And my son?"

The apparition shrugged his scrawny shoulders. "The choice is yours."

"I'd choose my son."

"Then do so swiftly for the hour nears."

"I believe you are false and exist only in my mind, so go and leave me in peace."

"I will go but someone else will come for your final answer, perhaps they will be more convincing than I." He raised his crook and immediately disappeared and almost as quickly a new form began to appear.

"Hello Rhys."

"Moira is it really you?" He held out his hand for her to come closer but she remained at the foot of the bed and out of focus.

"If you want to save your son then do as you're asked. Don't do as I did, when I ran off I condemned my unborn child, but you have it within your power to save Elis. I know you would have done for me what is asked, but for me it is too late, grant Elis the life I so readily forsook.

"For Elis I'd do anything, and for you I'd do more if we could be together again."

"Do as you're bid and we will be for ever I promise."

"Then so be it, I can't lose you again."

Rhys woke with a start. "C'mon Morgan rise and shine." The warder withdrew the hand from his shoulder. "Christ you was dead to the world, put the wind up me you did."

Rhys experiencing a sense of disorientation blurted. "I must have nodded off." An explanation more for his own benefit, having fought to stay awake all night he must have fallen asleep

Elis wondered how long before they took more than a passing interest in him, he'd been questioned several times, sometimes with weeks between each session. Most of the time he'd been confined to a small cell with three other prisoners, in the basement of the headquarters, initially in Calais and then Caen. They were aware of the fierce battles getting nearer as the gunfire grew louder and the vibrations from the impact of the shells grew stronger. Periodically they were bundled into a truck and transported to a new location, where the sound of gunfire was distant once more. The first time he'd thought perhaps he was to be handed over to the Gestapo, but instead his captors repeatedly required him to retell his story of how he a poor baker had been travelling the area looking for a supply of flour, as there was an acute shortage in Dieppe, and when he'd come across what he'd assumed as an allied invader he'd intended to apprehend him if possible. They'd treated him as of no consequence and he hadn't experienced any of the brutality he'd been warned to expect. He was relatively unscathed apart from a few minor beatings which were to more satisfy the guards desire to inflict pain than to extract information. He attributed their indifference to possibility they were more than occupied by the thrust of the invasion force. In the last week it had become almost a daily occurrence that he and a dozen others were ordered into the back of a lorry and taken to a new location, but today there was a distinct change in the attitude of the guards, something he couldn't define, if he were a woman he'd have called it intuition.

Chapter Twenty Five

Friday 23rd March 1945

The court rose as the judge entered, and not for the first time Rhys reflected on his fate being determined by a man who came to work in dress more suited to a carnival clown, than an arbiter of life and death. Once seated the jury were summoned by the usher, who shuffled from the jury room into their seats. All noticeably avoiding any eye contact with Rhys, who made a point of analysing the body language of the eight men and four women.

The clerk asked, "Have you agreed a verdict?" This was just a formality, a procedure that had to be observed, the whole court was aware they'd been deliberating for two weeks and the likely hood of a unanimous verdict had been abandoned days since.

The foreman shook his head as he spoke. "No Your Honour."

The judge posed the next question his self. "And do you consider that you are near to such a verdict, and given more time an agreement amongst you could be reached."

"No Your Honour."

"Is that an opinion on which you are all in accord?"

"Yes Your Honour." The other jury members nodded in unison, it seemed they could agree on something.

"In that case I have no option other than to discharge the jury, and thank them for their commitment in attempting to resolve this difficult case. A date will be set for a new trial."

"Have you decided what you're going to do now love?" Gwen knew the futility of the question, they'd been over it a hundred and one times, and there wasn't a solution.

"No, Mam, I can't think, there's nothing we can do is there? My marriage has been annulled and Geraint's not allowed to be Edmund and Kathryn's dad.

"Bloody police, Barrelle promised Tudor he'd keep it quiet, instead they used it as another motive for Rhys to kill Pryce the bastards."

"Mam!"

"Well that's what they are, don't care how many lives they ruin. The only one who hasn't had to suffer being humiliated and vilified by the newspapers is bloody Pryce. He may be dead, but it strikes me our lives won't be worth living either."

"They certainly took you to pieces, made it look like you led Pryce on. I blame myself if I hadn't told Catrin."

"That little bitch, after all Rhys and Nerys did for her."

"Well she's done for us all, she'd better keep out of Geraint's way when he comes home or there'll be another murder in the village."

"Geraint won't be able to stay here not now."

"I've arranged with him to stay with Tudor."

"He can't stay there, not in that mess."

"Where else, Mam? Me and Sara are going over today to give it a good clean, he'll only have to sleep there. No chance you and Tudor?" She looked quizzically at her mother.

"No, I can't forget what he's done." The answer emphatic.

"Well he didn't turn his back on you, he could have walked away when you were pregnant, he's a good man Mam and he loves you."

"And I love him, if I didn't I wouldn't care so much at what he's done."

"Then give him another chance, neither of you are happy."

"And if it all goes wrong for Rhys what then, do I say it's all your fault Tudor but never mind you had good intentions?"

"No, Mam, you cross that bridge when you come to it, if you come to it. Are you going to court today?"

"No not much point Nerys and Huw will be there to see bail refused once again, whoever heard of bail being granted in a murder case?"

"He's gotta try, stranger things have happened."

"Let's hope."

"What time is Geraint coming tomorrow?"

"I'm meeting him off the two thirty in Bridgend station."

Gwen raised her eyebrows. "Better if you didn't."

Mari immediately became defensive. "And why not why shouldn't I meet him?"

"Better to play it cool and not draw attention to yourselves or both of you could land in prison, you know what the lawyers said, and now the blood ties are public knowledge the slightest sign of an incestuous relationship and you'll be in deep trouble"

"You make it sound dirty, we're the same people it's no different to how it was before, and what about the kids how do I explain to them?"

"It is different because the whole world knows and the whole world thinks it's perverted, not just wrong."

"You can't stop loving someone just because some old judge says so."

"You have to, otherwise the law will put Geraint in gaol, don't fool yourself it won't, and there's plenty of people round here who'd enjoy setting the police on you."

Gwen's final sentence convinced Mari of her only option.

Rhys wondered why his solicitor had insisted he be present at the bail hearing, he'd lost count of how many times the ritual had gone ahead without him, but one more day away from gaol wasn't to be scoffed at. He glanced around the near empty gallery trying to smile confidently at Nerys and Huw, while unable to recognise the only other spectator sitting right at the back. Vernon Howe spelt out his case for approval for the application as he had several times before. Stating that Rhys wasn't a danger to anyone, he wasn't a hardened criminal, hadn't at anytime previously been brought to the attention of the constabulary, and until now he'd been considered simply as an honest hard working man, who'd gone conscientiously about his business providing for his family, only this time he added.

"For anyone to spend nearly fifteen months in prison without conviction and then to have to contend with the prospect of a long delay while a new trial date was set is unjust." Then he played his ace. "Your Honour the brother of the deceased in the case, Mr Joshua Jenkins a well known and respected business man, local councillor, and former town mayor, a man of undisputed integrity is prepared to stand surety and provide accommodation in his own home. There by guaranteeing that Rhys Morgan will duly appear as and when required to answer the charges against him."

"Is Mr Jenkins in court?"

"He is Your Honour."

"Mr Jenkins step forward." The man seated at the back stood and made his way from the public area to the front of the court.

"Are you well acquainted with the defendant?" The judge already knew the answer; the questions were about determining Joshua's character.

"No sir, of course I know him but not well, we've met on no more than half a dozen occasions."

"And yet you're prepared to stand surety and risk what I would consider to be a large sum of money, to help a man you hardly know who stands accused of murdering your brother."

"Yes sir I am. It was my late stepmother's intention to provide every assistance to Mr Morgan, and I feel obliged to carry out her wishes. I consider myself to be a good judge of character and what I know of Mr Morgan I think he's an honest man who can be trusted to honour his promise."

"Thank you Mr Jenkins. Mr Morgan it is highly unusual for an individual to be granted bail when committed to trial for such a serious crime as murder. I am of the opinion that a person charged with such a crime should be held in custody until a jury of his peers decides on his guilt or innocence. The prosecution have objected to bail on the grounds that you may abscond or interfere with the witness'." Rhys glanced at his solicitor whose attention remained focused on the judge. This was it then, refused again same as last time.

"They do concede however should you be granted bail you are unlikely to commit any further crime. It is my belief that if you were released into the charge of Mr Jenkins the possibility of you interfering with any of the witnesses would be extremely remote, and the probability of you taking flight even more so, but the court must be absolutely certain on you having no such intentions."

Rhys felt any glimmer fading, they always do it people in authority, raise your hopes then dash them.

"I must also take into account the assurance offered by such a venerated gentleman as Mr Jenkins. It is therefore my decision that the application be granted with an assurance that you will confine yourself to remain within the boundaries of Rhydamman, and will report to the police station twice daily, morning, and evening before sunset, you will not under any circumstances attempt to approach any witness either personally or by proxy, and provided Mr Jenkins is prepared to stand guarantor to a bond of fifteen thousand pounds you will be released into his charge.

Nerys hadn't come prepared, or she'd have brought a suitcase with clothes for her and Rhys.

"Don't worry, Mam, I'll sort that, just tell me what you need."

"Oh anything, I don't know ask Mari to pack something," she blurted as a fresh panic gripped her. "Where is he? The judge has changed his mind, he's keeping him locked up."

Huw grasped her shaking arms. "No don't be silly they're just completing the formalities."

"Before we go Rhys we have to get one thing clear."

321

Grateful as he was Rhys wished Joshua would get on with it, Nerys was waiting.

"Don't get the idea I'm sponsoring you because I like you, or I believe you're innocent, whether you're basically an honest man I have no concept, but my stepmother's appraisal of character was usually very good. You may have or may not have killed my brother, and to be honest I care little either way. I'm surprised his past hadn't caught up with him sooner but that doesn't mean I condone murder."

Reminiscent of his brother Joshua stretched his neck as if trying to gain height while fingering his clasped lapels. "I'm doing this out of respect for my mother and her wishes, personally speaking you could rot in gaol and my conscience would not give you a second thought. So if you fail to satisfy my expectations let alone the courts you'll find yourself back in prison faster than you can say Joshua Jenkins." Rhys hadn't felt so humble in years, nobody had talked down to him like this since his school days except Pryce, and now his brother was taking up the reins.

To Gwen the house seemed quiet without Nerys, both Mari and Geraint had gone back to Rhydamman, Geraint staying with his parents and Mari in Plas Amman with Lowri and the evacuees. Sara and Huw were at work all day which was when the isolation felt most prevalent, hopefully when Geraint reported back to his unit Mari would come home. When the knock came at the door she didn't speculate on who her caller could be, and was considerably surprised to see Tudor in his Sunday togs.

"I'm sorry, I'm sure I'm he last person you expected," he apologised.

"Sara put you up to this?"

His face reddened slightly and he stumbled over his words, "No, no, I, I'm not here to cause any fuss," he stammered.

"Good job Huw's not here, he'd soon send you off with a flea in your ear."

"I said I'm not here to argue, or to plead with you to come home."

"You better come in then, the neighbours have seen enough, their little minds will be to working overtime." Tudor crossed the threshold as nervously as the first time he'd called on her.

"Sit down I'll make you some dinner, look at the state of you, you look like you borrowed someone else's suit." Her offer eased his mind somewhat, perhaps she didn't hate him after all, and words spoken in anger weren't always heartfelt after a little time.

"Ta, I don't have an appetite for eating alone."

"You lived alone for years."

"That's was before you."

"Gone soft that's your trouble." She rattled the frying pan on the hob. "Won't be much mind, a bit of fry up I was saving."

"I got coupons you can have, food and clothes."

"Thanks but they're only good if there's stuff in the shops." The pan hissed as she emptied the basin of cold mashed potatoes and cabbage into the minute puddle of melted dripping. "So why are you here?"

"I need you to come to the railway station with me."

She turned towards him slightly surprised. "What for?"

Joshua had every intention of selling Plas Amman, his own house was smaller and less grand but ideally situated in the centre of town, where Plas Amman was much too large and on the outskirts, and he'd asked Lowri to remain as caretaker until a buyer could be found. As the war was in its final throws Elizabeth, Joan, Barbara and Thomas were due to go home to London very soon, much to Emlyn's sadness, he was going to miss the evacuees especially Thomas. His attempts to persuade him into staying with Siân and himself a little longer were unsuccessful, and he felt ashamed at his selfishness, of course the boy would want to go home and be with his own family. For all the affection Emlyn felt he had to accept that Thomas was someone else's son.

"I'm going to miss those children a lot," he confessed to Mari. "And I expect you'll be taking Edmund and Kathryn back to Pentre soon?"

"If they want to stay for a while they can, if you and Siân want them that is?"

"No need to ask, leave them as long as you like."

"Were you and Geraint serious, you know what you said about after the war?"

"I expect it was a shock learning me and Ger shouldn't be married."

"That we'd got used to since it came out in the trial. It's what you said about vanishing as soon as he's demobbed."

"What choice we got if we want to be together, we'll find a place where no one knows us and we'll be forgotten about."

"Will we see you and the children?"

"When we're settled."

"And how long will that take?"

Mari stayed silent for awhile. "To be honest I don't know, couple of months, couple of years, as long as it takes for people to lose interest.

Nerys and Rhys found it hard living with Joshua, Rhys tried to disregard his continual scrutiny saying, "You can understand him keeping an eye on me, if I mess up he could end up bankrupt. All the same he is a pain"

"Yes, but he doesn't have to make it so obvious he thinks we're rubbish, just because he's got a big house and been mayor of this tin pot town doesn't make him any better. He's so overbearing and has to be right about everything, he really gets my back up, can't think why Gwen, why anyone would want to do business with the likes of him."

"I know he's a pain but be fair, if it weren't for him I'd still be locked up, and beggars can't be choosers, and it's a better prison than I've been in."
Neither of them were aware that Joshua' wife Rebecca had entered the room.

"You may think this is a tin pot town, but Joshua is a good man, he can be direct, abrupt, even rude at times, but he is what he is, and beneath his prickly exterior is a kind gentle person."

Before they could recover from their embarrassment she'd left the room, with Nerys in apologetic pursuit.
"Rebecca I'm sorry, that wasn't for you to hear."

Rebecca turned from the doorway she was about to enter. "So am I, I've never met such an ungracious pair, if I could I'd ask you to leave, but I know the man you can't stand wouldn't hear of it because he's committed himself to help you. Alright it may be because he feels he owes it to his stepmother but that's Joshua for you, loyalty counts. How dare you call him overbearing and self opinionated when you don't know anything about him."

"I can only say I'm sorry, it's the strain of the new trial starting soon, this'll be the third one, everything is getting on top of me, I am really sorry." Rebecca disappeared through the door and closed it firmly. Nerys pondered on following and thought better of it, perhaps tomorrow Rebecca wouldn't be so irked.

"It's going to be a shock for him." Gwen grabbed the door and pulled herself from the car seat.

"And them," added Tudor,

"You could have phoned and let them know."

"Do you think they'd have come to the phone once they were told it was me?"

"You got a point, though you could have left a message, if I have time I'll ring them from here."

"Trains due any minute."

"You can meet him while I phone."

"Suppose that'll be alright, being as he don't know anything yet."

Gwen set off in search of a telephone calling back to Tudor, "And don't you say anything."
Elis stepped from the train, looking up and down the platform in search of a familiar face. They spotted each other at the same time, Elis' face lit up and Tudor smiled, something he hadn't done naturally for a while.

"How are you lad?" Immediately wishing he'd omitted the lad.
"Fine Tudor I'm fine, how are you?" Elis' eyes continuing to scan the platform.

"Only me and Gwen I'm afraid, she'll be by the car."

Rebecca entered the room her face stern and her body language said I've something to say. Rhys and Nerys prepared themselves after all they deserved it.

"I've just had a phone call from Gwen," she said her expression giving nothing away. "Her and Tudor are coming, they should be here in an hour or so." She paused to give Nerys time to spill out the words that filled her mouth.

"What's wrong? Must be something wrong for Gwen to be coming, and with Tudor."

"I would think Tudor's just bringing her or how else would she get here?"

"Oh God what's happened?" She turned to Rhys expecting he should know.

"Nothings happened, I've some good news, their bringing your son, Elis." Neither heard her added warning. "And I think you should keep well away from Mr Gruffydd when they arrive."

Chapter Twenty Six

Tuesday 8th May 1945

V.E. Day. The Morgan household didn't feel like celebrating, maybe Hitler had been finally defeated, and perhaps no one else would die because of Germany's ambitions. No more would young men be crippled, or as Iwan have their lives snatched from them. Compared to those that had been burned, blinded or ended up blubbering wrecks Huw was virtually unscathed. The Morgan's had a lot to be thankful for especially for Elis who'd come through without a scratch, yet all their cause for rejoicing was outweighed by the legacy of Dafydd Siencyn-Pryce. The continuous ringing of church bells drew the inhabitants into the village square and the merrymaking took on a dimension unseen before in Pentre, the doors of both pubs the Bell and the Miners Arms were thrown open and remained so in defiance of the drinking laws. Petty differences were set aside as neighbour hugged neighbour, friend or otherwise, with the exception of one household where the world hesitated respectfully on the street side of the threshold.

Nerys was still in shock and had been for the past five days, her mind unable to vacate the picture of the judge. What he'd said hadn't registered, until he'd reached for the black cap and placed it on his head, and then her world had frozen. Huw and Elis had between them carried her from the court, and it had been Gwen who'd prevented Huw from assaulting Tudor, who'd stupidly and selfishly tried to apologise and exonerate his self. Then Gwen hit him herself, with a punch Joe Louis would have been proud of. He tumbled backward down the steps of the court building, and sat cradling his head sobbing. Cameras clicked as Huw managed to deliver a passing blow with his good leg, giving the assembled hacks the front page story for the next edition.

"All's not lost yet, Mam." Elis referring to the prospect of an appeal as he helped his mother into the back seat of the car. "I'll go and see Mr Stanley maybe he can help."

Nerys nodded unable to expound the horror that supplanted the original hollowness. What his former boss could do Elis didn't know, they already had a top solicitor and barrister but anything was worth a try.

Gwen decided they were keeping Tudor's car so Mari and the children could be driven to Rhydamman, and he could like it or lump it, after all she had as much right to it as him and he hadn't had much use for it of late. Huw had driven several miles without either him or Mari attempting to initiate a conversation, so avoiding the one topic that dominated all else. Even the children remained silent, aware that now was not a good time to try and grab the limelight.

"I didn't think Sara would have moved back with him." Huw finally spoke making no attempt to disguise his loathing for Tudor, which he also now assigned to Sara.

"He's her dad like Rhys is yours."

"He's a bloody no good back stabbing Judas, and that's the best I can say about the rotten bastard."

"Whatever your opinion he's been good to her and me, and don't swear in front of the children."

"My fathers been bloody good to you and all, you've forgotten that have you?"

"Don't be stupid I love Rhys like he was my father, how could I forget? Now change the subject I'm going to Rhydamman to get the children away from all this ill feeling and bitterness."

"It's a heck of a lot more than ill feeling."

"You ranting and raving doesn't help your mother or mine, Tudor's done what he's done, and now we've got to concentrate on the appeal."

The revellers in the villages of Gwaun Cae Gurwen and Glanamman were passed virtually unnoticed.

"Their both sleeping," Mari turned her head back from the children spread out on the rear seat. "They always do it when we're nearly there."

"I'm sorry Mar don't let's fall out."

"Don't expect me to hate Tudor, I hate what he's done and I know he regrets it. But the thing that really hurts is he did it for me, so I'm the reason Rhys is where he is."

"No one blames you, you didn't ask him to do it."

"He did it because he loves me, how can I hate him?" Taking a hanky from her pocket she wiped her eyes and blew her nose. "And if I hadn't been so open with Catrin then Tudor wouldn't have had to choose, so I'm as much to blame as him."

"No." Huw said angrily stopping the car sharply in the centre of the road. "You didn't deliberately do anything, but Catrin and Tudor did,

330

they both knew what they were doing. Tudor knew when he changed his statement he was helping to send my dad to," his knuckles whitened as he tightened his grip on the steering wheel. "The gallows. Every time dad did a good turn he got shit on, he saved Pryce's and Catrin's lives and look what it's cost him, where's the justice in that?" Slumping forward his head buried in his arms he wept uncontrollably.

Gerald Stanley shook his head. "You know the system Elis, you already have excellent legal representation what could I possibly add to their expertise? As a friend of course I'll look through the evidence but I'm not a criminal lawyer, I may have been instructed on a few minor cases of theft but nothing on this scale, as you know this firm specialises in civil and family matters."

"But you have a sharp eye and fresh mind and if anything's been overlooked you might spot it."

"As long as you don't expect a miracle, because that's what you're seeking."

"I've had my share of those I'm afraid." Gerald Stanley raised both eyebrows encouraging further comment. "It's a long story I'll tell you about it one day."

Stanley nodded asking. "Are you staying in town or are you going back home?"

"Staying tonight and visiting my father tomorrow."

"Then come to dinner this evening, and we can go through these papers together. Better still stay the night with us, I'm sure Mrs Stanley would be delighted."

The offer took Elis completely by surprise. "I had another engagement arranged for this evening, but of course I'll cancel thank you."

"Hope the young lady won't be too disappointed."

Elis shook his head. "I think she'll understand." He'd know thirty seconds after leaving this room."

Violet managed a smile that didn't absolutely disguise her disappointment.

"I am sorry there's nothing I'd rather do, but I haven't a choice, he's my father's only hope." Elis truly regretted having let her down. "Can we make it tomorrow night instead?"

Violet's face brightened. "Of course."

The full impact of what she'd done had finally struck home. Rhys was going to hang because of her actions, but she hadn't known that when she'd revealed Mari's secret to the police. It wasn't all her fault, she hadn't an inkling they could use it against Rhys. All she'd wanted was to knock some of the smugness out of Mari. The self satisfied cow had had it all, she'd never had to do anything she detested, like sleeping with Owain or Mostyn. Her family had always looked out for her, she had children by the man she loved, not by a man who'd bought her for a pound of butter or a few pork chops. It had been Geraint this and Geraint that until she was sick of hearing about him, and that's why she'd done it. Rhys had never been in the equation he'd saved her life and cared for her, she loved him so much and he didn't know and never would, not now. Nerys had guessed, that's why she'd wanted her out of the house that time, she'd never deserved him, she didn't appreciate the man he was. But then Nerys hadn't betrayed him either it had taken her Catrin Thomas to do that, and she knew by the gaping hole from where her heart had been ripped out that jealousy was a killer, and she couldn't bear it. This time there was no Rhys with his strong arms to grab her, no Rhys to tell her everything would be alright and he'd look after her. Yet he was there, his arms outstretched inviting her to join him in an everlasting embrace, her insides pounded and her lungs felt they would explode as she came within reach of all she'd ever desired, his arms folded around her and drew her to him in an eternal union, while the last ripple folded over her head.

"Mr Stanley was always a long shot, but the appeal will still go ahead if he fails to come up with anything." Elis tried to be cheerful Violet deserved better than his long face and despondency.

"You've done all you can, Mr Stanley still might find something and perhaps the barrister has a card or two up his sleeve."

"I don't think so Mr Stanley didn't seem too hopeful, and if Mr Rothsey had any reserve ammunition he'd have used it in the trial. Our only chance is the trial judge wrongfully allowed the housekeepers evidence, the legality of which was disputed at the beginning but the judge ruled it was admissible, we contend he was in error and hope to win a retrial."

"What are the odds?"

"Not good. I'm sorry Violet perhaps this wasn't a good idea, I'm not the best of company right now." He leaned forward to rise from the settee and but she pulled him back by his jacket sleeve.

"I don't mind I'm a good listener and we can stay here, we don't have to go out." He turned about to say she didn't need to be burdened with his problems, but before he spoke her lips were pressing against his.

His emotions on the train journey home ranged from bouts of guilt ridden depression to periods of euphoria. The memory of Violet's soft eagerly yielding body aroused a yearning that woke every tingling nerve, then he felt remorse, guilty for setting aside the wretched plight of his father while he quenched his carnal thirst. The other two men in the carriage were hidden behind their opened broadsheets from which neither endeavoured to venture. Elis speculated that whatever they found so absorbing would be a trifle compared to the pleasures of Violet, or the predicament of his father. Next week he'd journey back to Cardiff and visit both Mr Stanley and his father, and definitely Violet.

The shock paralysing Nerys' consciousness finally thawed and Gwen's anxiety eased slightly, while still keeping a watchful eye on her sister's morose demeanour.

"You sure you don't want me to come? I've nothing better to do."

"No Huw is taking me, and only immediate family are allowed in."

"If they say I have to I don't mind waiting outside."

Nerys attempted a smile, the first in last couple of weeks. "I'll be ok Elis will meet us there."

Gwen nodded. "Let's pray Mr Stanley has positive news for Elis." Truthfully she had dwindling expectations.

"I pray all continually.

"There's something I wanted to ask you." Gwen wavered. "Of course if it'll upset you I won't do it." She paused again. "Only it's Catrin's funeral on Friday and I thought I'd..."

"Do as you want, I got no feelings about her."

"I'll just pop in and pay my respects to the family."

"Your choice I'm not your keeper." The quiver in Nerys' voice contradicted her previous claim. "I'm going to lie down for a while." She rose from her chair and a woman twice her age shuffled to the door.

Gwen knew once Nerys locked herself in her room she wouldn't emerge until the next morning.

"I don't suppose you'll be going back to the service except to get demobbed, so don't forget there's a place for you here when you're ready."

Elis took the offered hand. "I've compassionate leave until, well you know. Give my regards to Mrs Stanley."

Gerald Stanley held out the file. "Sorry I couldn't have been more help."

Elis remained stony faced. "Thank you for trying."

Gerald Stanley put his arm on Elis' shoulder as he escorted him to the door. "Has a date been set."

Elis stopped abruptly surprised by the man's insensitivity. "The executions set for eight am August seventh." The pain of his statement penetrated Stanley like needle, and his face flushed. "I'm so sorry I meant a date for the appeal."

He'd only had time for a quick word with Violet as he left the office and arranged to meet her later. When he arrived at the prison his mother and Huw were waiting outside the huge oak gates.

"I'm sorry I was longer with Mr Stanley than I intended."

"What did he say?" Nerys visually challenging him to demolish her last and slenderest of hopes.

Unable to sustain eye contact he bowed his head. "I'm sorry, Mam, he tried his best."

When he'd been on remand Rhys had dressed in his everyday clothes and visits had taken place in the communal visiting area. Now he dressed as the other prisoners, and because of his forthcoming

335

engagement with Albert Pierrepoint special conditions applied, allowing his visits in a private room away from the other convicts. If he only had himself to be concerned about he'd have laughed at the irony, in having committed the most serious crime he was receiving preferential treatment, such as a cell to his self while others had to double up. The knowledge of Nerys forcibly coming to terms with the inevitable sickened him, how would she cope when the day came? For come it would he was certain, even if he was given leave to appeal there was an almost inevitable chance of failure. Nerys was placing so much hope in the judgement being over ruled that hope had turned to blind expectation, would Gwen, Huw and Elis be enough to carry her through.

They were already seated when he was escorted into the room; the prison officer retired to the far wall, trying his hardest to convey an impression of total disinterest. Rhys hugged the three in turn starting and ending with Nerys then seated himself across the table from her. Nerys gripped his hand so tightly he felt his fingers were in danger of crushing.

"You ok? He asked gently cupping Nerys' grasp with his free hand. "I hope you two are looking after your mother," he said lightly in an attempt to soften the mood. Elis smiled and Huw nodded.

"How they treating you?" Nerys always asked and always received the same reply.

"Fine, as well as they can, not the Ritz mind you."

They talked about the family, the war with Japan being almost at an end, how they'd celebrate when Rhys won his appeal, they spoke of anything and everything apart from what Rhys considered inevitable.

Huw and Elis left the room in order to give Nerys and Rhys fifteen minutes alone.

"He seems to be in good spirits." Huw said while they waited on a bench in the corridor.

"All an act for mam, he's crumbling and trying not to show her."

"When will we hear about the appeal?"

"If it's allowed to go ahead, Rothsey says there's less than a fifty-fifty chance of that because we're not introducing new evidence, and two judges have already ruled against us on the very point we're contesting."

"So we might not even get to appeal?"

"That's what he says, and Mr Stanley agreed with him."

"We'll get a new barrister then."

"And then what, he won't be able to change the law will he?"

Chapter Twenty Seven
Monday July 23rd

Gwen's revulsion of Catrin's actions hadn't been tempered by the sorrow she felt at seeing the Thomas family's anguish. Yet she couldn't help thinking if it hadn't been for Rhys the daughter they'd once disowned would have perished long ago, and they wouldn't have their granddaughter Nia. She hadn't seen Tudor in the weeks since the funeral, and then only through the window as he'd declined an invitation to join the mourners in the house, remaining outside with Mostyn, Owain, and a group of other men waiting for the cortège to depart. She wondered how he felt knowing Rhys' application for an appeal had failed, did he know? Sara had probably telephoned him from Rhydamman, where she'd gone to stay with Mari and Geraint's family to get away from Huw's constant sniping. Sara needn't have bothered as Huw had taken to spending all his waking hours in either the Bell, or Miners Arms, belligerently blaming the world for all his woes and on several occasions had returned home with cuts and bruises, evidence he'd lost the physical argument, the residue of his time he spent sleeping off his alcoholic stupor.

Elis had stayed overnight in Cardiff and was due to visit his father today with Mr Howe the solicitor. No matter how much she'd been coaxed Nerys hadn't left her room since returning from visiting Rhys the previous Friday. Gwen had left her meals outside her door, they'd been barely touched but as long as the tray was disturbed she knew Nerys was ok. Her mind unable to settle with the constant agonizing over Nerys, Huw, Rhys, and the knowledge Geraint would soon be home, and he and Mari planned to disappear to God knows where. Her mind leaping from one problem to another and back again, Gwen found herself contemplating yet another outside the door of the house she'd once so blissfully called home.

Unsure whether she should knock she tried the latch, the door with its peeling paint and rotten threshold squealed eerily open on its un-oiled hinges. The lack of care so evident outdoors continued inside, she caught her breath as the stale air rushed past her in an effort to rejuvenate itself outside. She sought the hanky tucked in her sleeve and placed it over her nose and mouth.

"Tudor, Tudor you there?" Unsure whether to proceed or retreat Gwen waited and listened, she'd begun to turn when she became aware of a faint buzzing coming from the kitchen. "Tudor," she called louder, making her way along the hallway towards the source of the sound. She halted at the kitchen door aware that the stench was significantly greater, but that wasn't why she stopped. She knew what she'd find on the other side by the seething black mass that bubbled on the inside of the half glass door, she dropped her hanky and fled.

Newly promoted Detective Sergeant Moyle handed Gwen an envelope. "It's addressed to you. I'm sorry under the circumstances I had to open it, but only I have read it."

Gwen took the letter and unfolded the two handwritten pages.

'Dearest Gwen,

You once wrote me a letter saying how hard you found it to write, so you know how difficult this is for me as I've never been one to exhibit my feelings. I don't expect you to forgive me for what I did, why should you when it's impossible for me to live with Rhys' death on my shoulders. I've written to him, he's refused to see me in this world, I expect we'll meet shortly when he joins me in the next.

The one reason I had for living was the hope that one day even if you couldn't forgive me you'd understand and come back, and help me to live with the terrible thing I've done. I realise this will never be because the ghost of Rhys will always be between us. Along time ago you said if you could change a mistake you'd made you would, so would I, but we both know no matter how much we long for a chance to make amends it's not always possible. I confess my mistake by far outweighs yours, as yours brought life into this world, and the consequences of mine is a good man having his life taken from him. But I think I must love you a lot more than you me, for I was able to put aside your indiscretions and you are unable to come to terms with mine. I love you, always have from our days together in school, it broke my heart when you married Gomer yet I could see how happy you were and that made it bearable. Each moment knowing you despise me my heart is savaged from my chest, and I can bear this torture no longer without you. I care not what others think of me the only opinion of importance is yours. Try not to remember me by the terrible thing I have done but by the good times

*we shared together, and carry with you the knowledge that the time we
were together I was the happiest man since Adam found Eve. I love you
Gwen and if I die a thousand times it cannot alter that, only my pain will
cease.*

*Goodbye and do not hold yourself responsible for what I do, you can no
more control your feelings than I can mine.*

I love you so much, now and forever.

Tudor.'

Vernon Howe walked away a saddened man, he'd grown to like
and respect Rhys, and deep down the feelings of having somehow let
him down weren't justified. The appeal to the Home Secretary for
clemency would undoubtedly not be granted as Rhys' plight hadn't
generated a great deal of public sympathy, and the case no longer made
the papers let alone the headlines. The press concentrated on Japan
being close to the brink of defeat, and celebrated the prospect of peace
bringing an end to the years of killing, one death early on an August
morning would pass virtually unnoticed.

Elis went to the sink and washed his cup, took his jacket from
the back of the chair and slipped it on. He glanced around the flat Violet
wasn't the tidiest person, perhaps that was part of the reason he loved
her. Adorning the floor and settee were her clothes, the ones he'd
hastily removed last night. The memory simultaneously warmed and
disheartened him, would he tell his father he was to be married with a
child on the way, his first grandchild he'd never see? With plenty of time
to spare he decided to walk to the prison. It was a sunny day yet cool
for the height of summer, not one of the swans nestling on the banks of
Roath Lake stirred it's periscope neck as he ambled by, he wondered if

he'd had bread to throw for them would they have taken notice. He sat on a bench and observed a man fishing from a small boat, his eyes watched while his mind speculated on why his father had asked him to come alone?

Violet finished typing the letters and arranged them in a neat pile ready to take into Mr Stanley for his signature. Maintaining her concentration this morning had not been easy, accomplishing her tasks in automatic mode. Last night she'd been apprehensive about telling Elis she thought she was pregnant, not because she feared his reaction, that he might discard her, that hadn't crossed her mind. She loved him and him her of that she was certain, nevertheless he had enough on his plate at the moment and it couldn't have happened at a less opportune time. His reaction to, '*I think I'm pregnant.*' had surprised her, she hadn't expected him to welcome the news with such enthusiasm, hugging her tightly and twirling around until they were both dizzy they collapsed laughing on the settee, his problems momentarily consigned to second place. Then there were her parents to consider, they'd been less than happy when Violet had told them of Elis, or more to the point about his father. Now their grandchild would also be the grandchild of a convicted murderer, well like it or not they'd have to accept it, because soon she, Elis and the baby would be a family, and that she yearned more than anything.

"What's the secret why did you want to come alone?" Elis got straight to the point.

Rhys shook his head. "No big secret, Huw came last week, and I'd like you to arrange for Mari to do the same."

"Alone like this, why?"

"So I can say goodbye, and spend the remaining visits with your mother."

Elis nodded, so that's why Huw had taken to the bottle, his way of coping, only he wasn't.

"And there is something I want to ask you, don't ask me why I need to know just accept I do."

Elis wondered for a split second if he knew about Violet and the baby and immediately dismissed the idea, he'd have to be psychic.

"What's that then, Dad?"

"You never explained how you escaped from the Germans."

"That's it, that's what you want to know?" Elis smiled. "I thought it was some dark secret you'd imagined I was hiding."

"I hope not, it's partly because of secrets I'm here."

"Did you do it, Dad, did you kill him."

Rhys levelled his eyes to meet Elis. "Not intentionally I didn't set out to do it, we argued and there was a struggle he fell and hit his head, I didn't hit him he slipped as I've told you before. What I never mentioned to you or anyone is, he was lying there looking up at me with this inane smirk. Believe me I didn't know if he was dead or not and at that point and I didn't care, I picked up a big clock from the mantelpiece and threw at his head just to wipe the stupid grin off his face."

Elis sat silent for a moment absorbing the confession. "Then why have you always denied ever being there you could have claimed it was accident?" Elis asked incredulously. "You could have admitted manslaughter, you'd have got a prison sentence but you'd have been out in a few years."

"I lied because I wasn't thinking straight, I wasn't sure if I'd killed him with the clock. And I did leave him with his head in the fire I hadn't done anything to help him, then I thought nobody had seen me

343

so it would be better if I knew nothing. Then it got to a stage where I couldn't change my story, if I admitted lying why should anyone believe me then?"

"We'll the result couldn't have been worse could it?" Elis' tone changed from bewilderment to anger.

Rhys shrugged. "Too late now, maybe I should have told the truth it's easy to be wise after the event. I did what I thought was best and I was wrong, there's no going back now. I'm not sorry for Pryce I'm glad he's dead no man deserved it more than him. I am sorry for the distress I've brought on our family especially your mother. I've accepted my fate and soon it'll be over for me, but your mother's going to suffer for the rest of her life."

"Does she know you did it?"

"I never told her about the clock, but she guessed I'd done more than I admitted though she never said so. I know Gwen had her doubts to."

"I'll do all I can for mam you know that."

"I know you all will, but what if it's not enough."

"You don't think she'll harm herself."

"Promise me you'll keep a close eye."

"I promise, I'll watch over her just as you would."

Rhys nodded. "So tell me how did you get away?"

"To tell the truth it was all a bit strange, and I still find it hard to believe myself, it was so incredible I begin to doubt it happened."

"Is that why you haven't spoken about it? One thing I've learned is not to dismiss anything, the more implausible the greater the likelihood it's true."

"You know there was a plan to drop decoy parachutists to keep Jerry thinking the main invasion force was concentrated on Calais." Elis chuckled. "Fooled me as well, thought one of the decoys hanging from a tree was an allied soldier and I went to help him, didn't find out it wasn't until I had a rifle stuck in my back."

"But you were interrogated?"

"Yes but not as robustly as I'd been trained to expect, luckily my story if not totally believed didn't stir any significant suspicion. I think they believed I was just another French allied sympathiser that they would deal with, and fortunately I wasn't handed over to the Gestapo."

"Even as a kid you were always damn lucky."

"Aye, well you got to remember the Germans had a lot more on their minds than few dissident peasants. As the allies advanced we were moved from place to place, each time we expected to be transferred to the SS. Finally about a dozen of us were put in the back of a lorry, we were made to get out and line up in a clearing in a wood."

Rhys said nothing though he'd have been able to describe every German soldier, every prisoner, every tree, every blade of grass and everything that happened next.

"They opened fire with a machine gun from the back of another lorry, we didn't stand a chance."

"You did."

"That's what I can't fathom. When they opened fire some tried to run, I was knocked to the floor when the head of the man next to me exploded and he fell on me. I lay with his brains splattered all over me feigning death. Then the officer in charge to make sure we were all dead started shooting one round from his Lugar into the head of each prisoner, each time he fired I expected to be next and I felt his footsteps as he came by me. I could hear him breathing, and smell the polish on his boots, I lay there petrified unable to move. Elis stopped, reliving the scene while searching for an explanation. I knew the next bullet would be mine, but for some reason I've never been able to understand he carried on past me and fired into the next man. They made no attempt to hide the massacre, so I laid there until they left and crawled into the wood.

Rhys continued his silence, finally convinced his dreams were more than imaginings and soon he'd enter that world for perpetuity.

No one had slept, and nobody had tried, Mari hadn't been able to stay in Rhydamman and had come home to visit Rhys one last time and had remained with the family, she needed them as much as they needed her. Each one of them sneaked glances at the clock when they thought they were unobserved, collectively they ignored the sweep of the hands, yet individually they were aware of each passing second. Nerys sat quietly fondling the ring on her left hand, the plastic smile held on her face convinced Gwen that she was no longer in command of her faculties, her remarkable surreal serenity could be attributed to the injection Dr Richards had given her. Gwen hoped it would last and wished she'd had one herself, rubbing her hand across her face she stole another look at the time, seven thirty, thirty more minutes. Would he change his mind or would he remain adamant in his refusal to see a priest, she hoped he'd make his peace with God.

Elis sat with his mother, wondering how his father would pass his final minutes, and questioned if he done all he could? Perhaps he could or should have done more, exactly what he didn't know but instead of being so wrapped up in himself and Violet he should have thought of something It was too late now, the one time in his life his father needed him he'd let him down. His father's parting words kept spinning round his head. 'It's down to you now son, you're stronger than Huw you'll have to see to the family.'

346

Huw sat alone in the kitchen, there was no one left to hate, both Catrin and Tudor had got what they'd deserved. He'd surprised everyone by attending Tudor's funeral, and shocked the mourners at the graveside when instead of dropping a handful of soil onto the coffin he gathered a mouthful of saliva and spat into the grave. He reached across the table for the near empty bottle, and ignoring the unused glass sat beside it he gulped down the remaining single malt.

Sara cuddled closer to her mother, she was having difficulty in controlling her emotions, Gwen's arm circled her as the restrained tears crept down her cheek, fearing she'd break down at any moment, she pulled away and fled the room.

"It's time." The governor said solemnly as he accompanied by four prison officers and a priest entered the cell.

Rhys picked up the photograph standing beside the carved wooden box, visually caressing the image before he pressed his lips against the glass for the last time. He remained silent commanding his rubber legs to support him as his hands were bound behind his back. Firm hands gripped his arms as his hands were tied behind him. The priest chanted the Lord's Prayer and he was escorted gently the short distance to the scaffold and a hood was place over his head. His absolute belief that whatever lay beyond Moira would be there to greet him didn't waver. As he felt the rope around his neck he uttered his final words. "Gomer you were right, they always win."